METAL BONES

KATHLEEN CONTINE

METAL BONES

Printed in the United States of America
Cover Design and formatting: J.M. Ivie
ISBN: 978-1-7342316-0-1
First edition: March 2020
10 9 8 7 6 5 4 3 2 1

To Virginia

1

Thwap thwap thwap.

Leo Spearman's hair stood on end at the sound of rain hitting metal. It dripped off the side and pooled in the grass, soaking into his shoes. His drenched, ashy hair stuck to his skin as he stood outside his father's old spaceship, watching his brother, Gaeth, hug his mother goodbye. Not one friendly face was visible among the crowd of townspeople surrounding them.

The downpour intensified as Gaeth pick up the mud-caked suitcases, but his mom pulled him back into a hug. She immediately withdrew with a yelp and Leo knew she must've been poked by a piece of metal sticking out of Gaeth's arm. Gaeth pulled his sleeve down so no one would notice, but it was too late.

"Get that thing out of here!" someone from the crowd yelled.

Leo tried his best to ignore them. He jogged to his mother and brother, the water soaking through his shoes, and grabbed one of Gaeth's suitcases.

"Mom, it's okay." Gaeth patted her on the back.

"I shouldn't have agreed to this. We should have found a different way," she said through tears.

Leo brought the suitcase to the ship where their father waited. He stared at Leo with sad eyes and let out a long sigh.

"You seem alright for someone who won't see your son again," Leo said, crossing his arms.

"Don't make this harder than it is," his father replied without glancing his way. "I'm glad they agreed to let you take Gaeth. I can't imagine a skinny nineteen-year-old on a freighter by himself."

"He'd be terrified. Of course I'm taking him," Leo said. "If I had my way, he wouldn't be going at all. I always thought it was a bad idea."

Was it him, or was the crowd moving in closer? The quicker they got off Earth, the sooner they could get Gaeth away from all these people. Leo's stomach turned as he thought about how they spat on Gaeth as a child and ran from him as if he were a monster. If it had stopped when they grew older maybe they could have stayed on Earth. It wasn't Gaeth's fault he was sick, after all.

Leo's father motioned to the townspeople. "Do you see everyone out here, gawking?"

They all stared at Gaeth like predators ready to strike.

"If Gaeth stayed, who knows what they might do to him. I don't want him to go through any more pain."

Leo looked away. He knew his father was right, but he didn't want to admit it.

"I don't want him to be in pain either," Leo said.

"Then help him."

Gaeth finally wrestled himself free of his mother's grip and walked toward them. His clothes had soaked through, and his wavy brown hair slicked down across his forehead. His green eyes widened with worry as he glanced frantically at the crowd who had started up a chant.

"Hell no! Hell no! Robot kid has got to go!"

The rain poured down; the *thwap* sound Leo hated so much grew more irritating. Gaeth stood in front of their father. "Bye, Dad," he said quickly.

Their father hugged Gaeth, and even though he wasn't making any noise, his quiet shaking screamed louder than any wail could have.

"Get a move on already," a man's angry voice carried above the others. "I haven't got all day."

Leo flipped the man off, to which his mother scolded him. "Leo, what did I tell you about talking to anyone but us when we're doing this? Act like a twenty-one-year-old for gosh sakes."

"They shouldn't be saying those things."

"Hey Leo, you forgot to pack this in case your brother gets a loose screw on the way over." Through the rain, someone threw a small object. It smacked Leo in the chest and splashed in the mud at his feet.

He picked it up and wiped the grime off. A screwdriver. Leo didn't care who threw it or who said the joke; he sprinted at the crowd, not knowing what he would do when he got there. A bloody nose or two, at least. The crowd cheering drowned out his parents' shouts as he collided with a man. The people nearby gave them room as they sent mud in all directions.

Leo threw his fist into the man's face. Anything resembling flesh he wanted to destroy. The crowd around them erupted, Leo managing to land a few solid punches before several hands grabbed him and threw him back toward the ship.

"You could infect me, you contagious freak," the man Leo attacked shouted, a trace of blood dripping from his nose.

"Don't insult my brother then, asshole," Leo shouted back. He walked back to the ship, where his family talked low among themselves.

"Send it to Oblurn already!" The crowd rushed toward Leo's family. Out of the corner of his eye, Leo spotted someone holding a metal bat.

Leo ran toward the ship as his parents rushed Gaeth aboard. The crowd closed in, jostling Leo every which way as they shouted in unison, "Hey, hey! Ho, ho! Robot kid has got to go!"

A policeman managed to grab Leo and push him through.

His father grabbed him and shoved him up the ramp. "Take care of your brother and send us a message to let us know you're okay."

Leo fell back into the ship, where Gaeth already sat in the copilot seat. The crowd surrounded them, banging their fists on the hull, still chanting.

Leo sat in his own seat. He watched through the window as the same policeman lead his parents through the crowd, stopping a safe distance away. Leo's heart sank for his brother. He knew he would be coming back, but Gaeth? How could Gaeth possibly feel right now, knowing this would be the last time he'd see them?

Gaeth had thrown his bags in the back with the cargo. Leo shivered in the cold, the dim lights not helping their spirits. He didn't know what to say as he sat in his own chair. The rain slid down the large front window as he went through the routine checklist he kept between the seats. Outside the police shouted at the crowd to back away.

"Fuel tanks?"

Gaeth checked the gage. "Check."

Leo took his time checking it off the list. "Escape pod?"

"Still there," Gaeth said.

Leo rechecked it, even more slowly. "Emergency thrusters?"

"Leo, just let me do it." Gaeth's voice shook as he said it, his face remaining solemn. He grabbed the checklist and finished the routine in less than a minute, not paying attention to Leo. After shoving it back between the seats, Gaeth sat back in his chair and sighed.

Leo carefully turned the ship around, the crowd now running away from the heat of the engines. His back pushed into the seat as the darkness of space filled the window. After a few moments, they were operating in silence except for the occasional beeping.

The ship's computer buzzed. "Please enter coordinates."

Leo glanced at Gaeth, still searching for words of comfort before typing in Oblurn's location. There had to be something to make him feel better. But what do you say to someone being sent away from their planet for something they can't control?

"Setting course for Oblurn," the computer chimed.

Gaeth remained silent. Leo put the ship on autopilot and leaned back in his seat. "How are you feeling?" he asked.

"Stiff, cold." Gaeth paused, not able to say the words. He eventually forced them out, "Wishing I could stay home." His voice was barely above a whisper.

"I wish we could go back," Leo said.

"So we're really doing this." It wasn't a question, more of an accusation. He kept his eyes forward, playing with a loose thread on his chair.

"You saw the crowd. If you stayed home, it would only be a matter of time before they made you leave anyway." Leo realized it wasn't the right thing to say. "Think about it like going away to camp, except in space."

"Yeah, a camp I can never come back from, and no one can visit." Gaeth sighed. "And if you go, everyone thinks you're some sort of monster. I'm surprised you aren't afraid of catching Steel Elbow."

"If I did, we'd be stuck in Oblurn together. Wouldn't that be fun?" Leo snuck a glance at Gaeth, who rolled his eyes. If he could get him to laugh a little, it would be a small victory. "If it's so bad and you don't think you can stay there, we'll figure something out. It's the best thing for you, though."

"Best thing for everyone back home," Gaeth muttered, pushing the heat button on his seat. "Why aren't you worried you'll catch Steel Elbow?"

Leo thought for a moment. It was true he should be scared of his brother. After Gaeth had given their neighbor Steel Elbow, all their friends had turned on him. But the way the crowd had treated Gaeth, Leo didn't want to leave him.

"If I caught your virus and it meant we were going to live together for the rest of our lives, then I'd be okay with that. It's what family does," Leo said.

"But I could cover everything sticking out of my skin like I have, and no one would be any the wiser. I could build a house in the countryside in the middle of nowhere, and no one would bother me. The only reason I have to leave is that everyone found out about it."

"How about this: if we both agree it's so bad you can't live there without being miserable, I'll take you away from there."

Gaeth faced Leo for the first time since they took off. "You better not be joking."

"Why would I joke about something like that?" Leo shot Gaeth a look that said *I'm serious*.

"You swear?"

"I'll even help you build a house in the countryside."

Gaeth held up his pinky finger. "You have to pinky promise."

"Gaeth, I promise I'll do it."

"No. You need to pinky promise." Gaeth wouldn't break eye contact.

Leo exhaled. "Fine." They wrapped their pinky fingers and shook them up and down. Gaeth nodded, sitting back in his seat, happier than before.

It was rare Gaeth smiled and it made Leo happy whenever he did. His heart sank as he realized it might be the last one he'd ever see. He didn't want to get Gaeth's hopes up, but if he could keep him in a good mood until they got to Oblurn, then he would at least keep his word to his parents.

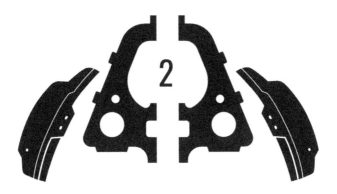

2

There could never be a more perfect day to practice killing.

Tank snuck through the trees; he knew where to step, making as little sound as possible. His green scales helped him blend in, but he was always paranoid about being sighted. A stick broke behind him. He tucked his tail in, trying to make himself smaller. It was hard given his size, but he might be able to catch his target off guard. Whatever was walking through the woods wasn't trying to be quiet.

Ducking behind a rock, he pulled out his blaster from the holster around his waist and waited. A few more seconds and it would walk right by him. Three. Two. One.

Baring his fangs, Tank jumped out with a roar, pinning the creature down with a clawed hand, the other shoving his blaster under its neck.

"Whoa! Whoa! Whoa! I thought we agreed we weren't using blasters." The creature desperately tried to escape his grasp.

"Naf, if you keep stomping around like that, you don't have a chance at winning the Ceremony." Tank climbed off to let him up.

"Let's be honest, I'm not winning the Ceremony. I can't even aim a blaster."

Nature had been unkind to Naf. Instead of the typical dark green scales Sovichs usually had, Naf had been born with bright orange ones. And while Tank always towered over his friends, Naf barely reached his elbow. The other Sovichs had picked on Naf since the day they started talking. Perhaps that was why Tank found himself always trying to help Naf out. If he could help Naf stick up for himself, then maybe he wouldn't be picked on so much.

Because of Naf's size, it gave him low odds of winning the Ceremony, so the older Sovichs hadn't tried to train him. Tank knew the older Sovichs were right, but he didn't want Naf to be hard on himself.

"If you keep thinking that way, you won't be," he said. "We've been practicing long enough, let's head back."

Tank led the way through the forest along the worn-out path. It had been there for as long as he could remember. He would live here if he were allowed. He loved how dark it stayed underneath the trees no matter how bright it was outside. The sun poked through, giving them enough light to find their way, but the air was still cool.

They came to a small river. The bridge running across it had collapsed long ago, the splintered wood thrown in a pile on the bank. Tank heard time and time again it would be fixed, but it never had been. The only safe way to get across now were by stones jutting out of the water. Tank took a running start and skipped from one rock to the other, landing on the other side. He waved to Naf, who focused on his feet.

"Come on, Naf!" Tank shouted across the river.

"Why don't I just go around?" Naf shouted back.

"It's faster this way. You can't walk around it forever."

Naf shot him a stare.

"Just do it how I did it," Tank said.

"I'm going around." Naf backed away.

"I'm leaving without you then." Tank turned around, walking away from the river. "I'll see you when you get back to the village."

"Hey! That's not fair. Wait a second, Tank."

There was a yelp and a splash as Naf tumbled into the water. He grabbed a rock and clung on, yelling Tank's name until he finally came back.

Tank reached in and yanked Naf out by his neck. "What will you do when the Ceremony starts? I can't save you then," he said with a hint of annoyance. "It's everyone for themselves."

He helped Naf the rest of the way across the river, and they made their way to the path toward the helibikes.

"You'd save me if you needed to," Naf said, shaking the water off and getting Tank so wet he might as well have fallen in the river too. "If it were between me and the necklace, what would you choose?"

Tank thought for a moment. If he were honest with himself, he would have no problem shooting Naf in the face to win the Ceremony. He had been training for it for so long he wasn't about to let anyone take it from him. Of course, he would never tell Naf. What if he did and Naf tried to kill him when the Ceremony started? *Don't kid yourself. That would never happen.*

Tank went for the diplomatic option. "It's meager chances we'll both be fighting for the necklace at the end, Naf."

"Pretend for a second, somehow, out of sheer luck, we manage to make it to the end. It's you, me, and the necklace. What do you choose?"

"I can't tell if you're being serious or not. Is this how you deal with nerves?" Tank asked.

Naf groaned. "Just answer already."

Tank sighed. "The whole reason I've been training for this is so I might have a chance to find my father."

"So that means you'd pick your dad over me?"

Tank stopped and turned around to face him. "Naf, I don't mind helping you practice for the Ceremony, but you have to think about what you're saying. I haven't heard from my father in years—he could be dead. But if I win the Ceremony and leave the village, maybe I can find him and bring him back. If it means having to punch you in the snout to do it, then I will."

Tank turned and kept walking down the path, not bothering to wait for Naf's response. He shouldn't have said anything. If Naf wanted to strategize, then he just figured out if he needed to worry about Tank or not. But after a few moments, Naf caught up.

"If it were between you and winning the Ceremony, I think I would let you win." He stared up at Tank expectantly. "Let's be honest, there isn't a reason for me to leave the village. I couldn't tell you the first thing about surviving on my own. I can't even cross the river without needing you to come save me."

"Are you trying to make a pact with me?" Tank asked, tilting his head.

He'd heard of others making pacts before the Ceremony, promising they wouldn't kill each other until they were the only ones left. It was a good strategy until you realized your friend might betray you, and Tank wasn't about to take any chances.

"You've helped me a lot with training when no one else would. No, I'm just saying if we're the only two left, then I'll give it to you because you want to find your dad so badly," Naf said, putting his hands up in defense.

"Naf, when the Ceremony starts, it's every Sovich for himself. You can't let your emotions get in the way. That's how you lose," Tank said. "Even when the Ceremony is over, you shouldn't feel bad. This is what we've been training to do for years. We all know what we're getting into."

"I'll still feel bad if I kill you," Naf said.

"Well, you won't have to worry about that happening because you aren't a good hunter and you aren't good with a blaster, so dream on." Tank was getting more uncomfortable the longer this conversation went on. "And I helped you train because everyone should have a fighting chance going into the Ceremony."

"Who trained you?" Naf asked.

Tank paused for a moment. "No one. They thought I was too weak to train. I had to learn it all on my own."

They came into the clearing, where their bikes waited, and stopped and bowed.

"Make sure you thank your bike before getting on it, Naf," Tank said.

"Thank you for your aid," Naf said as he mounted his helibike.

Tank sighed as he climbed on his own helibike. Naf always forgot to thank the technology they used.

Tank held on to the metal handlebars as he settled into the seat, his feet resting on both sides. It took them a moment to power up, but the wheels spun faster, perpendicular with the ground, sending leaves flying in all directions. Soon they hovered a few feet off the ground. Tank sped off toward their village without another word, Naf trailing behind him. The cold wind blew against his scales, refreshing after sitting in one place all morning. He darted in and out of the trees, the sun becoming brighter as they got closer to the forest's edge.

"Be careful!" Naf yelled.

Tank laughed. "Lighten up, would you?" He pushed his helibike faster. It groaned under strain, but he pulled away from Naf toward the opening of the trees. They shot out of the forest, slowing as they passed under the wooden gate of their village.

Several fires had already been lit, and the smell of cooked meat wafted through the air. A group of younger Sovichs wrestled nearby but stopped as Tank and Naf approached. Others walked out of their mud huts to see who was back, but Naf and Tank kept flying forward. They passed the wooden platform in the center of the village.

Tank glanced at the flagpole sticking up from its center. No flag. They were free from a long speech today.

Several Sovichs stood in their path and Tank slammed on the breaks, stopping just before hitting them. The largest one gave his bike a small kick.

"If you hit me with that piece of junk, I would beat you so hard, you'd sleep through the Ceremony," he said.

"Shut up, Roaz," Tank spat.

"Yeah. We don't need to hear it from you," Naf chimed in.

Roaz stared at Naf for a moment before erupting in laughter. "Kargul, Thorn, are you hearing this?" He wiped a tear from his eye.

They continued laughing, the other Sovichs around them watching to see what would happen. Kargul approached Naf, whose grip tightened on his handlebars.

"Easy to talk tough when Tank is here, isn't it Naf?" He grabbed Naf by the neck, pulled him off his bike, and forced him on the ground where he swiftly kicked him in the side. Naf let out a yelp of pain as Roaz and Thorn laughed harder. "You'll be the first one to go when the Ceremony starts."

With a snarl, Tank leaped off his bike onto Kargul's back, clawing at every inch of scales he could dig in to. Claws dug into Tank's shoulder, and someone dragged him away. He turned to look for the culprit only to be met with a blaster inches from his face. Roaz smirked.

Before he could say anything, several older Sovichs ran over. They pushed everyone apart, scowling at each of them.

"The Ceremony hasn't even started, and you're acting like this? I thought you were better than this," one of them said.

"They started it," Thorn said.

"And I'm finishing it," the Sovich said. "If Prylek saw you all fighting you would be beaten. Tank and Naf get on your bikes. You other three be on your way. Roaz, you know better than to have your blaster out in the middle of the village. The Ceremony is tomorrow and you're already trying to kill each other."

Tank and Naf slowly got on their bikes and rode away. Tank smiled to himself at the sound of the Sovich's voice yelling that followed him and Naf all the way to his house.

They pulled up next to Tank's hut, dismounted, bowed, and went inside.

"Tank, I thought you'd be back later." A female Sovich sat at the table. She had a blaster in one hand and a spoon in the other. The liquid dripped down her chin as she ate from a large metal bowl.

"You should have told me you were going to visit today, Mom." Tank sighed. "We got back early. We've had enough training for the Ceremony today."

"Naf have some food." She motioned to the bowl.

Naf sat across from her with his own spoon, shoveling the food into his mouth. Half of it splashed onto the table.

"You'll do fine." She put her spoon down, wiping her mouth with the back of her claw. "Your father won when he entered."

"Where did they send him?" Tank asked, edging closer to her, his tail twitching back and forth.

"They never told me." She stood and put her scaly hands on his shoulders. "I hate thinking about what might have happened to your father."

"Mom, it's been years."

"Don't say that." She held him firmly. "He's out there somewhere, he just doesn't have a way to get in contact with us. If you win, you'll have the necklace and you'll be able to leave the forest. You can go find him." She shook Tank slightly. "If you win, promise me you'll send me a message when they send you away."

"Of course I'll send you a message." They were the exact same words his father had said to them the day before he won. They were told he had been sent on his mission without a chance to say goodbye. Tank's mother hadn't been the same since. If he won, he would get a message to her somehow.

"Good." She smiled, her fangs showing in the light. "I'm going home. I'll see you off tomorrow. If there's a speech come get me."

"The flag is down, so you don't have to worry." Tank waved his hand.

Naf was still shoveling food in his mouth. Tank walked over to where he kept his blasters, eyeing them carefully. If he were going to win the Ceremony, he would need his best weapons.

He thanked the one he used that morning and put it on the shelf, inspecting the others. That one was too slow. This one didn't fit in his holster the right way. He hadn't used that one enough to determine if he liked it yet. There were so many variables that could sway the turn of events. His tail flicked back and forth.

"How many are you taking to the Ceremony?" Naf asked.

"Two," Tank said, rubbing his chin. "But whenever I look at them, each one has something wrong with it."

"Well, think about what you like about them and pick that way."

Tank sighed and examined the blasters again. The one he used that morning had never steered him wrong. He grabbed it and put it in his holster before eyeing the others. There were so many things he didn't like, it was hard to pick something he did. The slow one was easy to hold, but if he needed it in a pinch, he would be dead. The one that didn't fit right in his holster was a good shot, but if he couldn't pull it out right away, he wouldn't win.

That left his new blaster he didn't have much experience with. He picked it up, flipping it over a few times. It was light, but not too light. He held it up to the ceiling to get a better view. If he could practice with it one more time, he would be more confident in his choice. His body still ached from practicing with Naf that morning, but if it gave him an edge, he would do it.

"I'm going to take this in the forest and practice some more. I just want to make sure it's the right one." He put it in his other holster and walked out of the hut. Just as he reached the helibike, a loud horn sounded from the center of the village. A flag slowly rose from the platform, causing Sovichs to flock to it. Some walked out from their huts, others flew through the gate on their helibikes.

If he could sneak out through the commotion, then maybe he could make it to the forest on foot. If anyone found out Tank purposely missed a speech, he would be in huge trouble. Perhaps he'd even be taken out of the Ceremony, but this was for his father, he had to do it. Tank started toward the gate when a clawed hand gripped his shoulder.

"Some people are saying Prylek is starting the Ceremony now," Naf whispered. "And whatever you have on you is what you have to use as your weapon. All I have is my spoon."

The horn still rang over the village, calling everyone to the center like bees to honey.

"He wouldn't do that. He's been our leader for so long, he wouldn't change the rule now."

They elbowed their way to the front of the emerging crowd. Some Sovichs desperately whispered to each other; others scanned the group to find their loved ones. The horn stopped abruptly, and a large, hunched-over, dark blue Sovich with saggy scales walked onto the platform.

The crowd erupted into cheers before he waved for them to quiet. "Thank you, my family."

Tank once asked his mother why he hadn't passed his position on to a younger Sovich, to which she replied no one dared to challenge him. He was too powerful.

Prylek continued, "I am so happy to see all your smiling faces, especially the younger ones who have come of age to take place in the Ceremony. For some of you, it will be the last time you spend the day with your family and see our beautiful planet of Whukogantu, for others, you might be lucky enough to escape with your life."

The crowd stayed silent as they hung onto his every word. He walked back and forth on the platform, his gaze lingering on each of them in turn.

"But we must not dwell on that. For we must honor those who came before us. Those who found this land we walk on, those who had to survive when all seemed lost. They fought for their freedom with nothing but their claws and teeth."

He stopped in front of Tank, his gray eyes boring into him.

"I noticed today that the Sovichs who are taking place in the Ceremony were fighting in the middle of the village."A stiff wind traveled throughout the crowd as Prylek snarled."It seems you have all been trained so well you can't wait to kill each other tomorrow."

Tank held his breath as Prylek held his gaze.

"Which is why the Ceremony will commence now. Whatever you possess at this moment are your weapons. The guards will take you to your starting positions."

The crowd erupted in protest, but Prylek held his hand up. "How can we honor our forefathers if we do not try to live as they have lived? They couldn't prepare. They fought for this forest with the weapons they had at their disposal, and they were still triumphant. The rules of the Ceremony are simple."

Prylek paced back and forth on the platform.

"Make it to the center of the forest from your starting position before any of the other contestants and reach the necklace." Prylek held up a crystal dangling on the end of a rope. "This will allow the winner to leave the forest and go on their pilgrimage. The winners before you have gone on theirs and found honor and meaning to their life. I hope the winner of the Ceremony can do so as well. To prove that you are strong like the Sovich before you, you must kill whoever you come into contact with.Good luck to all of you."

A covered metal carriage with two guards walking on both sides rolled into the village. Its ramp slammed into the dirt, causing several nearby Sovichs to flinch.

One of the guards stepped forward. "I will now call out the names of the Sovichs who will partake in the Ceremony."

"First is Thorn."

Thorn, pushed on by his mother, moved forward. He thanked the guard and boarded to polite applause.

"Second is Kargul."

Kargul rushed forward with a shout, knocking several others out of the way before making it to the ramp. He waved to the crowd before entering.

"Third is Naf."

Snickers followed Naf as he walked to the carriage. He didn't bother facing the crowd.

"Fourth is Roaz."

Roaz marched through the crowd, nodding to others as they gave him room. When he made it to the carriage, he gave a flourishing bow, which several people clapped to, and then disappeared in the darkness after Naf.

"Lastly, we have Tank."

Tank held his chin up as he strode toward the carriage. Sovichs stared at him as he walked by, someone patted him on the back, and his mother's muffled voice barely registered in his ears.

"Good luck, Tank!"

He forgot to wave.

———◆———

Tank's eyes never adjusted to the dark, and with every bounce, Naf kept shouldering him. The stuffy air didn't help the situation, and the presence of the other Sovichs made it tense and awkward. What do you say to someone when you've been training to kill them for the last year?

"So how have you all been?" Roaz said from the corner.

"Could be better," Kargul answered.

"Ready to be crushed?" Roaz replied. Whatever air had been in the carriage before disappeared, replaced by nothing but the cold realization of what they were about to do.

Tank breathed deeply. He could do this; he *would* do this. Naf bumped into his shoulder again, and he couldn't help thinking these might be the last moments they spent together as friends. After all these years, they had to be okay with ending the other's life. They had to forget all the good times they spent together. He shook the thought away.

"So what weapons were you all carrying when Prylek said the Ceremony was today?" Thorn asked. Tank scoffed under his breath. It was a silly question to ask. Who would reveal what weapon they would be using?

"Tank has two blasters," Naf said.

"Wow, I thought you and Tank were best friends," Roaz said.

"We're in the Ceremony now," Naf said with a note of finality.

Tank's heart stopped. They were all thinking the same thing. Tank had a massive target on his back.

"Too bad the Ceremony hasn't started already, huh Tank?" Thorn said.

A ball of rage settled in Tank's chest. If Naf hadn't opened his stupid mouth, they'd think he was starting on the same playing field as them.

Tank spat. "Naf has a spoon."

The rattle of the carriage came to a sudden stop. The ramp slammed down as a guard stood in the doorway, arms crossed.

"Tank, this is where you get off."

As Tank went to the door, the others stared at him, trying to get a good view of his face.

"Better watch out, Tank," Kargul called out.

In one motion, Tank pulled out his blaster and aimed into the carriage. Everyone ducked, and someone let out a scream.

Tank smirked. "Better watch out for me." He walked to the guard, who motioned him to get closer so the others wouldn't overhear.

"Tank, this is your starting point. You're not allowed to move until the flash goes up in the sky. Good luck." The guard climbed back in the carriage, and it drove away.

Tank stood there, taking his surroundings in. He had never been this far into the woods before. The sun was high above the trees, but his eyes had trouble adjusting to the darkness. His heart beat faster as the silence settled in, his hands going to his blasters every so often to make sure they were still there. He took one more deep breath.

I can win . . . right?

3

Tank scanned the area around him. Rocks, trees, shrubs. Everything could be used to hide in. Anytime something moved or made a sound, he pulled his blasters out. As he put them back in his holster, he thanked them silently for what must have been the fiftieth time.

Relax. It hasn't even started yet.

A flash went off suddenly, lighting up the woods. An outline of someone appeared in the distance, their head turned, and he immediately dove toward the nearest rock. If someone had already spotted him, he wasn't going to go down easy.

Shots blasted off in the distance. He poked his head out from behind the rock. They were gone. Were the woods quiet or had his ears suddenly stopped working? No, they were working because his heart pounded against his chest so hard it had to be giving his position away.

There was a rustle nearby, and Thorn passed him, heading toward the Center. He didn't have a weapon and seemed to be confused.

An easy kill.

Tank followed a ways behind, pulling out his blaster in case he turned around. Thorn walked between the bushes, rustling the leaves as he passed, sticks snapping under his feet. He approached a path, stopping to peer down each way.

This was it.

Tank took two leaps and wrapped his arm around Thorn's neck, pulling him back into the brush. Thorn struggled for air, reaching back and clawing at his face. Tank tightened his grip and shoved his blaster against Thorn's head. There was a bang, a splatter of blood, and the young Sovich went limp in his arms.

Tank set him on the ground, making sure he stayed out of sight. He did his best to wipe Thorn's blood off his arms but gave up after a bit.

A nearby yell reminded him of what he was doing. He sprinted across the path. The roar turned into a bloodcurdling scream. Tank tried to ignore it and keep moving, but a small cliff stopped his progress. He took a deep breath, reached up, and started climbing. As long as he got to the Center first, he would be okay.

The scream continued as he climbed, almost spurring him to go faster. When he reached the top, he peered over the edge to make sure no one else was there. He pulled himself up, just as the screaming stopped. Tank froze. What could possibly cause someone to stop screaming like that?

He didn't have time to think about it as someone tackled him from the side. They rolled a few times before Kargul had Tank pinned underneath him. Kargul reached for the blaster in his hand as Tank clawed at his face. The blaster flew several feet away.

Kargul pushed Tank into the dirt and raced over to it, Tank tried wildly to grab him, but he managed to get out of his reach. Kargul scooped up the blaster, turned, and aimed.

Tank dove just as the shot went over his head. He fumbled with his second blaster, trying to dodge a second shot. Finally, the blaster was free, and Tank pulled the trigger.

It missed.

They ran at each other, Tank hoping to catch him off guard, but Kargul punched Tank in the face, sending him to the ground again. Kargul pushed his foot into Tank's neck, aiming the blaster at his face.

He opened his mouth to say something, but an orange blur appeared on his back, clawing at his face. Kargul fell back, trying to grab Naf, but he was so small it did nothing. Tank aimed his blaster. He shot two times. One hit Kargul in the shoulder, the other in the face. His opponent stumbled and inched closer to the edge, falling over the cliff with Naf still on his back.

Kargul lay in a crumpled heap at the bottom of the cliff, blood already puddling around him. Naf rubbed his head nearby, glancing up at Tank.

Tank gave the thumbs-up, and Naf returned it. He held up Tank's blaster as if to say, *Do you want this back?* Tank waved his hand and mouthed *Keep it.*

Anything to help Naf stay alive a little longer. Tank turned and kept heading toward the Center. As he trekked through the forest, the same thought kept going through his mind.

Two down.

He made it to a path going in several directions. They seemed to be trying to throw him off. The left and right both looked the same. He knew he had to get to the Center, where the flash of light had gone off. Going straight would be the best option.

He didn't run into anyone for a while. The paranoia set in. What if Roaz made it to the Center and he ended up being the last one? Or maybe he was waiting for him to get there so they could ambush him? The shots and screams stopped. The trees thinned out as he got closer to the Center. He tried to hide behind rocks and in the brush, but they weren't big enough for him.

Finally, he saw it: the Center. The sun beamed through the trees, calling out to Tank to come closer. The coolness of the forest suddenly didn't seem as comforting as it always had. He pictured the light hitting his scales as he walked through the entrance. The warmth surrounding him as he won. He shook his head, trying to keep his thoughts clear.

He couldn't make out anything beyond the entrance to the clearing. Was he about to do it? Was he actually going to win the Ceremony? What would he say to his mother when he won? What would she tell him?

Tank walked toward the clearing when a deep, sharp voice rang out behind him. He whipped around and aimed, searching for the cause of the noise, but nothing appeared. The light from the clearing lit up everything in front of him. The voice sounded close, but no one was around. Tank held his blaster steady, searching for any sign of movement. A deep laugh rumbled through the trees.

Tank's heart sank. Roaz. Tank knew if he wanted to win, he would have to take him out. He took one last look at the Center, its bright light so inviting, and snuck toward Roaz's voice. As the voice got louder, he realized he was talking to someone. It was a Sovich he didn't recognize.

"You didn't see him anywhere?" Roaz asked.

The young Sovich rubbed his hands together, his eyes darting around. "No, I searched, but he must have slipped past me. I'm just one Sovich, I can't cover the whole forest."

Roaz put a hand on the younger Sovich. "Do you not remember what Prylek promised you if you did this for him?"

"I wouldn't have to be in the tournament."

"Do you remember what happened if you didn't do it?" Roaz tilted his head to the side.

"Not really." The younger Sovich shrank under Roaz's stare.

Roaz squeezed the younger one's head and tore it from his body, staring at its eyes which were still open wide with horror. The body slumped to the ground. Roaz smiled as blood ran down his arm. "That's what," he said, tossing the head aside.

Tank's tail twitched.

Fuck.

As though he could hear Tank's thoughts, Roaz turned around and caught sight of him, all his fangs showing as he flashed a wicked grin and charged toward him.

Tank fired. It found Roaz's shoulder, but he kept going as though it hadn't even touched him. Tank shot again, this time hitting his chest, but it still did nothing.

Roaz punched Tank in the snout. The world went fuzzy as he fell to the ground. He managed to look up just in time to see Roaz raising his foot.

Tank rolled out of the way as he stomped it on the ground and shot again. It had no effect as Roaz swiped at the blaster.

Tank raised his arm just in time for Roaz's sharp claws to dig into his scales. Cold blood ran down his arm. He backed away as fast as he could, trying to regain control. He rolled onto his stomach and sprinted toward the Center.

Roaz grabbed him by the tail, pulling him back.

Tank flailed and kicked to no avail. He was so close. He couldn't make it this far just for him to fail. This was his ticket out of here. He held his blaster steady and aimed at Roaz's hand. It hit right in the center.

Roaz growled and shook his hand, trying to get rid of the pain. Tank took the opportunity to jump up and tackle him to the ground. As Roaz gasped, Tank shoved his blaster in his mouth and fired.

The blast echoed throughout the woods. As Tank released him, he flopped to the ground and remained still, the hole in his head still smoking.

Nothing stood in Tank's way now. He didn't bother looking back as he ran through the trees. The sun was almost on his face. He would do it. He would be the winner. The clearing was so close. He practically fell through the opening in the trees.

A pedestal rested in the center on a small grassy hill, the necklace waiting for someone to take it.

Tank approached it when a single shot rang out, and fiery pain exploded in his shoulder. He dropped his blaster and looked frantically for where the shot came from.

Naf stood there, shaking and aiming Tank's blaster at him.

"Naf, put it down." Tank held out a hand, keeping himself between Naf and the necklace.

"Why should I?" Naf's eyes darted every which way as though he were searching for an answer to their situation that wasn't sitting in his hand. "I made it here first."

"Because I let you have the blaster," Tank said through clenched teeth, blood dripping from his wound.

Naf held steady. "I could have done it without it too."

"Why are you putting up a fuss now? You even said you didn't want to be sent away. You should be happy, it's just us." Tank held on to his shoulder. Why did Naf have to be a good shot when he was aiming at him?

"I never get to be the best at anything," Naf pled with Tank.

"We talked about this. We agreed to it. Don't go back on your word." There was a pause as they stared each other down. "You wouldn't shoot me, would you Naf?"

When this whole thing started, Tank was sure that Naf would get killed or if he was lucky, seriously injured. Ever since their conversation in the woods, he didn't think he would have to worry if, by sheer luck, it ended up being just them at the end.

But here they were. And now Tank doubted himself. Naf might actually kill him.

Naf stared at him. The blaster shook slightly in his hand. The seconds ticked by as neither one spoke. Naf finally threw the blaster at his feet. "No, you're right. You need to find your father." He breathed a sigh of relief. "Take it."

Tank held out his hand. "Shake on it."

Naf nodded.

They shook hands and made their way to the necklace. It sat on its pedestal, the light bouncing off its surface, giving it the illusion that it glowed. It was much smaller than Tank thought it would be. He lifted it off the stand and held it above his head. A loud horn blew throughout the woods.

He had won.

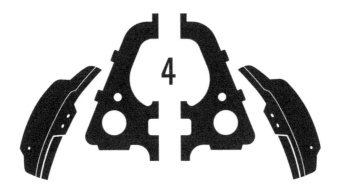

4

A loud beep followed by bright lights awoke Leo. The pit in his stomach started to spread. Why did he suddenly feel like this was a bad idea? He looked over at the still sleeping Gaeth. His chest wasn't rising, but that was normal for someone with his virus. The metal in his bones made it hard for him to move.

As the ship flew closer to Oblurn, Leo looked out the window to a small brown world, dark and devoid of any civilization. Had he been given the wrong coordinates? There was nothing but sand for miles. As he typed on the computer, a small dot appeared in the sand.

"Now approaching Oblurn," the computer chimed.

The ship landed roughly with a thump.

I thought Dad fixed the landing gears.

Gaeth had woken up and stared out the window. A giant domed building awaited them. The sun bounced off its rusty iron exterior, giving it the effect of a giant bug sitting in the sand. He turned to Leo with a wide-eyed, exasperated look. "This is where I'm living?" He sighed, slumping into his chair.

"Maybe it's an underground facility?"

Gaeth groaned, burying his head in his hands. "Are you sure there isn't some way for me to stay on Earth?"

Leo didn't know what to do. They had already landed, and if they took off now, Oblurn would know. Everyone on Earth watched them leave, and if they came back together, there was no telling what would happen to Gaeth.

Before Leo could say anything, there was a knock on the side of the ship. He checked the cameras and saw a human woman in a white lab coat. She smiled up at the camera and waved.

How creepy.

Leo sighed. "We can't leave now. But I'll keep my promise, okay?"

Gaeth nodded, not saying anything as he lowered the ramp where the woman waited.

"Welcome to Oblurn," she said, giving them a short bow. She spoke softly, but her voice carried an air of authority. "You are Gaeth Spearman, correct?"

"That's me," Gaeth said. He stood close to Leo as though if he ventured too far, he would be snatched away.

"We are delighted that you have decided to come to stay with us. If you would, please follow me." She turned and walked toward the domed building without looking to see if they followed.

Leo and Gaeth trailed behind. She led them to the front of the dome and placed her finger on the screen of a keypad that blinked

and beeped before going silent. The entryway
it rose slowly, sand raining off it. They walked in
large door. Before Leo could say anything, the
plunging them into complete darkness.

"Please wait while the decontamination pro   ⌐..⌐," a
smooth female voice said from some sort of speaker.

What sounded like massive hair dryers turned on all around them. A roaring wind whipped around them, almost knocking Leo to the ground. Gaeth grabbed his brother to keep them steady. Whatever sand had managed to make it in the chamber with them flew in all directions, stinging as it hit his skin. The air howled, pulling on Leo's clothes until he realized it wasn't being blown at them, it was being sucked out of the room. As soon as it started, it stopped.

"Decontamination process complete. Please proceed."

The door in front of them opened, and Leo shook his ashy hair out of his face.

"The decontamination is to get rid of the sand and other bacteria that might harm our guests. Filters line the wall in the chamber that helps us keep it out of the dome," the woman said matter-of-factly.

"You can't make a quieter process?" Leo asked.

"Nope." She flashed that weird smile she had used on the camera. It reminded Leo of a doll someone wanted to look like a human but couldn't get right. The woman continued, "For every new citizen of Oblurn, we offer a tour to help you get familiar with our facility. Please follow me and I'll take you to the first part of the tour."

"I don't know about this Leo," Gaeth said, rubbing his arm.

"Give it a chance, we haven't been here that long. Look at the positives. You know you'll be living in a clean place," Leo said.

They walked out of the chamber and into a plaza overlooking the whole dome. Everything from the floor to the ceiling was spotless. People of all ages walked through the plaza, going about their day. In the center stood a giant statue of a man, his entire body except his face covered in metal and wires. Before Leo could get a closer look, Gaeth pulled him to follow the woman in white. She led them to a door that blended in with the wall and held it open. Inside was a dark room with nothing but two chairs next to each other in the center.

The woman pushed them into the room and motioned them to sit. "After you complete the tour, I will come back and instruct you on what to do next." She hurried from the room.

It went completely dark, and the same voice from the decontamination chamber came on over speakers. "Welcome to Oblurn. If you're hearing this, then that means you've made your first step in creating a better future for yourself and your loved ones."

On the wall in front of them, in big blue letters, it said *Oblurn*.

"Our founder, Dr. Oswald Moon, was a scientist who loved to perform experiments. It was because of this curiosity that the Steel Elbow virus was born."

As the voice spoke, the blue letters turned into a blue figure picking up different vials. It drank one, then frowned. The tour zoomed in on its arm and showed its bones turning into metal.

"Once the people in his town found out about Steel Elbow, they became apprehensive that it might affect them too, and it did."

Blue figures appeared around the first one, and the bones in their arms turned to metal.

"In retaliation, they decided that Dr. Oswald needed to leave. But it wasn't enough to leave the town he lived in, they wanted him to leave the planet. So he did, and he found our planet, devoid of civilization, and built Oblurn for us."

The blue figure hopped in a spaceship and flew up to a planet, where it landed.

"Ever since then, anyone contaminated by the Steel Elbow virus is sent to Oblurn."

The tour zoomed out to show spaceships flying between Oblurn and Earth.

"We strive to make sure that any guest who stays with us will be taken care of in the best way possible. This means every day, you will go to sleep happy and healthy."

The planets turned into a little blue figure sleeping with a happy face.

"Because we are so dedicated to the well-being of our guests, we use a state-of-the-art decontamination process for everything coming in and out of our facility. Unfortunately for you and your loved ones, this means we try to have as little traffic into Oblurn as possible. After the initial tour, our guests aren't allowed any visitors."

The blue figure waved goodbye to a group of blue figures as he entered the dome.

"Every day, you will be given carefully crafted meals and take part in physical and social activities." The tour showed the blue figure eating food at a table, running, and talking to other blue figures with a smile on its face.

"If for some reason you are unable to take part in these activities, you will be taken to the medical wing to be evaluated." The scene morphed into the character sitting on a bed, frowning while a doctor examined it.

"We hope you enjoy your stay here at Oblurn as much as we enjoy having you here. If you have any questions at all during your tour, please don't hesitate to ask your tour guide. Before you continue, please make your way to the door on your left. Your tour guide will initiate the process of stopping your virus from spreading."

The blue lights disappeared, and a spotlight shone onto a metallic door on the other side of the room.

Leo glanced at Gaeth, his gut clenching uneasily. The voice in his head screamed for him to take Gaeth away from this place and never come back. But where would they go? They couldn't go back home, and how would they start a new life on another planet if they didn't want anyone to find out about Gaeth's Steel Elbow?

He stood and walked toward the door, but the presence of Gaeth next to him was missing. Leo looked back at his brother, still sitting in his chair, head down, playing with his hands. The silence in the room pounded in Leo's ears. He was so bad at making people feel better.

"Gaeth, in here." He pointed to the door.

"I want to leave," Gaeth whispered.

"It'll stop your virus from spreading," Leo said as he reached for the door. "If you won't do it for yourself, do it for Mom."

Gaeth stared at him, sighed, then ambled to the door. Leo gave him a reassuring pat on the back. The door opened, and they both stared in horror.

A surgical table waited for Gaeth. They tried to make it seem less intimidating with a pillow and several blankets on it, but there could be no ignoring the numerous instruments on the table or the bright light hanging overhead.

The woman in white appeared in front of them. "Lie on the table please," she said.

Gaeth shook his head. "I'm not sure about this anymore."

"It is required of all guests in Oblurn. It is a simple injection that will stop your virus from being contagious. Once it's complete, we will show you to your living space." She gave Leo her plastic smile.

"If it stops him from being contagious, he can come home, right?" Leo asked.

"I'm afraid not," she said. "We have had cases where the virus came back after we gave the patient the injection. It's safer for everyone if Gaeth stays here. Please wait out there, we will only be a moment."

She pulled Gaeth into the room and slammed the door in Leo's face. He pushed his ear against the door, trying to hear anything, but all the sounds were muffled. Walking back to the chairs, Leo collapsed. The gnawing feeling remained in the back of his mind. Everyone seemed so happy when they arrived, so why did he think Gaeth wouldn't be?

Perhaps because Leo knew he wouldn't see him again or because he had never been here before and wasn't sure how they

would treat Gaeth. His brother could be sensitive, and it was difficult for him to adjust to new situations. Leo put his face in his hands
and sighed. No point in overthinking it.

A scream erupted from the room.

Leo bolted toward the door and grabbed the handle, but it didn't
budge. He pounded on the door with his fist, screaming as loud as
he could. "Open this now."

He should have listened to Gaeth when he said he didn't want
to come. He should have just turned the ship around and gone
somewhere else. Leo spun around, searching for something, anything, that he could use to break the door open. His eyes fell on the
chairs, the only other thing in the room. He grabbed one, went back
to the door, and smashed the chair against it as hard as he could.
Once. Twice. Three times. It didn't do anything. Leo kicked it, knowing it wouldn't be effective either.

The door slammed open, and Gaeth stumbled out, clutching his
arm. Inside the surgical room, shattered glass lay on the floor in a
puddle of strange liquid. The woman in white didn't seem the least
bit worried.

"I can't do that." Gaeth stared down the woman with narrowed
eyes.

Leo moved Gaeth to stand behind him, his jaw set.

"That was only the medicine that stops it from being contagious.
I should have warned you it might be painful," she said firmly. "But
you will take the rest after you gather your belongings."

Leo pushed Gaeth back, putting as much distance between his brother and the woman as he could. He should have listened to Gaeth when he had the chance.

"We'll go get his things. They're still on the ship."

"I'll escort you." The woman tilted her head and flashed her annoying smile once more.

———◆———

Leo pushed Gaeth ahead of him as they walked to the ship. The woman had guards behind her as she followed them, as though they were summoned out of thin air. It was like she could read Leo's mind and knew what he planned to do next.

As they arrived at the ship, Leo's mind raced. How was he supposed to get Gaeth out of here while avoiding two Oblurn guards and the woman in white? The ramp on the ship lowered.

"After you." The woman in white motioned for them to go first.

Shit.

Leo walked up first with Gaeth following right behind him. When he reached the button to raise the ramp, he looked back to make sure Gaeth was with him. He wasn't expecting the woman in white to be boarding the ship too. She had likely followed to make sure he wouldn't do exactly what he planned to do.

He led her to the back where Gaeth's things were. Luckily Gaeth packed a lot, so they all had to carry something. She picked up a bag, Gaeth picking up a particularly big box, while Leo trailed behind them. Gaeth took his time walking back to the entrance of the ship. His eyes were wet as he looked around the ship one last time before following the woman down the ramp.

As Leo stood at the top of the ramp, he watched Gaeth follow the woman. His mind spun. He missed his chance, and now there was no going back. But if these were the last few moments he spent with Gaeth, then he'd make the most of them.

Before he had a chance to start down the slope, Gaeth held the box over his head and threw it as hard as he could. It hit the woman in the back of the head, and she tumbled the rest of the way down. Gaeth raced back up toward Leo, but a guard managed to grab his foot.

Leo grabbed Gaeth's hand, pulling him toward the top of the ship as hard as he could. It didn't help Gaeth's metal bones made him more cumbersome. The guard didn't let up, pulling harder.

Leo searched for anything that could help him. The ramp button hung on the wall. He reached out to touch it, but it stayed just out of reach. Gaeth kicked at the guard, desperately trying to escape.

The guard's hands slipped, and Gaeth became free. Leo pushed the button, and the ramp slowly began to rise. He pulled Gaeth back into the ship and pushed the button for the emergency door to go down, trapping the guard between the ramp and the door. The door shut with a satisfying click and Leo jumped into the pilot seat. With nowhere to go, the Oblurn guard pounded on the door.

Leo didn't bother with the routine checklist as his hands darted across the controls. The engine roared to life, and the computer beeped. "Safety issue. Person in ramp area. Please remove before liftoff."

"We can't put the ramp down," Gaeth said in a shrill voice. "Who knows how many guards they might bring back by the time we lower it?"

The banging on the door and the guard's muffled yelling on the other side didn't help the situation.

Leo shut his eyes and took a deep breath. "I can override the warning."

"But the air will be sucked out, and he'll die," Gaeth said.

As if the guard could hear their conversation, his screams became more frantic.

"It's that, or you stay here." He didn't bother listening to Gaeth's answer as he typed furiously. The warning disappeared, giving him the clear to take off. "Sit down," Leo demanded.

Gaeth jumped in his seat as they shot off, leaving a cloud of sand in their wake.

5

The necklace stayed warm against Tank's scales as he and Naf marched into the village.

As they approached, a young Sovich spotted them. His eyes went wide, as he yelled, "They made it back! Tank has the necklace!" A moment later Tank couldn't tell what was going on as numerous Sovichs rushed at him. Some shouted their congratulations, while others patted him on the back before yelling to their friends they had touched the winner.

Tank and Naf were separated as Tank was pulled into the crowd, the flag already flying high on the speech platform. Prylek waited for him with open arms, his fangs showing through his broad grin. Behind him stood a few guards, waiting to help Tank up. The villagers cheered with every step he took, the necklace swung gently from his neck.

Tank's heart was pulled in two separate directions. He was going to go on his pilgrimage. He was going to find his father and bring him back. Tank had trained so hard for this moment and now it was all becoming a reality.

But over the cheering, he could make out the crying of other Sovichs. They would never forgive him for what he did today. He kept his eyes on Prylek.

"Tank." Prylek beamed. "You have proven to not only yourself, your village, but your ancestors before you, that you truly have what it takes to be a Sovich." Several villagers roared at his words.

"You have the strength, wisdom, and courage holding our people together. For that, you were able to make it to the Center and retrieve a piece of our ancestors. Please hand it to me."

Tank stood up and pulled the necklace over his head. Prylek's claws wrapped around it as he gazed at the stone.

"Tank, after tonight, your pilgrimage begins. You will be sent away from our village to find your reason and give the necklace away. Do you accept this?"

"Yes," Tank said.

With one hand, Prylek held the necklace above his head, and with the other, he grabbed Tank's hand and held it up. "Our yearly ceremony has once again come to an end. While over the next few days we will search the woods for the dead, tonight we celebrate Tank."

The Sovichs roared in unison, some chanting Tank's name, others jumping up and down. Tank scanned the crowd for his mother or Naf but couldn't find either of them. He would search for them later.

The night was consumed by celebrations. Tank was bombarded with the best cooked meat and his cup of water was kept full while he told the story of how he won over and over again. The other So-vichs listened tentatively as they sat in a circle around one of the many lit fires. Many were perplexed Naf was the last one to make it with him. Tank wasn't sure how to explain the truth, but someone would say something like "he probably tripped and ended up in the Center." Tank laughed it off, never mentioning how Naf singlehand-edly saved him from Kargul.

As Tank walked back to the platform where the food had been laid out, he spotted one of the younger Sovichs playing with this blaster.

"Thank you."

"I know you want to give your father the necklace. Even if you don't find him, I'm still very proud of you, alright?" She patted him on the back before walking back into the crowd.

Tank held tight to the necklace, watching her leave. He didn't want to disappoint her.

The night grew dark, and fires were lit around the village as the celebrations continued. All night Tank kept an eye out for Naf but he couldn't find him. He eventually found him eating away from the others. "What are you doing here?"

"You wanted to soak up all the attention, so I figured I'd let you." Naf took a huge bite of his food, keeping his eyes down.

"You know this is what happens when someone wins the Cere-mony." Tank laughed. "We do this every year."

"But this could have been my year," Naf said through a mouth-ful of food.

Tank sat next to him. "Naf, every time we've trained in the woods, I've always beaten you. The only reason I'm doing this is to find my father."

"Is it?" Naf spat. "You're having a lot of fun for someone who's being shipped off on their pilgrimage tomorrow."

"So I'm not allowed to have fun before I leave? Is that it?"

"I was this close to winning and you took it from me." Naf finally looked Tank in the eyes. "I don't care you want it more than me. I made it to the Center first."

"What happened to our conversation in the woods?" Tank's shoulders tensed, and he waved his arms around. "What happened to the Naf who said if he had to pick between me and winning the Ceremony, he would choose me? You told me you would let me win."

Naf stood and walked away, but before Tank could follow him, someone had grabbed his shoulder and pulled him back toward the crowd. "We can't keep partying if we don't have you!"

After a while, Prylek got on the platform again. "It's time for the festivities to end. Another Ceremony is complete."

Everyone clapped and said their goodbyes. Tank slowly made his way to his hut amidst everyone still congratulating him. He had half a mind to find Naf, but his muscles were too sore.

If he wants to be like this, let him.

He entered his hut, which was full of gifts from the villagers. Different food and weapons they wanted him to take on his journey lined the wall. He smiled again. The thought that he had won crept back into his mind, making him sigh. He collapsed on his bed, falling asleep to the thought of walking through the gate of the village with his father, straight to his mother, seeing her face when she realized who he was. He had never been happier.

Bang!

Tank shot up and looked around. The fires had been put out, the moon being the only source of light. He reached toward his blaster, listening for anything outside. Nothing.

Someone isn't ready to stop the festivities.

He laughed to himself, laid back down, and closed his eyes.

There was a loud knock on his door as two of Prylek's guards walked into Tank's hut. They held their blasters out as though worried someone might start shooting. Tank already had his blaster aimed at them. No one moved for a moment before one of the guards spoke.

"Prylek wants to speak with you before your pilgrimage in the morning."

"What about?" Tank asked, searching for an answer in either of their expressions.

"I don't know." The guard's tail twitched back and forth. "We were just sent to come to get you."

Tank finally lowered his blaster. This was probably another test of some sort to make sure he was ready to go on his pilgrimage. "Where are we going?"

"We'll fly you there. You don't need to bring any weapons."

It's a test.

Tank put his blaster back on the wall and followed them out of his hut where two helibikes were already on and waiting. Tank squeezed into an attached sidecar before they took off. At first, he thought they were going to Prylek's hut, but they turned toward the gate and headed into the woods. The lights from the helibikes bounced off the forest walls as they zipped between trees and brush. Perhaps because it was nighttime or because they had gone so far, Tank couldn't recognize anything. He had been there so many times he felt he could navigate it with his eyes closed, but the guards were flying through places he'd never been.

They'll probably want me to find my way back in the dark.

The trees opened up to a small moonlit clearing. The guards flew to the center, and the helibikes landed. It was then Tank realized how quiet the woods were. How alone they really were. He hopped out and walked around the clearing, taking in his surroundings. If he was going to have to find his way back to the village, then he needed to figure out the easiest way to do so.

A third helibike flew into the clearing. It was Prylek. He set his bike down a few feet away. The guards grabbed Tank on either side and forcefully held him down to the ground. A guard pulled his head up and Prylek marched toward him, holding a spike blade. His heart started racing as he realized this wasn't a test.

"Prylek, what's—"

Prylek kicked him in the face, and he fell backward. The world went dark as his vision blurred. Tank's head throbbed as he shook it, trying to regain his sight.

He finally did, just as the moonlight caught the spike blade Prylek held over his head. Tank rolled to the side, but he wasn't fast enough. Blinding white pain filled his senses. Nothing else existed but pain. The noise that escaped him was so loud and agonizing, he was sure someone would come find him.

My hand. My hand.

He looked over to assess the damage. Blood gushed out of where his hand used to be, the tendons hanging limply in the air. His mangled scales littered the ground around them as the guards picked him up under the arms to face Prylek.

"The party was fun," he said, flicking a piece of Tank's flesh off the spike blade. "Did you feel special? Excited to go find someone to give the necklace to?" He grabbed Tank's chin and yanked it up. "Look at me, Tank."

Tank's eyes fluttered as they focused on Prylek. "Is this part of the Ceremony?" he managed, hoping against hope his leader would say yes.

Prylek laughed. "Did you hear that? He still thinks this is part of the Ceremony." He let Tank's face drop and moved closer, whispering, "You and I both know you're more observant than that Tank. Look around you."

Tank's eyes shifted in the darkness. Prylek stared at him, the spike blade hanging loosely at his side. Neither guard said anything; the only sound was the low hum of the helibikes as they floated above the grass. The helibikes—if he could just jump on one, then he could fly out of here.

"Still nothing?" Prylek asked.

"I don't know," Tank said. Anything that might give him more time to think.

"Tank, I'm going to kill you," Prylek said matter-of-factly. "I kill all the Sovichs who win the Ceremony. How do you think I've been the Sovich leader for as long as I have? Get rid of the strong ones every year."

"But that would mean my father is—"

There was a rustling in a bush nearby, causing Prylek's head to snap up; he motioned to one of the guards. As the guard walked toward the noise, Naf fell out of the bush, then clumsily picked himself up and wiped the dirt off himself.

He stopped when his eyes fell on the scene in front of him. The spike blade in Prylek's hands glistened with crimson blood, the two guards holding Tank down on his knees, his arm bleeding profusely.

Prylek threw down his blade and pulled out a blaster.

Naf just stood there, still glancing between Prylek and Tank, apparently unsure of what to do. "I heard everything. I know what you were going to do to him."

Prylek held his blaster steady. "Come here and let me talk to you for a moment."

Tank struggled against the guards' grip until one of them punched him. "Naf, he'll try to kill you. He's killed every winner of the Ceremony. He killed my father. He would have killed you if you had won."

Staring at Tank, Naf slowly inched toward Prylek. Naf finally closed the distance between him and Prylek. He lunged for the blaster, trying to wrestle it out of Prylek's hands, causing a shot to go off into the sky. The guards dropped Tank and rushed to help Prylek.

Tank forced himself to his feet and ran toward the nearest helibike. He jumped on, shooting through the woods. One wrong move and there would be nothing left of him for Prylek to find. There was a flash of light behind him; the guards had followed him. The lights of the helibikes flickered in between the trees as they darted through the forest. Tank held on as best he could, his right hand tightly on the handlebar, his left arm tucked under his chest.

The side of the helibike smashed into a tree, the bark scratching his shoulder. The front wheel started wobbling, but he steadied himself. He couldn't tell if he was heading toward the village or somewhere new. Rocks and brush stuck out as if they were all trying to grab him. He flew down a small hill and saw the trees open up into another clearing.

Had he circled back around?

A blast rocketed over his shoulder, hitting a nearby tree and sending splinters in every direction that left smoldering holes. Tank pushed the bike to go faster. It groaned under strain. He would take his chances.

The clearing wasn't a clearing at all but a giant field. He raced across the grass, trying to push his bike faster. The guards' voices became louder. The booster light suddenly lit up, and he pressed it. The helibike shot forward.

But there was no more ground in front of him. He pushed the brakes, but it was too late. He careened over the edge, losing his grip on the bike, his arms flailing as he fell to the junkyard below.

He landed on the side of a junk pile, rolling the rest of the way down, until he plopped in a mud puddle with a splash.

Tank lay at the bottom, not moving. His body was in so much pain. He opened his eyes, trying to bring the world into focus, blinking a few times. The helibike was utterly destroyed, he was at the bottom of a pile of metal debris, and the guards' voices carried over the junkyard from the top of the cliff. If he could stay still and wait for them to leave, maybe he would be okay.

"You think he made it?"

"No way. He wouldn't survive that fall."

"Should we check for him? At least bring a body back to Prylek?"

Tank tried to move. He needed to keep moving if he didn't want to be found. But the guard's voices faded away as his body pulled him into unconsciousness.

———◆———

Tap. Tap. Tap.

Tank opened his eyes. The sun hadn't come up yet, and he couldn't see anything in the dark. He let his head rest back on the ground where it sank into the mix of mud and blood.

He didn't even care. His leader, his way of life, everything he'd ever known. It had all been a lie? Did this mean his father was really dead? Did his mother know? He held his arm up, staring at the place where his hand had been. It was hard to look at, and thinking about it made it worse. Tank cradled his arm to his chest and growled to himself. How could he have missed Prylek's intentions? There had to have been signs. But the pain was all that clouded his vision.

Tap. Tap. Tap. Tap.

The rain fell harder now, sinking him further into the mud.

What had he done wrong? All the times he had practiced hunting with Naf in the woods, picked out the perfect blaster, made sure to study every aspect of battle he could to get to the Center. And now here he was, at the bottom of a junkyard.

"It didn't matter." Tank covered his eyes.

Taptaptaptaptaptaptap.

He shot to his feet, the mud sticking to his scales, and gasped when he peered up and saw the top of the cliff was so high it was surprising he was still alive. The guards chasing him were nowhere in sight either.

But that didn't mean they weren't still searching for him.

A faint light shone on the opposite side of the junkyard. Tank stumbled through a jungle of metal and forgotten spaceships. All he could think about was Prylek.

No. He couldn't go back and tell the entire village everything Prylek had ever told them was a lie, or the Ceremony they celebrated every year was set up to keep their leader in power. What if in a moment of weakness he had let Naf take the necklace? Naf might be dead right now.

Tank growled at the thought.

He would come back. And he would make sure everyone knew what was really going on. For now, he needed to get out of this hole. He was injured, trapped, and without a weapon.

A small blanket hanging on some scrap metal caught his eye. Tank wrapped the cloth around the stump where his hand used to be, anything to soak up the blood. It was hard to make out the color as it was caked in mud. Then he ripped off a piece and used it to tie the blanket in place. The pressure didn't help, but he kept walking.

The faint light was brighter now, taking up the sky. It was barely visible as Tank reached the edge of the crater, the junk piling to the top. He took a deep breath, bared his teeth, and dug his claws into the metal pile, pulling himself up.

It wasn't as easy as he thought it would be. The pile wasn't steep, but little pieces of metal kept poking his feet. He made his way slowly, every so often glancing up at the glowing light past the edge of the crater.

The pile became steeper, and he reached for a slim pole sticking out right above his head. It smoothly slid out of its place. Tank tried to grab something with his other hand, only to remember he no longer had another hand. He tumbled backward down the slope, landing with a thump at the bottom.

Taptaptaptaptaptaptaptaptap.

He stared up through the rain at the taunting bluish glow, determined to find out what was causing it.

"Stupid light," Tank said he eyed the hill and backed up, giving himself a lot of room. With a running start, he sprinted toward the mount and climbed up, barely touching the hill.

Just like the river.

The lights at the top grew brighter. Tank was almost there, and a small voice in his head pushed him to move faster. He grabbed the edge of the crater and pulled himself up.

Ahead of him in the distance, a shining city illuminated the night sky. A small ship flew into it, lost in the hundreds of others darting in and out of the buildings. Tank stood there dumbstruck. How had this been near his home all this time, and he had never known? Well, there was probably more Prylek hadn't told them.

He had been walking toward the city for a while, the junkyard far behind him, when he spotted a large ship landing just outside. It had a green B on the side of it with the saying *Bisekt! We are your home away from home*. Two pilots walked away from the ship into a nearby store as a worker from the refueling station pushed a hose into the vessel.

I need to get on that ship.

The woman walked away from the hose and Tank snuck up the ramp. It was big. He could easily find a hiding spot. Racing to a large storage area in the back, he ducked between the different boxes and containers, making sure he was comfortable before leaning against the wall.

There were a few moments of muffled voices, and then the ship rumbled. If it weren't for the fact that the blanket tied around Tank's arm was soaked through with blood, or that he had been running on adrenaline and his blood was pumping faster than usual, he would have been excited he was flying on a spaceship for the first time.

Instead, he passed out.

6

After escaping Oblurn, Gaeth had fallen asleep in his seat. Leo let him sleep and kept checking the monitors for any sign that Oblurn was sending someone after them. If they appeared, he wanted to be ready to jump into hyperspace. He tapped Gaeth on the shoulder. "Hey. Wake up."

Gaeth looked up at him, stretching as he looked out the window. "What's going on?"

"We need to figure out where we're going now."

Gaeth's eyes widened. "I thought we were going home?"

Leo sighed. "I told you we can't go back home. They'll make you go back to Oblurn. I promised Mom and Dad I would take you there, and if they found out you didn't go, I'm not sure how they would react."

Gaeth's eyes narrowed. "So we find another planet to live on."

"What happens when they find out about your virus? You think they'll be okay with it?" Leo asked. "We can't take the chance, especially if Oblurn's guards are looking for you."

"So what do we do then?"

"Well," Leo said slowly, "I've been doing some research while you were sleeping and there's a place where we can go and not have to worry about Oblurn chasing us. Anyone part of the law can't chase us." He searched Gaeth's face for a reaction.

"You mean, become a criminal?" Gaeth asked. "That's what you're saying, isn't it?"

"Not a criminal, just a couple of jobs to make some money. Then maybe we can look for a planet off the grid that you can live on," Leo said matter-of-factly. "I've been thinking about it, and it's the only way to keep you safe, and Mom and Dad happy."

"A couple jobs doesn't mean running errands. We could end up doing something dangerous," Gaeth whined.

"But it's that, or we go back to Oblurn," Leo said.

That shut Gaeth up. "I'm not going back to Oblurn," he whispered.

"The nearest place I could find was a station called New Star City. Not too far." Leo glanced at Gaeth, who was playing with the thread on the seat again. "Are you okay?"

"I'm fine."

"I heard you scream, you know."

Gaeth crossed his arms and pinched the bridge of his nose. He kept his head down, trying to make himself as small as possible. "She had two needles. She said the first one would stop the virus from being contagious. I like to think I'm not a hypochondriac, but it was the most painful thing I've ever gone through. I don't know if it's because I'm . . ." He stopped, unable to find the right words. "Because the Steel Elbow makes it harder for the injection to work or what, but it was terrible."

Leo's throat went dry. So they went through that whole tour, the woman in white flashing her stupid smile the entire time, and in the end, they treated Gaeth like some experiment.

How real was everything on the tour? Would they have given him "carefully crafted food" or was that bullshit too? The more he thought about it, the happier he was that he had taken Gaeth away from that place.

"So you got the first injection then? You aren't contagious anymore?" Leo asked. Maybe they could convince their parents to let him live at home. If he wasn't contagious, why would that matter?

They'll hunt him down if they find out what he is.

His heart sank as he remembered his father's words.

"Yeah, but it still hurts where she put it." Gaeth rubbed his arm. "I'm glad you came in when you did. I don't think I could have taken the other one."

Leo smiled. "I promised I would get you out of there if I thought they weren't treating you right."

They kept on flying in silence. Soon they were near a red planet with a large space station orbiting it. There were several domes on it with towers sticking out of them. The bottom of the station was completely dark, except for what looked like millions of little lights sprinkled throughout it. The spaceship shook as it passed through their shield. They flew around New Star City up to a landing pad jutting out of the station. Leo landed perfectly, and they were pulled inside. Once all the way in, the gate shut behind them.

A small man ran up to the ship with a sign that read*Free Parking*

"I guess we'll just stay here then." Leo shrugged. "Free is free right?"

Gaeth went to the back of the ship. "It's probably best if we wear different clothes," he said. "And try to cover yourself as much as possible so no one can see your face."

Gaeth settled on a leather jacket and gloves with long pants and boots. His turtleneck covered everything up to his chin. He grabbed a beanie and pulled it down to his eyebrows.

"It won't be snowing in there." Leo raised an eyebrow. "You sure you need all that?"

"Can't be too careful," Gaeth said. " You should put something on too so no one will recognize you."

Leo rummaged through the back and found a jean jacket and a scarf. He threw them on and looked at Gaeth. "Good?"

"Yeah. Pull it up a little so that your mouth is covered." Leo did so.

When they were ready to go, Leo pushed the button for the ramp.

The door slid up, the ramp lowered, and the Oblurn guard's body rolled down until it landed roughly at the bottom.

"Shit."

Gaeth moved to pull him back into the ship, but Leo stopped him. "He'll stink up the whole ship. We should hide him."

"You think no one will notice a body smelling up the place?" Gaeth replied.

Leo looked around the hangar. The man with the *Free Parking* sign had gone back to his chair in the corner and had somehow fallen asleep in the time it took them to put the ramp down. The hangar was big enough for one ship, and no one else was there. He spotted the entrance where they had come in. The expanse of space looked like a wall of black against the white interior of the space station.

Leo pointed to the entrance. "We'll throw him out."

"What if someone sees him?" Gaeth looked around as though waiting for someone to catch them in the act.

Leo threw a glance at the sleeping man. "Do it quick before anyone sees it."

They picked up the guard by the arms and legs and carried him toward the entrance. They stood next to it, the void strangely calling to Leo. With three big swings, they tossed the guard through the shield, and he floated away from the station, still not moving.

"Never tell anyone." Leo shook a finger in Gaeth's face.

"About what?" Gaeth asked.

"Exactly."

They crept by the man, whose snores echoed in the hangar, to an elevator made entirely of glass that opened automatically. There was one button on the wall. Leo pushed it, and his stomach flipped as they shot downward. Lights flashed by faster and faster as they zoomed through a tube when they came out on the edge of a building, overlooking New Star City.

Buildings stretched on for what looked like miles. Cars zoomed back and forth on the crowded streets at horrific speeds, but it was nothing compared to the horrid stench that assaulted his senses when the doors opened. The smell stopped Leo in his tracks as a mix of oil and body odor filled his senses. People walked by, trying to get to their destinations, men wearing suits, women carrying strange animals, a few aliens with blasters bigger than Leo's head draped over their shoulders.

"We'll just ask one of these people for a job, and they'll give us money, and we'll be on our way," Leo said, trying to keep the mood up.

"Hmm," Gaeth answered.

"Shut up." Leo rolled his eyes. The neon lights made it hard to see anyone. Everything seemed so chaotic, he didn't know where to start. No one spared them a glance as they walked by.

A Kekzin, a giant cockroach creature, dressed in a green tailored suit wandered up to them. He went up to Leo's knees, but he gave off the vibe of someone that towered over everyone else.

"You want something, fella?" he asked Leo. "You've never been here before, I can tell."

Leo wasn't sure what to do. "We have, we're just looking for a friend."

"What's his name? I know everyone in this city." The Kekzin's eyes bulged out of his head as he focused on Leo.

"Oh, I think I see him over there." Leo walked away, motioning for Gaeth to follow.

They walked down an alleyway, the neon lights giving it a soft pink glow. Gaeth caught up to Leo, slightly out of breath. "We haven't even been here a minute, and already someone's suspicious of us."

67

"Let's try this place," Leo said, determined to prove Gaeth wrong.

They entered a dark building, whose own neon sign barely lit up. Gaeth followed him through the door, and their eyes adjusted to the darkness as the loudness of the streets turned into the ruckus of the patrons in the bar laughing and talking over one another. Some yelled for more drinks, while others showed off their blasters. A large circular table sat in the center of the bar where most of the patrons stood as they watched a tiny alien move different cards back and forth to several tense players.

"Put your bids up," the dealer said. He had ten eyes, all of them were pointed in different directions. One stayed on each of the players, another scanned the crowd, and one focused on the card in front of him. "Bids done, cards played. Dealer up." He pulled a card out of the pile next to him and put it face up on the table. The crowd cheered as one patron stood while the dealer pushed a massive pile of tokens toward him, his eyes never stopping.

Booths were built into the wall along the back of the bar with heavy curtains on either side. The people sitting in them leaned into each other, whispering. A hand completely closed the curtain on either side of the booth. In the corner, a man played guitar and sang in a language Leo never heard before.

A waitress walked up to them with a giant smile on her face. "Would you like a normal seat or private seat?"

"Private?" Leo said a little too slowly.

She looked him over once before motioning them to follow her.

She led them past the table where the crowd let out a groan. A tall blue patron with webbed hands slammed his cards on the table and pulled out a blaster, pointing it at the dealer.

"That was fixed! There's no way you would get two numbers three times in a row!"

The dealer pulled out his own blaster and shot the patron in the face. He fell on the table, sending blood and tokens in every direction. The other patrons dove for them, tearing at each other to get as many as they could. The dealer signaled to someone and a few moments later an alien identical to the dealer, but much taller, took the dead patron away.

Another alien took the empty space, the green suit catching Leo's eye. The Kekzin they had run into earlier sat down at the table.

"The usual amount, Scril?"

"Do you even need to ask?" Scril replied.

The dealer pushed a large number of tokens toward him and started the game again.

The waitress held the curtains open for Leo and Gaeth. When they sat down, she tied the curtains back so they wouldn't be in her way. "So what'll you have today?"

Leo glanced at Gaeth, who looked just as confused as he felt.

"We'll both have the . . . uh special?"

"Uh-huh. I'll have it sent to you in a second." She smiled as she let the curtains shut, her heels clicking away.

"Do you have money to pay for this?" Gaeth asked Leo. "And how is this supposed to get us a job?"

"I'm trying to figure it out right now, let me think," Leo snapped.

"Leo, why would you tell them to seat us when we don't have any money?" Gaeth whispered frantically.

"We could try to play a game." Leo motioned toward the table.

"Did you see what happened to that guy?" Gaeth looked down at his hands. "Maybe this was a bad idea."

The eerily quiet booth made Leo tired, the only light coming from a single bulb above them, giving it a faint glow. He glanced down at the table. There were burn marks and a bullet hole. He noticed a stain he couldn't categorize, but he didn't want to think about it.

The curtains flew open. The waitress was back, empty handed with a scowl on her face.

"I'm going to have to ask you to leave," she said with a stern voice. "We don't serve people who can't pay."

The waitress held back the curtain for Leo and Gaeth and motioned for them to follow her. Behind her, the table of patrons let out a groan as Scril stood on the table, pulling more tokens toward himself.

"I didn't know this was beginner's night," he said, stuffing tokens in his pockets. "I was hoping for some sort of challenge. Should I charge for lessons? I can't promise you'll get better seeing how abysmal you've all been playing." The others rolled their eyes at him.

Leo and Gaeth followed the waitress past the table of patrons who were still cheering but stopped when Scril's voice rang out over the bar.

"I know that face. I've seen it too many times. That's the face she makes when someone can't pay." Scril hopped off his stool and stood in front of the waitress. "I just won a decent pot, and I'm feeling a little generous. Give them their food and put it on my tab."

"I'm already taking them out, Scril," she said.

"We can get it to go," Scril replied.

Scril snapped his fingers, and two monstrous aliens appeared on either side of Leo and Gaeth. Scril made his way to the door and before calling over his shoulder. "Make sure you send it to Vanish's office please."

Leo had barely any time to wonder who Vanish was or what was going on when a muscled alien grabbed Leo firmly by the arm and pushed him through the crowd. The man was still playing his guitar with no one watching as they walked into the artificial brightness of New Star City. Scril stood in the street, tapping his foot. "Today was supposed to be my day off," he said, playing with a token. "But you want to know what happened?"

Leo glanced at Gaeth then back to Scril. "What happened?"

"You two showed up and threw a body out of a hangar." Scril threw the token on the ground. "I had the day all planned out too."

"You know about that?" Leo tried to think of anything he could say to make the situation better. "I'm sorry," he finally said.

"Me too," Gaeth chimed in.

Scril's eyes narrowed. "Well, we're taking you to Vanish. She wants a word."

He stomped down the road, the guards pushing Leo and Gaeth after him. Leo tried to look over his shoulder to see if Gaeth was nearby, but the guard smacked his head forward.

Scril stopped at a wall and pushed a button Leo hadn't noticed before. They must have passed it the first time they walked by. The wall dinged and slid open to reveal a hidden elevator. Before he could stare too long, they were ushered quickly inside. The elevator descended on its own. No one spoke.

When it stopped, the doors opened to a room with a glass floor. Leo's stomach did a flip as he looked through the glass floor at the expanse of space below him, the nearby red planet being the only visible object. The room barely held any furniture except for one chair at the end, upon which sat an older woman. Numerous pieces of jewelry weighed down her body, the red planet's light bouncing off her rings and bracelets.

Scril motioned to the woman as they walked toward her. "May I introduce Vanish?" he said with a flourish. "She runs this space station."

Vanish leaned forward to get a better view as they came in. "Leo Spearman and Gaeth Spearman," she said slowly. "I wondered when you would show up in my office."

"How do you know our names?" Gaeth asked as they came to a stop in front of her.

She smiled. "Nothing on New Star City is really free, hon."

"That's illegal," Leo said, annoyed.

"Not here." Vanish smirked. "And next time you get rid of a dead body, maybe don't do it in a hangar with security cameras. This is a space station after all; we still care about safety. It was ridiculously easy to follow you." She took a sip of water. "I understand Gaeth has a bit of a secret. How long have you had Steel Elbow?"

"Since I was young," he said.

She gave a small laugh and then motioned to the guard behind them. He stepped forward and grabbed Gaeth's arm. He pulled his glove off, where the metal visibly pushed against his skin.

"I can tell you're telling the truth. Well, you've probably come here looking for work, and by now you've figured out finding it on a space station full of criminals isn't as easy as you thought." Her eyes lit up. "I'm feeling charitable today, so you can work for me."

Leo didn't like how easy this seemed. They just walked in and were offered a job like that? Something was weird about it.

"How do you know all of this?" he asked.

Scril laughed next to him.

"Honey, I don't think you get it yet," Vanish said. "You flew to a space station housing the most dangerous people in the galaxy, threw out a dead body in plain sight of cameras, and you think we wouldn't tail you? Scril found you as soon as you were on the street."

The elevator dinged again, and the waitress from earlier walked in with a bag of food. She set the bag on a nearby table and disappeared as quickly as she had come.

Leo and Vanish locked eyes for a while, each waiting for the other to say something. When it was clear Vanish wouldn't speak, Leo said, "We'll look for jobs elsewhere."

Vanish smirked, raising an eyebrow. "Then I'll just make a quick call to Oblurn and tell them one of their patients is in New Star City."

Leo glanced at Gaeth, who eyed the room nervously. The whole reason they had come here was to find a job, and now that it had landed in their laps, he should be thankful.

"Fine, we'll do it," he said unenthusiastically.

"Good." She smiled at them. "Your first job is to kill the alien spreading lies about me at the spa. His name is Felgi, and he works for the Sol Empire. There'll be a picture of him on your ship, so you know what he looks like. Use whatever means necessary. As long as he's dead when you come back here, you'll receive your payment."

Scril jumped in front of them. "Sonja is there too; she's been collecting information on the Sol Empire for us. We're picking her up."

Gaeth stared wide-eyed as they talked. "The Sol Empire?"

"You've never heard of them?" Vanish peered between the two. "Tell me you two have at least heard of Onyx?"

Leo shook his head.

"Oh, boy." Scril rubbed his head. "You're in New Star City. How do you not know? It's Onyx's home base."

"It doesn't matter." Vanish waved a hand in the air, her jewelry clinging together. "Congratulations. You're part of Onyx now. We work to stop the Sol Empire from trying to take away our freedom. If it weren't for us, they might already control everyone in the galaxy."

"You're talking to the leader of Onyx." Scril pointed at Vanish. "She's been doing this for years."

"We've been able to stop them in smaller ways," Vanish said. "Intercept messages, switch some of their people to our side, and even capture a small ship. But I want to do something on a big scale. Something that will really put a dent in their plans. Which is why we need you two to help. No one has met you yet. It'll be easy for you to get close to Felgi."

"We'll still get paid?" Leo asked.

"Of course."

Leo sighed. "We'll do it."

"I know," Vanish said. She nodded at the guards, who ushered them back to the elevator. Scril squeezed in with them, straightening his tie, and escorted them all the way back to their ship. As Leo and Gaeth boarded, they realized he followed them onto the ship.

"Did you think we would let you fly off the station alone?" Scril asked to their astonished faces. "Get going."

The pain in Tank's arm jolted him awake. He hissed, reaching for it, only to find his arms chained down, keeping him sitting on the concrete floor. Confusion set in as the metal bars surrounding him came into focus. A strange smell filled his nose. Clean, but too clean. A machine outside the cage glowed and moved as if it was breathing in and out. A tube traveled from the front of it down to Tank's left arm.

His heart raced. What was that for? He fought against his restraints. The machine's soft beeping turned urgent. The door to the room flew open, and a woman in a lab coat rushed in. Instead of going to Tank, she walked to the machine, touching a button and turning several dials. Tank's body cooled before his heart slowed down.

The woman faced him as she waited for him to catch his breath. "I wondered when you would wake up," she said. "Do you remember when you came here a few days ago?"

Tank shook his head.

"Well, they found you bleeding out. We were able to stabilize you, and now you're here." She smiled at him.

"Where?" Tank pulled on his chains.

"I'm afraid that's a question for Miss Ruba," the woman said. "I'm just here to make sure you get better."

Tank tried to move again. He finally gave up, waiting for the woman to do something.

"I'll let Miss Ruba know you're awake." She left him alone.

Tank pulled with all his might on the chains, but they didn't budge. They weren't going to keep him locked up like some fearsome creature. The machine's soft beeps weren't helping. They were a constant reminder of his situation.

You're stuck. You're stuck. You're stuck.

He growled. Everyone in the village would love this. The almighty Tank. Bested by a chain. He gave up and sighed. He couldn't help but wonder what Naf was doing. Was he even alive? What had Prylek told him after Tank ran away? What would Naf say now if he saw Tank?

The door opened, and the woman from before was back, accompanied by a short woman with curly gray hair in a business suit. She waved to Tank, giving him the same smile as the nurse.

"Hello, I'm Enzu Ruba." When she realized Tank wasn't going to say anything, she said, "What's your name?"

Tank only stared at her.

Enzu came closer and bent down so they were at eye level, the bars still between them. "Why did you get on my ship?"

Still, Tank said nothing. He didn't know this woman, why would he give her any information?

"Alright. If you don't want to talk, then you can stay in there a few more nights." She stood and brushed herself off.

"Miss Ruba, I would highly advise against this. Even though we have his vitals under control, we need to find out if he needs more medical care. His arm clearly needs more attention," her assistant said.

"We'll find out in a few days, won't we?" Enzu said. Her clicking heels faded as the room plunged into darkness again.

He tried to sleep, but being forced to sit on the concrete made it difficult. The one window in the room barely let in any light. All Tank had were his thoughts and how he would get out of this place.

Was he on a different planet? How was he supposed to get back home to warn his family about Prylek?

Tank flinched as the door slammed open, light spilling into the room. Enzu and her assistant walked in and stood in front of the cage once more.

She crossed her arms. "What were you doing on my ship?"

"Escaping my planet," Tank said.

"I wouldn't consider the Sovich's planet a volatile place." She narrowed her eyes at him.

"Me either," Tank mumbled.

Neither said anything for a moment until Enzu broke the silence again.

"Well, you've officially trespassed on Bisekt property, and I'm afraid I'll have to give you to the authorities."

"Great," Tank said. *Bring it on.*

"However," Enzu said. "Seeing as I'm the CEO of Bisekt and this is my home, I don't think I'm going to."

The nurse tapped Enzu on the shoulder. "Are you sure that's a good idea, Miss Ruba? We don't know what kind of power Sovichs are capable of."

"That's why he's perfect." Enzu turned back to Tank. The bars of the cage separating them obscured her face. "Have you heard of Bisekt before? We make luxury spaceships for people throughout the galaxy."

Tank shook his head.

"Well you're going to work for me now. You are going to be my son's bodyguard. Well, adopted son."

Tank laughed. It wasn't a soft laugh either, but a genuine guffaw. "I'm not guarding a kid."

"Sovichs like weapons, don't they? I'll give you your very own. Customized and everything."

Tank perked up. "My own weapon?"

"Bisekt certified. They're top of the line. And you'll have clearance to the entire mansion."

"Miss Ruba," the assistant started, but Enzu ignored her.

"If I don't?" Tank asked.

Enzu tapped the side of the cage. "You don't mind small spaces, right?"

Tank growled. He would rather do anything than sit in a cage all day, but guarding some kid? He didn't do grunt work. On the other hand, if he did get clearance to the whole mansion, then maybe he could find a way to escape and get back to his village. He needed to warn everyone else about Prylek.

"Show me the gun, and I'll think about it."

Enzu smiled and held out her hand to her assistant. "Hand me the instrument please."

"Miss Ruba, I strongly urge you to wait until we have further information on him. At least let me give him a sedative so you don't have to worry about any harm coming to you." She reluctantly placed the instrument in her boss's hand.

"If we do that, how can he trust me?" Enzu opened the cage door and walked in. She knelt in front of Tank. "I need to take measurements of your left arm, so I'm going to unchain you, ok?"

The nurse grabbed the bars. "Miss Ruba."

Enzu held her finger on the lock, and the chain fell away from Tank's left arm.

For a split second, he saw himself knocking her out. He didn't need his hand to kill someone. If he swung his arm hard enough, the force would do the trick. He cursed the chain holding his other arm down. He would still be stuck in here, so he didn't do anything. Enzu pulled out a metal device with long prongs from her lab coat and motioned for him to hold out his stump.

Tank growled and reluctantly held it out for her. He didn't like this place at all. Enzu held the instrument along his wrist and arm. It lit up, showing numbers on its screen that she wrote on a clipboard.

"So how did this happen?" she asked.

"I found out something, and I had to leave my village." Tank kept his eyes down.

"Why?"

A voice in the back of Tank's mind told him not to tell her anything. She could use the information on him later. On the other hand, she promised him a weapon.

"My leader started a ceremony and told us it was to pick the strongest Sovich. The winner was sent on a pilgrimage. But he was really killing the winners so no one would challenge him to be the next leader."

"What's the Ceremony?"

"A yearly ritual where Sovichs who are of age compete to get to the center of the forest. We train for years because you can do anything to get there. A lot of us die in the Ceremony. Some are lucky, though."

Enzu kept measuring as he talked. "So what's the necklace for?"

Subconsciously, he reached for it, the chain going taut as it stopped him. "It's what I got to keep when I won."

"Hmm." Enzu put the instrument back in her pocket. "Get him cleaned up and bring him to the lab," she said to the nurse before turning to Tank. "You can meet Myca then too; he's having breakfast soon."

Once Tank was cleaned and had convinced the lab assistants he wouldn't attack them, they led him down the hall to the lab—although they put handcuffs on him just in case. It smelled clean like the cage, the bright lights making him squint.

He stood in a large circular room, with machines scattered throughout the area used for different experiments. Men and women shuffled around him in lab coats, checking charts and different screens on nearby terminals. A lab assistant gestured for Tank sit on a large table in the center of the room.

Enzu entered, and everyone said, "Hello, Miss Ruba," before going back to their tasks. She walked through the lab, checking everyone's work before stopping in front of Tank. "I put your measurements in our computer; your weapon should be done soon."

"That fast?" Tank asked.

"This is Bisekt. We mostly make luxury spaceships, but we can do anything," Enzu said.

Tank nodded, trying to understand.

After hours of more measurements and exercises, Enzu had him stand in the center of the room. A few lab assistants pushed out a cart covered with a large cloth. They stopped in front of Tank and an ecstatic Enzu.

"Here it is," she said, removing the cloth to reveal a metal cannon as big as Tank's arm. "State of the art, never been made by Bisekt before. First of its kind."

Enzu turned the cart so the hole where Tank put his arm faced him. She motioned for him to put it on. "It won't hurt," she said, waiting for him.

As everyone around him watched, Tank hesitantly put his arm in the cannon. He didn't know what he expected. The inside tightened as the barrel lit up and a cooling sensation traveled from his wrist to his shoulder. The neon orange glowed brighter, and he lifted it from the cart. It wasn't as heavy as he expected. Tank aimed it around the lab, scattering the assistants. Enzu smiled.

"Feels funny," he admitted. He wasn't sure how else to describe it, plus he didn't want to anger the person who'd just handed him the most powerful weapon he ever owned.

"Good. That means it's working like it's supposed to. You'll get used to it after a few times." She glanced at something on her clipboard. "The reason I asked you down here was because I wanted you to practice your cannon shot. It's much safer down here than if you let it go off upstairs."

Tank nodded.

Enzu walked him into a glass room where a man with clear goggles waited.

"If you're going to be protecting Myca, I need you to be able to shoot," she said.

"I won the Ceremony on Whukogantu. I trained with blasters my entire life and killed other Sovichs for a necklace. I can handle an arm cannon."

"Alright." Enzu motioned to a man in goggles, who set up a target on the other end of the room. He rushed out and locked the door behind him. "I want you to shoot the target."

A dummy with a target painted on its chest stood at the end of the glass room, no more than a few feet away from Tank, smiling with a poorly drawn mouth. He smirked to himself and raised the cannon.

Nothing happened.

"You need to really think about it. Think about the target being hit."

Tank raised the cannon again and aimed it at the dummy. A soft orange appeared on its sides, but as quickly as it appeared, it vanished.

"Think about someone who makes you angry," Enzu encouraged. "Do you have someone like that in your life?"

"Yeah."

"Look at the dummy and think of that person and try again," Enzu said sternly.

Tank carefully stood and looked around the lab. Every single person had stopped and stared, not saying anything. He took a deep breath and readjusted himself, holding the cannon steady. The image of Prylek with a spike blade popped up in his mind. Prylek acting all high and mighty as he told Tank he was about to kill him. The cannon's sides glowed bright orange as it charged, sending a tingle throughout Tank's left arm. With a flash of light and a ferocious bang, the cannon fired, the kickback shooting Tank backward, glass shattering around him. The dummy was gone.

"What do you think?" Enzu asked.

Before Tank answered, one thought shot through his mind: Prylek begging and kneeling before him as he aimed the arm cannon right at his heart, forcing him to tell the entire village what he did. And Tank watching his face as the life drained from it.

"I'll take the job," he said.

8

"We're on our way to kill someone—this is getting too real, Leo," Gaeth said as they flew out of New Star City. The bright red planet in front of them looked different now that they were on a mission to kill someone there. More ominous. "I don't know if I can do it."

Leo fiddled with the computer to make sure the ship was on course. "When the time comes, I'll do it." His hands shook as he typed on the dashboard. "Hey, you never gave us the coordinates," he yelled back to Scril.

"Well, don't wake up the whole galaxy over it," he yelled back, jumping onto Leo's lap and typing the coordinates in. "I'm just here to make sure you don't do anything stupid."

"Course set for Iotis," the computer chimed as the ship turned toward the red planet next to New Star City.

"No offense, but aren't you a little small to be making threats?" Gaeth asked.

He jumped on Gaeth's shoulder and stared at him, inches from his face. "Listen here. If you ever find yourself walking alone in New Star City, you better be scared. Before you know it, your knees will be shattered and you'll be on the ground face to face with my blaster, begging for your life as your tongue flops next to you." He squinted at Gaeth. "And that's if I take it easy on you. It's kill or be Scrilled in this galaxy. Got it?"

"Got it." Gaeth stared at him with wide eyes.

Scril jumped off his shoulder. "Just because we aren't in front of Vanish anymore doesn't mean she won't know exactly how you do on the mission. Anything you do wrong I'll have no trouble telling her."

"We'll do whatever we can to make her happy," Leo said, trying to cut the tension. "By the way, do you want us to call you Scril? I overheard them calling you that in the bar."

"Sure," he said. "Don't think we're friends because you know my name."

Scril scampered to the back of the ship and curled up on the cargo. "Just think of me as the eyes and ears of Vanish. Anything I see, she sees. If you mess up, she'll know before we get back to New Star." He put his hands behind his head, staring up at the ceiling.

Leo spun around in his chair, gripping the sides until his knuckles were white. "We won't mess up."

"We'll see," Scril said.

Leo liked Scril less and less. How were they supposed to get the mission done when he sat there acting all high and mighty? They had just been ordered to kill a person, something neither of them had ever done before, and Scril was giving them a hard time. Leo could squish him if he wanted to. But that wouldn't help Gaeth.

Leo sighed and turned back to the console. They were approaching the planet fast. Gaeth was playing with the thread on the chair again.

"You all right?" Leo asked.

Gaeth sighed. "I just want to get this over with."

"We'll be fine," Leo said, hoping his brother would believe him. If he was honest with himself, he had no idea if he was okay with what they were about to do either. But right now it was either this or Scril telling Vanish they were running away.

A swarm of snowflakes engulfed the spaceship as they entered the planet's atmosphere. The ship bounced back and forth, the cockpit window completely white. Leo grabbed the controls and pulled back. As they flew lower, he could just make out a building built into the side of the mountain. A platform stuck out over the edge of the cliff where Leo landed smoothly.

"Who would go to a spa all the way out here?" Leo asked.

"Someone who doesn't want to be followed," Scril said.

The wind howled as Leo and Gaeth stumbled toward the entrance. Scril held on tightly to Leo's back as it threatened to blow him off. The door to the structure was covered in snow, and Leo's hand stuck to the handle as he tried to pry it open. They stumbled inside, warmth washing over them like a warm blanket.

They were in the lobby of the spa where shelves lined the hallway with different-colored oils and treatments. Lavender, cinnamon, and honey wafted through the air, the combined smells making Leo's head fuzzy. Puffy blankets, cushions, and towels covered several nearby chairs. A large desk sat at the end of the hallway, and behind it a woman sat waiting for them. Her face lit up as they approached.

"Welcome to Star City Spa. I'm Sonja." Her voice was soft, and it matched her brown eyes that smiled as she talked. Leo couldn't stop staring at them. "Are you Leo and Gaeth? You have an appointment, correct?" Her brown hair fell over her face as she looked down at her computer.

Leo and Gaeth looked to Scril, who was perched on Leo's shoulder, shaking the snow off his suit. "Their appointment should be today," Scril said.

She stared at Scril, who gave a miniscule nod. "Yep. Your appointment starts soon, actually." She flashed a smile again before pulling out a bathrobe and slippers from the desk for each of them. "Please change into your robe when you get to the changing room. When you're done, exit the other door, and they'll start your treatment."

"Treatment?" Gaeth's eyes darted between Leo and the woman.

"That's what we call it when you come to the spa." She smiled. "Enjoy."

They walked past her into an empty locker room. Every locker was made of wood, and thick steam made it hard to see. A shower ran in the corner.

"So we're supposed to just wear the robe?" Gaeth asked.

"Yeah. Just take everything off and put the robe on," Leo said.

"What if someone's able to tell I have Steel Elbow?" Gaeth held tightly to his robe.

"Don't worry about it. No one walks around a spa staring at other people." Scril stood on the sink, looking at his teeth in the mirror. "Just walk around like you own the place, and no one will bother you."

Gaeth didn't look convinced as he went to a changing room, closing the curtain behind him.

Leo rolled his eyes. If there was one way to make Gaeth more worried about people seeing the metal poking out of his skin, it was telling him to pretend they weren't there. Gaeth opened the curtains and stood in front of the mirror with his robe on, fidgeting with the collar. The back of his neck was clearly visible, metal pushing against his skin. Sensing his brother's unease, Leo grabbed Gaeth's collar and pulled it up.

"There. It looks a little funny, but it does the job." Leo nodded.

Gaeth shrugged him off, straightening out the robe himself.

He put his own robe on, and something in the pocket pressed against his leg. He reached in, and his eyes went wide as he realized it was a blaster. He looked at Gaeth whose hand was in his own pocket.

It was suddenly more real. They were going to kill someone. For money. Could he do it? What would happen if the time came and he chickened out?

"You two find the presents in your robes yet?" Scril smirked. "You won't get the job done with your bare hands, will you?" He jumped down and looked up at them with his hands on his hips. "Now get out there and don't come back until you have a body count."

"What about you?" Gaeth asked.

"My job is to make sure you do your job. You worry about you." Scril waved them away. "Good luck."

Leo and Gaeth stood in front of the door that read To Spa. It looked plain, but Leo was still afraid to touch it.

"Well, let's do this." He opened the door.

The spa was small with a shallow pool in the center surrounded by extravagant chairs covered in cushions and towels. Several bowls of fruit were scattered throughout the room with a button for different foods to order. Leo sat at the edge of the pool and dipped his feet in. Gaeth grabbed a piece of fruit.

Another door opened, and the alien from the hologram walked in. Felgi. Leo's blaster suddenly weighed heavier against his leg.

Felgi spotted them and held out his arms. "How long did you save up to come here? I've never seen such a piece of shit parked outside my spa before." He laughed, his belly jiggling with every guffaw. "I'm kidding. I pay top dollar to get people to come here, but it's when the commoners like you come that I'm interested. They always have the stories. Businessmen just want to talk about business."

He said business like it was a dirty word.

"So tell me where you're from. What stories do you have for me?" He slid into the pool, making the water splash over the sides.

"We're brothers from Earth," Leo said. His throat had gone dry. The same thought kept racing through his mind. The living, breathing being in front of him would be dead soon. And Leo would be the one to end his life.

"Earth? No wonder you came all the way here to relax." Felgi laughed again, showing rows of yellow teeth. "Their businessmen always try to get a discount. What kind of business is that? If more people were like that Enzu Ruba, then I could retire tomorrow. I have no reason for a luxury spaceship, but I would buy one knowing it's coming from her."

Felgi splashed around the pool as they talked.

"Enzu Ruba?"

"Owns Bisekt. Every time she comes here, the staff get good tips, and I don't need to worry about being underpaid." He splashed water on his face with a yellow calloused hand.

"So how often do you get treatments?" Gaeth asked.

"I never liked spa treatments. Someone else touching me? No." He cringed. "But everyone else loves it, so there's money there, right? And if there's money to be made, then I'm there."

"Has it worked out for you?" Leo asked.

"For the most part," Felgi said. "But what I'm about to tell you is going to stay between us, ok?"

Leo and Gaeth nodded.

"There's a space station just above this planet where some bitch named Vanish lives. Thinks she can take my money because my spa and her space station have similar names."

Leo tried his best to look shocked. It must have worked because Felgi tapped him on the shoulder and said, "Right? How does that make sense at all? Now, I'm not pretending I'm part of New Star City —you wouldn't catch me there if it was the last place in the galaxy.

But just because I'm not part of her little fantasy group doesn't mean she can steal money from me."

"Fantasy group?" Gaeth asked.

Felgi sighed. "She has this crazy idea that the Sol Empire wants to take over the galaxy and control everyone."

"What do they actually want to do?" Leo asked.

"They want to use their power to enrich the galaxy. They have the smartest people and the best technology, so why wouldn't they use it to make everyone's lives better? It's too bad Vanish can't see that. If she should be mad at anyone, it should be the Volnea for doing business with Enzu instead of her." He froze for a moment, glanced at Leo and Gaeth, and then regained himself.

"I know you boys won't go telling anyone else that." He forced out a laugh. "So how did you find this spa if you're all the way from Earth? Don't you have your own?"

"We've traveled all over Earth trying different spa treatments; it was time to find something new," Leo said. "You were one of the first places we found when we were looking for a new spa and your reviews are great." The lies flowed smoothly from his mouth, but he still felt like he was about to explode.

"Sounds fun. Not my cup of tea, but if that's what you like, then do it." Felgi shrugged. "So what are you here for? Neck pain, back pain, all the pain?"

"I have some neck pain, and my brother is here for some shoulder pain," Leo said.

Felgi hopped out of the pool and stood in front of Gaeth, whose eyes had gone wide.

"Let me see which shoulder and I can start your treatment," Felgi said, reaching for Gaeth, but he took a step back.

"No, that's okay. Just tell me where I need to go." Gaeth pulled his robe tighter around him.

Felgi laughed again, except this time it seemed to be more out of nerves than out of finding Gaeth humorous.

Leo's heart pounded against his chest. Felgi was paying attention to Gaeth. This was the perfect opportunity. He slowly reached into his pocket and wrapped his hand around the blaster.

"Okay then. At least let me fix your robe for you."

Leo had his blaster halfway out of his pocket. Just another second and he could do it. Before he could react, Gaeth slapped Felgi's hand away and shot him in the face with his own blaster. Felgi stumbled and fell back into the pool before his blue blood started oozing in the water. Was he dead? Had Gaeth killed him or would he wake up in a few minutes and call someone on them?

Leo and Gaeth stared at him, unsure what to do until a door opened.

"Dad?" An alien that looked similar to Felgi, but much smaller, ran to the edge of the pool and took in the scene before her. Her gaze traveled from the blood to her father's body floating in the pool, and finally, to Leo and Gaeth both holding blasters behind him.

"Security!"

Before he could see if anyone was coming, Leo grabbed Gaeth's arm and pulled him back to the door they came in. Scril waited for them with a lumpy bag over his shoulder.

"Get going," he said, shoving the bag into Gaeth's hands and jumping on Leo's shoulder.

They rushed toward the front door. More angry voices echoed in the spa as the guards found what Gaeth did. A blast went off behind them, and Gaeth ran ahead of Leo toward the entrance. They threw themselves out of the locker room. Sonja stood behind the desk, aiming a blaster at both of them.

"Get out of the way," she yelled.

A guard ran out of the room. Sonja shot between Gaeth and Leo, hitting the guard square in the chest. She collapsed to the ground.

They raced outside, shooting behind them, trying to keep the guards at bay. Gaeth and Sonja climbed on the ship while Leo kept firing at their pursuers. He hit one but missed the other and ran onto the ship after them.

Gaeth had already started the engines, and the snow howled outside. As the door slammed shut, Leo jumped into the seat next to Gaeth, and they took off through the snow.

9

"Myca's a little quiet, so don't be worried if he won't open up to you right away," Enzu said.

She waved her assistant down. Her clipboard was covered in scribbles, and she looked disheveled from the night of making Tank's cannon.

"Bring our new worker to the dining room. Myca should be eating breakfast shortly," Enzu said.

"Of course. Follow me, please." Just as Tank followed her toward the door, Enzu called after them, "Don't think I'm letting you off for not telling me your name. You have to eventually." She smirked.

Tank nodded. He caught up to Enzu's assistant as she led him out of the lab and down the white hallway. They made their way to a staircase Tank hadn't noticed before. He followed her up to a wooden door she held open for him.

"Please sit at the end closest to the window. Myca likes to look out the window in the morning as he eats," the assistant said.

"Are you coming too?" Tank asked.

"No. My job is to assist Miss Ruba in any way I can. I was only asked to bring you here, not to stay and supervise." She gave him a hard stare.

Tank sighed and walked through the door. A long wooden table sat in the center of the room with one chair on either side. A single window took up an entire wall on one side of the room.

Tank sat down and peered across the table at the empty chair. With it that far away, how did they expect him to have a conversation with the kid? Well, Enzu did say he was quiet, so maybe they wouldn't talk at all. Perhaps he would get lucky, and they would sit in silence every day.

He glanced down at his arm cannon. Who was he protecting this kid from and who was Enzu Ruba to be able to pull it out from thin air for him? Why did she want to know his name so badly? He wasn't about to tell her when he didn't think he could trust her yet.

A door across the room hissed open as a robot entered, leading a young boy. He was much smaller than Tank imagined, with a full head of bushy red hair and lanky limbs. The robot pulled the chair out for Myca, who sat down without looking at Tank. It was only after the robot left through a side door that he finally noticed Tank. He stared with big green eyes as he grabbed a fork.

"What happened to your arm?" Myca said through mouthfuls of food.

Weird first question, but ok.

"It was cut off."

"Are you my new guard?"

Tank huffed. "Yes."

"My mom said I would get a new guard soon, but I thought it would be another robot." He eyed the cannon again. "Where are you from?"

"Whukogantu."

Myca raised an eyebrow. "That's a weird name."

"There's no other way to say it." Tank set his jaw.

Myca took another bite of his meal, never taking his eyes off Tank. "How did you meet Mom?"

"Do you always ask this many questions this early in the morning?" Tank didn't mean for it to come out so abruptly, but he didn't like Myca interrogating him. "Sorry." He rubbed his face. How long had he been awake? "What's the question?"

Myca's face hardened. He shoved his fork in his meal and ate in silence, not answering.

Great.

For the rest of the morning, they sat there, Tank watching Myca eat. Myca keeping his eyes on his plate as he scooped his breakfast into his mouth while the sun beat on Tank's back.

So that's why Myca didn't want to sit at this end of the table.

Eventually, Myca finished and sat back in his seat, arms crossed. Tank was unsure if what he had said was offensive to the kid. Did it really matter?

The second he could figure out how to get out of here, he would be gone. It didn't matter what Myca thought of him.

The door to the dining room opened, and the robot from before walked in.

Its body was gray, stiff, and shiny, but its face was lifelike with wrinkles and saggy skin, lined with wispy white hair. It stood tall next to Myca's chair, staring at him with milky blue eyes.

"It's time for your lessons, Mr. Ruba," it said.

Myca pushed the chair out and with one last dirty look at Tank, strode out the room.

Just great.

Tank followed after him. He wouldn't let his opportunity go to waste because some kid threw a temper tantrum.

As he fell into line behind Myca, he couldn't help taking in his surroundings. The walls stretched so high Tank couldn't really tell where they stopped. The rooms were stuffed with furniture and decorations. Everything looked fragile like it had never been touched. A plush carpet covered a hallway with a door at the end. Numerous glass cases stood along the wall with different items in them. Tank eyed the glass cases as he passed.

"Miss Ruba likes to collect items from different planets," the robot said, noticing what Tank stared at.

Tank grunted in response.

They made it to the door, which had a small sign on it:Classroom.

The robot pushed a button, and the door hissed open. Myca reluctantly walked in. Tank went to follow, but the robot stopped him. "I didn't properly introduce myself. I am Arby Callington, model 325. I exist to serve Mr. Ruba, and I hope you understand if our goals conflict at times. It's all in my programming."

"If our goals conflict, don't worry about your goal." Tank pushed past Arby into the classroom. Myca sat in the only desk, facing the wall occupied by a massive rectangular hologram. Arby walked to the front of the room. "Are you prepared for your lesson, Mr. Ruba?"

"Yeah." Myca sighed, flexing his hand open and closed.

Probably nerves.

"Very well then, let's begin." At this point, Tank couldn't keep his eyes open. Even though Arby was a robot, his soothing voice led Tank to doze off. It felt like a few seconds, but it must have been the whole lesson because Arby tapped him on the shoulder and said, "It's time for Mr. Ruba's self-defense training."

Tank perked up. "I'll go watch."

"He is waiting in the hall." As Tank started toward the door, Arby grabbed his arm. "And I suggest next time you watch Mr. Ruba during his lesson, you don't fall asleep. You can't protect him when you're sleeping on the job."

"Right."

In the hallway, Myca was peering at one of the items in the glass case. He looked up briefly, then back down at his feet.

Tank sighed. This silent treatment was ending now. "What did I say wrong at breakfast?"

"Huh?" Myca's head snapped up.

"At breakfast, I asked you to repeat a question, and you stopped talking. Why?"

"I don't know." Myca stared at his feet again.

"Well, it's annoying." Tank crossed his arms, his cannon glowing slightly. "Just say why you're mad and get it over with."

Myca didn't say anything. They stood there for a moment with Tank looking down at him, Myca fixated on his sneakers.

"Mr. Ruba, you'll be late for your class," Arby said, coming out of the classroom. "Show your new guard where it is so he can take you there."

Myca pointed to a door that led outside. Arby pushed him forward, and they walked out.

Tank squinted as the sun hit his face; he hadn't been out in days. As he opened his eyes, he gasped.

The mansion sat in the middle of a desert, with nothing but sand as far as the eye could see. A faint shudder caused him to look up. A sheer bubble shield encapsulated the entire estate, giving them room to walk around the grounds just outside it, but small enough so they wouldn't be able to go far. Enzu told the truth when she said they were the only ones here. Green grass flourished from the mansion up to the edge of the bubble.

Myca had taken off, and Tank jogged to catch up to him. A man waited for them on the side of the mansion. He wore full armor like the guards Tank had seen board the ship when he came to Bisekt. The man smiled and waved when he saw them approach. "Is this your new guard, Myca?"

"Yeah. This is—" Myca pointed to Tank, lost for words. He hadn't asked Tank his name. Tank wasn't sure he wanted to tell him either.

"Well, I'm Kirk." The man stuck out a hand.

On instinct, Tank grabbed the man by the arm and flipped him on his back into the dirt, his cannon's orange glow bouncing off Kirk's helmet. Kirk held his hands up.

"Whoa. I was shaking your hand."

Tank glanced at Myca, who seemed remotely interested in Tank for the first time since breakfast.

"He's my instructor, he won't hurt you," he said.

Tank rolled his eyes, backed up, and held a long clawed hand out. Kirk eyed it wearily before taking it. Tank helped him up before sitting in the shade of the building to watch. Kirk shook the dirt off himself, motioning to Myca to start training.

"Show me your stances," Kirk said.

Myca held out one hand perpendicular to the ground and yelled, "Stop!"

Tank smirked to himself while Myca spun around and curled up in a ball on the ground.

"Perfect," Kirk said. "Last one."

What is he doing?

Myca rolled over on his back, spreading his limbs out like a starfish and shut his eyes while sticking his tongue out. "I'm dead."

Tank couldn't take it.

"What is this?" he asked, walking out of the shade. "This isn't effective against kidnappers at all. They'll just pick him up and carry him away."

"You let me worry about that." Kirk held out his hand.

Tank growled but went back to his spot in the shade. Did Enzu know Kirk was teaching her son ridiculous defense moves? Naf could defend himself better than that.

Tank plopped down and watched them go through the rest of the movements throughout the afternoon. The more they progressed, the harder it became to watch. With every "move" Myca did, Tank wondered if Kirk wanted to protect him at all. The bubble shield shimmered around the mansion as the sun rose high in the sky.

Arby appeared carrying a tray of food. "It's time for lunch, and then you are dismissed from your lessons for the day."

Myca left Kirk standing in the middle of the yard to scarf down the food from the tray. Tank's stomach growled as he watched him, but before he could think about asking for a bite, Myca had snatched it.

"Arby." Tank paused for a moment before asking, "Don't I get food?"

"Oh, yes. Your lunch will be given in the rover today, sir."

"The rover?"

"I'm so sorry," Arby said, "I must have forgotten to tell you at breakfast. Ms. Ruba needs your assistance when she goes to a meeting today. Kirk will be watching over Myca for the rest of the day."

"No worries." Kirk said, throwing a smirk at Tank. "We've got along without him this long, what's another afternoon?"

Tank growled under his breath. *What is this guy's deal?*

A cloud of dust appeared around the side of the mansion as a rover sped toward the front of the building. Tank stood just as it stopped. The dust settled, and a guard jumped out of the driver's seat and opened the back for him. The inside was decked out in rugs and wallpaper similar to the interior of the mansion.

Enzu sat on one side with a folder in her lap. "Tank! Arby sent me a message. Sorry, this is so last minute, but I have a business meeting, and I think it will go over better if you're with me."

Tank sat across from her, and the guard latched the doors shut. The only thing enabling them to see were the small lights swinging back and forth on the ceiling of the rover. A tray of sandwiches sat between them.

"So what do I need to do?" Tank asked as he grabbed one.

"Just stand there and look tough," Enzu said as the rover rumbled and started moving. "It should be simple for you. I'm trying to push a deal through, and I've heard through the grapevine they think they can swing it in their favor. How disrespectful can you get? I'm the CEO of Bisekt, and they think I'm going to agree to a ridiculous deal."

"If you don't mind me asking, what's the deal?" Tank asked.

"I do mind," Enzu replied.

Tank nodded. "I'll just stand there and look tough then."

"Good." Enzu opened her folder and began reading the pile of papers inside. The rover gently swayed back and forth, rocking Tank into a nap. There weren't any windows so he couldn't tell where they were or how much time had passed.

"So I meant to ask you"—Enzu's voice startled him—"when you finally shot the cannon, who were you thinking about?"

Tank didn't speak for a moment. The wound was still fresh; he wasn't ready to talk about it. "My leader," he said, not looking at her.

KATHLEEN CONTINE

Enzu nodded, not looking up from her papers.

Tank took another sandwich. "Why do you want to know my name so badly?"

"I know the name of everyone who works for me," Enzu said. "But mostly so I know what to call you."

"I'm still not telling you," Tank said.

"Suit yourself."

Tank sighed with relief. Not telling Enzu his name was the only thing he still had control over at Bisekt. He'd hold onto it as long as he could.

They sat in silence afterward. Enzu stayed absorbed in her papers, and Tank took another nap until the rover came to a grinding halt.

"This is the part where I put my CEO face on," Enzu said with a smirk. The handle clicked, and a rush of cold air entered the rover as the hatch opened. The guard held out a hand for Enzu as Tank climbed out after her.

They were in the middle of the desert. Millions of stars scattered the night sky. Three men in suits waited for them at the top of a sand dune, illuminated in the moonlight. Enzu nodded at Tank, who followed right behind her as they approached.

"Enzu Ruba. I'm glad you were able to make this meeting," the man in the middle said. "We've been hoping to talk to you about selling some land."

Enzu smiled, her gray hair shining in the moonlight. "Well first off you're trespassing on Bisekt property. I could have you arrested right now." She crossed her arms. "Or I could have my Sovich here blow all three of your heads off."

Tank took that as his cue. He lit up his cannon, illuminating the circle, causing the three men to flinch. Tank bared his teeth, and one of the men took a step back, making Tank laugh.

"Gentlemen," Enzu said. "I wasn't handed my business like it was some toy I could do willy nilly with. I built this business from the ground up, fighting tooth nail every step of the way. Now everyone wants a Bisekt luxury spaceship. Do you know why that is?"

When no one answered, she continued, "It's because I don't give handouts. If I were to sell you this piece of land on this planet I own, I would have to draw up regulations and contracts to make sure you don't break into my warehouses. And yet you would be getting a big chunk of land on my planet. Do you get my predicament here?"

"Perhaps we can pay you rent?" one of the men said. "Or we could give you a percentage of our earnings every month."

"Pennies." Enzu waved her hand at them. "The reason I even showed up here tonight was because I wanted to see if you would really show. Gentlemen, you're brave for coming here. Now get out before I shoot you myself."

"You can't just walk away," one of the men said. "We flew all this way."

He took a step forward. Tank aimed his cannon, but Enzu was quicker with her blaster. The man screamed, holding his bloody hand.

"Bitch!"

Enzu aimed the blaster at him. "I say it time and time again: I don't give handouts. If I ever catch you bragging about getting a good deal out of me again, then I'll make sure everyone knows how shit your company is. Understood?" The man didn't answer, cradling his hand.

"Get the fuck out of here and don't ever contact me again." Enzu pointed toward their ship. The men walked back to their ship and took off. Enzu watched them until they were out of sight and turned to Tank. "You did well. Standing there, looking tough was exactly what I needed."

"Are you sure you aren't part Sovich?" Tank asked.

Enzu laughed. "Let's head back."

10

Gaeth kept reliving killing Felgi over and over in his mind as they stood in front of Vanish. He couldn't believe he had gone through with it. That he was capable of it.

"I'm surprised at your success. Usually, people don't come back from their first mission." Vanish smirked as they walked into her office.

"You didn't think we'd come back?" Gaeth asked. Leo and Gaeth had changed back into their regular clothes in the ship after Scril pointed out they were in the lumpy bag.

Vanish looked him once over. "No."

Gaeth's eyes narrowed. "I'm the one who killed him."

A wave of snickers reverberated around the room from the guards as Vanish raised her eyebrows.

"You?" Her jewelry clinked together as she sat up straighter in her seat. "I wouldn't have pegged you for the killing type."

Scril cleared his throat. "It wasn't really on purpose, now was it?" He stared pointedly at Gaeth.

"Oh?" Vanish leaned forward in her chair. "How did you do it?"

All the eyes in the room bore into Gaeth. He hated it. Leo gave him a nod of encouragement. Gaeth pretended his voice didn't shake as he answered. "I pulled out my blaster and shot him."

Scril laughed as he jumped on Gaeth's shoulder. "More like he became so worried, he just went for it."

Vanish didn't say anything, her eyes staring into Gaeth's soul. He tried his best to maintain eye contact but had to break under her gaze.

"He almost touched me. He might have realized I have Steel Elbow." Gaeth stood as tall as he could, even though he had never felt smaller. "I couldn't let that happen."

"Why?" Vanish tilted her head.

"You're kicked off Earth if people find out you have Steel Elbow. Why would I let anyone else find out?" Gaeth said, a hint of annoyance flickered in his voice.

Vanish leaned back in her chair and tapped her fingers together. She nodded at a guard, who walked forward and shoved something into Gaeth's hand. He peered down at a small, harmless, metal chip. He handed it to Leo, who put it in his pocket.

"That should be enough to cover you for killing Felgi," Vanish said. "You can figure out how to split it among yourselves."

Scril pointed at Sonja. "Vanish, we still haven't talked about what Sonja found at the spa."

"You're right." She motioned Sonja forward with a finger. "I'm sorry you had to be around Felgi for so long."

Sonja clasped her hands behind her back. "Surprisingly, he opened up about the Sol Empire quicker than I thought. His personality made it easier to gather information on him."

"Anything of value?"

She nodded. "Felgi convinced the Volnea to transfer their business to Enzu Ruba. If we go to their planet, we could gather more information about Enzu and possibly the Sol Empire. Apparently, they've been working together."

"I knew it." Vanish rubbed her chin in thought. "The Volnea don't normally allow visitors. How do we get in?"

"Felgi visited them multiple times, and I obtained a landing code," Sonja said. She typed something on the watch on her wrist, and a hologram of numbers appeared. "All we have to do is send it to them when we get close to the planet, and they'll allow us on. It might be difficult to get information out of them though; they only talk in questions." She pushed another button, and the numbers disappeared.

Gaeth's mind raced. Were they being sent on another mission? Even though they had done what Vanish asked, why weren't they allowed to leave?

"I trust you'll be patient enough to get the information we need," Vanish said. "I want Scril and Leo and Gaeth to go as well. They have a ship you can use."

"Scril?" Sonja's lip curled.

"Problem?" Scril asked.

"No problem." Sonja's tight smile didn't match her words.

"I'll let you know when your ship is ready." Vanish waved at them as her guards herded them back to the elevator. The door slammed shut as the elevator shot up toward the city.

"I'm going to explore a bit," Gaeth said confidently. Something had awoken inside him. After killing Felgi and holding his ground with Vanish, he felt he could do anything

"You sure?" Leo asked. He had already taken a step toward Gaeth, ready to go with him, but Sonja put a hand on his arm.

"He doesn't need us, he can take care of himself." She smiled at Leo.

Leo's eyes shifted between the two of them, brows furrowing slightly. He finally sighed, eyeing Gaeth. "Fine. Just please be careful."

"I'm a big kid. Like Sonja said, I can take care of myself." Gaeth strolled away, leaving them behind.

He had never felt so free having the city open to him. He got to choose where to go and what to do. People walked by him without sparing him a single glance. He wandered around for a place to grab some food, feeling like he could fit in almost anywhere. No one noticing his Steel Elbow was refreshing. The bright signs all seemed to be calling him to come in and find out what secrets awaited inside.

Gaeth turned a corner and walked by street vendors, all of them yelling various advertisements at the passerbys.

"This is the best blaster this side of the galaxy. You want to protect yourself, don't you?"

"These bandages came all the way from Roturn. They're the best thing on the market. You won't even feel them on your skin."

"You hungry? I have food!" A short alien that looked like a slug held up food to Gaeth. It smelled of old socks and dripped with mucus; Gaeth decided to move on.

He strolled down the crowded street aimlessly, staring at the vendors before he got to the end where a strange vendor caught his eye. He sat in a chair, not yelling at anyone, with his nose in a book. His feet were propped up on the table; above him hung a giant sign.

Need money? Join the Sol Empire today!

If Gaeth could make some money in between jobs, then he could get his house faster. He stepped forward to the stall. Any job was better than no job at this point, and Vanish never said they weren't allowed to take other jobs, right?

"Excuse me, how much does joining pay?" he asked the man.

The man lowered his book and looked Gaeth once over. He raised an eyebrow. "You sure?"

"Yeah."

The man sat his book down and stared at him. "Look around you. What's one thing everyone has in common?"

Sure enough, everyone walking by either towered over Gaeth or carried enough firearms for four people. Gaeth looked down. "I still want to try."

The man nodded and disappeared through the curtains behind his chair. Gaeth stood there awkwardly as different people shuffled past him. At one point, someone stuck their head out from behind the curtain before going back into the room.

After a moment, the man came back out with a warm smile and said, "My boss wants to talk to you." He held back the curtain to let Gaeth through.

Without even thinking, Gaeth walked into the room. A voice in the back of his head told him it was a bad idea, especially if Leo knew what he was doing, but he kept walking like his feet had a mind of their own.

A small, windowless room lit with harsh lights greeted him. A large desk took up most of the space where a man wearing a dark suit sat in an oversized chair. He motioned for Gaeth to sit in the chair that was much smaller than his own. The air in the room felt suffocating from the closed curtain. It was clear this was someone Gaeth didn't want to be on the wrong side of.

The man stood, smiling, and shook his hand. "So good to meet you, good to meet you. We haven't had anyone in here in a while." He laughed. "I'm Sebastian Donnerstag. I help those who want to join the Sol Empire." He smiled again, showing off perfectly straight teeth. "I'm sure you've decided to join because it's the right thing to do?"

"Honestly, it's because the sign said I would be paid." Gaeth pointed to the curtain where the sign hung outside. "Vanish told me about it."

Sebastian's eyes flashed.

"Don't let her fill your head with silly ideas. It's the great empire that gives us all our freedoms. If it weren't for them, the galaxy would be overrun with all the nasty vermin who want nothing more than to steal everything from your pocket and leave you for dead."

"Oh." Gaeth wasn't sure what to say.

"My assistant told me there is something special about you. Let me see your hand." He glanced at Gaeth's hand as if he were a wolf waiting for its next meal after being malnourished for days.

Gaeth took off his glove. The pain increased every day as the metal tore his skin away from his body, but he felt as long as few people knew as possible, then he could keep it a secret forever. Unless it started traveling up his face.

Sebastian took one look at the skin being pushed up by the metal and smiled. "You have Steel Elbow then. We have special places in the Sol Empire for people like you."

"What do you mean?" Gaeth leaned forward.

"Do you feel like people are constantly telling you what to do? Maybe someone else is in control of your life?" Sebastian tapped Gaeth's finger where the metal had grown just below the surface of his skin. "There's a place called Sentrum. And everyone there covers their skin like you. No one would know you have it." He pushed a button on his desk, and the lights dimmed. A hologram of a white figure in flowing white clothing walked above them. "This is what people in Sentrum look like," Sebastian said with awe. "They control the galaxy, and no one knows what's under their masks. Don't you think it would be perfect for you?"

Gaeth stared as hundreds more joined the figure, all dressed in the same masks and the same white robes before finally disappearing. The lights turned back on, and Sebastian smiled at Gaeth as though he was ready to pull out a contract and have him sign on the dotted line.

"I'm not sure. I've never controlled anyone before. Not even myself, really." Gaeth rubbed the back of his neck. "Besides, my dream was always to get a house on a small planet my brother and I could live on."

"And what about your brother?" Sebastian asked. "Did he say he would stay with you in the house?"

Gaeth thought for a moment. Had Leo said that? He couldn't remember. But he thought they always said they would live together. There wasn't any other alternative.

"If you ask me"—Sebastian lowered his voice so Gaeth had to listen more carefully—"the second someone else comes into your brother's life, someone prettier than you perhaps"—he wiggled his eyebrows when he said prettier—"you might find him making decisions he wouldn't otherwise."

Gaeth scoffed. "Leo's smarter than that. We're brothers. The whole reason we're in New Star City is because of him."

Sebastian leaned forward eagerly. "If you joined the Sol Empire and came to Sentrum, you could destroy Oblurn." He pounded his fist on the desk. "Think about it, Gaeth."

Something in his eyes made Gaeth uneasy. He seemed too eager, too hungry for him to say yes.

"Let me try to persuade you another way." Sebastian leaned back in his chair, putting his fingers together. "What if I told you we could heal your Steel Elbow?"

"I wouldn't believe you," Gaeth said. "And I've already been given something that makes it not contagious, so it doesn't matter."

"Give me one chance to show you and I'll never bother you again." Sebastian opened a drawer and pulled out a needle.

"You just happen to have the cure for Steel Elbow in your desk drawer?" Gaeth scoffed, starting to stand.

Sebastian held up a hand. "It's a small amount. If you give me your finger, I can show you. You're still curious, I can tell."

Gaeth froze between the curtain and the chair. Sebastian could be lying to him. What if he poisoned him? It was probably all a trick. Gaeth reached for the curtain and stopped again. What if it really was the cure and he could be rid of Steel Elbow? He could go home, his parents wouldn't have to worry anymore, and Leo wouldn't have to take care of him anymore. He sat back down. A voice in the back of his mind that sounded a lot like Leo's yelled at him to leave. *You're being an idiot right now.*

Sebastian grinned. "Hold out your finger and I'll give it to you."

Gaeth took his glove off and hesitantly held out his index finger. He inhaled sharply as Sebastian poked him with the needle, the sharp prick catching him off guard. They sat there for a moment. Gaeth flexed his finger, still having trouble because of the metal.

"I'm leaving." Gaeth marched toward the curtains, but Sebastian spoke, stopping him.

"Before you go—" Sebastian opened a drawer in his desk and pulled out a white mask with black eyes and a small mouth. He held it out for Gaeth. "Take this as a souvenir."

Gaeth snatched it and threw the curtains open, not bothering to look back or say anything to the man at the front of the stall. He stomped down the street, the mask dangling in his hand.

What a waste of time.

Ahead of him, he saw a flash of red go around a building up ahead. It must be Leo and Sonja. He ran forward to catch up to them. The look on Leo's face when Gaeth told him what he just dealt with was going to be priceless. He might even let Leo look at the mask. He needed to find a spot for it on the ship. As Gaeth rounded the corner, he stopped.

Leo was handing the metal chip filled with their hard-earned money to Sonja.

Sebastian had been right.

11

The days ticked by as Tank went through his new schedule with Myca. Breakfast, school, defense lessons, more school. All the while, Tank had to keep going back down to the lab to do more training with Enzu.

She never seemed to be satisfied when Tank finished, but she always told him he did a good job. Sometimes he didn't train for days at a time. When he asked Arby about it, he would say Enzu had gone off-world to do business with someone. It was the strangest place Tank had ever been.

Enzu had finally finished Tank's room. She made sure it was right next to Myca's. Tank's heart swelled when he finally saw it. It was dark, his bed flat and hard like the one in his hut, and she had somehow made his room smell like the forest. That night he dreamed of his days before the Ceremony.

Every morning he woke up missing his mother. How could he know if she was okay?

I'll send you a message.

There had to be a way to get a message to her from this place. Enzu always talked about how they had the best technology and could do anything they wanted. If he could tell his mother what Prylek had done, then maybe she could tell everyone or at least get herself out.

He slipped his arm cannon on and made his way downstairs to wait for Myca. Arby always woke Myca and helped him get dressed. As usual, the young boy walked in with Arby and glanced down the table. A flash of disappointment crossed his face before he sat down, and Arby went to get his breakfast.

Now that Tank was part of the household, Arby had taken it upon himself to make Tank a proper breakfast too. It was usually a slab of meat on a large plate, and there were no utensils.

They ate in silence, as usual, when Myca spoke up. "What's the necklace for?"

Tank stopped mid-bite and put the meat down. "It's for my pilgrimage. I get to give it to someone who helps me find my reason for living. It can be a stranger, a friend, or family member. It all depends on who I choose." He grabbed his necklace subconsciously.

"Would you give it to me?" Myca asked.

Tank laughed. "Do you think you helped me find my reason for living?"

"No, I just want the necklace."

"Then, no."

Arby took the tray away. "I'm sorry, Mr. Ruba, but Miss Ruba won't be joining you for breakfast again. She said she has a lot of work to do. But if you want to schedule some time with her, she would be happy to do so. Would you like to reply?"

"No, it's okay." Myca sighed, putting his chin in his hand.

Tank cleared his throat. Should he say anything at all? Would Myca complain if he didn't try to comfort him? "You okay, kid?"

"No," Myca said, dropping his spoon in his bowl. "Mom never comes to breakfast. I don't know why I think she'll show up."

Tank shrugged. "It might be time to change your expectations."

"At least I know I can always find her in the basement." Myca sat back in his chair and crossed his arms.

Tank sighed and twisted the necklace in his hand. "I haven't seen my father in a year. I made a promise I would give this to him."

Myca seemed to be distracted from Enzu. "What will you do if you never find him?"

"Never give him the necklace." Tank stared Myca down from across the dining room table.

"What about your mom?"

"She's the one I made the promise to."

Myca nodded, as though reassuring himself of something. They continued on with their day to his lessons where Tank stood in the back of the room listening to Arby ramble on about the surrounding planets and how their alignment can affect older spaceship navigation systems. He started talking about proper procedure when navigation systems fail when Tank cut in.

"Is that true?" Tank asked.

"Of course it's true; it's right here in the book." Arby tapped the page. He pointed to the hologram on the wall, and a spaceship popped up. The bottom of the hull lit up orange as Arby touched it. "Do you see this, Myca? This is the most important part of your spaceship."

The hologram grew bigger.

"If the fuel tank dies, so does everything else. If there's so much as a hairline crack in the bottom of the ship, then it won't work."

"What about the backup tanks?" Myca asked, pointing to a picture in his textbook.

"Our older models didn't have backup tanks, which was an unfortunate oversight." Arby pointed to the ship where the backup tanks lit up.

"Big oversight." Tank rolled his eyes.

"Indeed," Arby said, turning back to the hologram.

———◆———

Myca skipped through the hallway as Tank walked beside him. For every few skips Myca did, Tank took one big step.

"Hey kid, has anyone ever tried to kidnap you?" Tank asked.

"A couple times, but Arby was there. Before you showed up, Mom said she wanted a stronger guard," Myca said.

"Interesting," Tank said.

They went outside where Kirk waited for Myca again. He never looked happy when Tank came around. Ever since their first interaction, he asked Tank to sit a few yards away while he trained Myca.

Tank thought it ridiculous, but he sat in his usual spot, silently making fun of Kirk's teaching methods.

How did Enzu approve this?

It made him wonder why they needed him in the first place if this was going to be his day-to-day life.

That night, when Tank made sure Myca's door was shut, and everyone had gone to bed, he snuck down the stairs as quietly as he could. He needed to get out of the house. The inside of the mansion was too stuffy, and he needed fresh air. It was hard finding the door in the dark as he still didn't know his way around yet. When he reached the door, he held his cannon up to it. It beeped and slid opened with a hiss.

Even though the mansion sat inside a bubble, the night air was still crisp and refreshing against his scales. A fountain sat in the middle of the yard with a stone spaceship in it, the water trickling down its sides. Several pathways snaked around the grass into tall hedges, making the yard look more prominent.

Tank closed his eyes and leaned against the stone railing. It felt good to be outside and not surrounded by walls or forced to stick to the same schedule every day. He went down the stairs to the yard. The grass cushioned his feet, reminding him of home. He tried not to dwell on it as he followed one of the pathways near the back of the yard. It led him away from the mansion, twisting and turning through the hedges until the house was out of sight.

As he walked, he couldn't help but think of the forest. He would give anything to go back. No amount of Enzu's research could recreate his mother, his friends, or his hand. Then he remembered why he was in his situation in the first place. Would home even be the same if he went back?

The pathway finally opened up into a clearing where a small spaceship had sunk halfway in the mud. Tank's heart beat faster. This could be his ticket out. He could escape right now.

He went to the back of the ship and with a bit of effort, pulled the hatch open.

"Thank you for your aid," he whispered.

A thin layer of dust covered the dashboard, not touched in years. Tank inspected it more, and everything seemed to be there— he just needed to figure out what he needed to power it on. He ran his hand over the chair.

Why would they leave a ship like this all the way in the back of the hedges?

He left the ship and headed back to the mansion, his mind swimming with ideas. If he could somehow get someone to fix the ship, then he could go home. Or at least somewhere that wasn't Bisekt. As he let sleep consume him, he could barely contain his excitement. This whole time there had been a way out of here, and he had just stumbled across it.

12

Leo and Sonja walked together through the entertainment district. As the lights danced around the street, every performer tried to grab people's attention. There were jugglers and dancers, aliens balancing blasters on their faces while walking on a tightrope.

"I'm still not used to it always being nighttime here," Leo said. "I constantly feel tired."

He glanced at Sonja. She watched a performer shoot fruit off a volunteer's head with blasters he juggled. The crowd erupted in cheers.

"I'm always tired here." She leaned toward him, glancing around the street slightly. "Don't watch the performers too long."

"Why?"

"You aren't paying attention to your pockets when you're watching something interesting," she whispered.

Leo shoved his hands in his pockets and held onto the chip. If someone stole it, he wasn't sure what he would tell Gaeth. It had been the first time he had let Gaeth go off on his own in a while, and he already regretted it.

What if something happened to him and Leo wasn't there to stop it? Or if Gaeth walked down the wrong road and couldn't find his way back?

"Do you want to sit down?" Sonja asked.

"What?"

"Do you want to sit down?" She pointed to a nearby bench. "You look like you're about to jump out of your skin."

"Yeah, sure," Leo said.

He let her walk him to the bench where they sat away from the crowd. Everyone passing by ignored them, their attention locked on the performers.

"People watching is fun, isn't it?" Sonja asked as she leaned back. "You notice a lot of things you wouldn't otherwise."

Now that he sat and watched from a distance, it was easy to spot the aliens darting in and out of the crowd, reaching into spectators' pockets as they went. The mix of aliens and people walking by didn't help his nerves as he thought about what Gaeth might be doing.

"Still thinking about your brother?" Sonja asked, her face scrunched with worry.

"Yeah. I shouldn't, but my whole life I've been worrying about him. It's hard to break the habit," Leo said, half laughing.

"You have to let him go sometime. It's the only way he'll learn," Sonja said. "And if he has a problem, you guys have Scril and me. He's not totally alone here."

Leo stared at her. "Why are you being so nice to us?"

"I wish someone had been nice to me when I first came here. Plus, I know you aren't staying forever. The sooner you leave, the better," Sonja said, watching several people push a hovering cart through the crowd.

Leo tilted his head. "What do you mean?"

"Come on, Leo. It has to be obvious by now; this is the kind of place you don't want to be stuck in forever."

"Well, no. Once Gaeth and I get enough money, we'll be gone."

"All I'm saying is it's harder to leave than you think. You might think what you two did back in the spa was dumb luck, but I can already tell Vanish sees potential in you two."

The crowd cheered as one of the performers did a flip, continuing to juggle the blasters as he landed. Sparklers went off behind them, lighting up the street.

"And what if we stay?" Leo asked. "If being here means Oblurn can't touch Gaeth, then maybe it's the best option."

"But the war between the Sol Empire and Onyx is here," Sonja said.

"How long have you been here?" Leo looked at her.

"Since I was little." Sonja stared at the performers, but Leo could tell she wasn't really seeing them. "I used to pickpocket until Vanish caught me and then I started working for her. I can barely remember doing anything else."

"Were you born here?"

"No."

The crowd grew larger as the performers started their finale. A musical number filled the street, and everyone clapped along. More small aliens appeared, darting in and out of the crowd.

They sat there watching the performers and pickpockets doing their tricks on the crowd. It almost seemed peaceful watching the people of New Star City go about their day, even though most of their days consisted of some form of violence.

Sonja stood suddenly and stretched. "I have a favor to ask you."

"Okay." Leo raised an eyebrow.

"Do you think I could borrow some money?" Sonja asked.

At first, Leo was offended. She knew what they were saving for and what they had done to get the money. Shouldn't Vanish be paying her as well?

"Didn't you just tell me to get out of here as fast as I could?"

"I did. But I need to report it," Sonja said, matter-of-factly.

"And you need money to do that?"

Sonja sighed. "I need money to call my informant, who can pass it on to the right people. Vanish isn't the only person who I need to report to. I'll explain as much as I'm allowed to, but all I need is money for this call." She took a step toward him. "You would be helping Onyx."

Leo rubbed the back of his neck. "I don't know. This is the money for Gaeth."

"I understand," Sonja said, backing away. "But you heard Felgi talking about the Sol Empire. If I can give what I found out to my informant, it'll get us much closer to stopping them."

Leo put his hands in his pockets, his fingers wrapping around the small chip. "I don't think I should. I'm not involved."

Sonja let out a frustrated sigh. "This will be the only time I'll ever ask. I promise."

Leo still didn't budge.

"If I give you my word, would you trust me? I'll even shake on it." She held out her hand, holding his gaze. "Helping me with this will help you get your brother out of here."

"How?"

"The more information our network has, the quicker we'll get jobs, the faster you'll make money. You want to help me," Sonja said.

Leo thought for a moment. Gaeth would be upset if he knew Leo gave their money to someone they just met. But Leo would explain he did it for both of them. He nodded and shook Sonja's hand.

The performers finished their dance, and the crowd erupted in one final round of applause. The lights bounced off the buildings around them.

"This way." Sonja walked alongside him as they traveled down the street to a row of callers. All of them were run down and beat up like everyone who used them had received bad news at some point and had taken it out on the machines. Sonja went to the one in the best shape. Its monitor didn't flicker, and it wasn't missing any keys. She quickly typed a code, and a message popped up:Please insert 10 credits.

Leo's eyes went wide. "Ten?" he asked, staring down Sonja. "You made it sound like you needed just a few."

Sonja waved her hands at him. "It's a long-distance call. I'm sorry."

"That's half of what we got from Vanish." Leo ran his hands through his hair, looking around.

"Maybe we should ask Gaeth if it's okay?" Sonja asked.

Leo's head snapped toward her. "He would never say yes."

Sonja's face turned stone cold. "If I don't get this information to Onyx," she said slowly, "the Sol Empire could take over the entire galaxy. Everything you know would be gone like that." She snapped her fingers. "Everything about yourself would be changed to fit their idea of how the galaxy should be. You wouldn't be able to be your own person."

"Why can't you ask Vanish for money?"

"The last thing I need is owing Vanish more favors." Sonja leaned on the console. "Please."

Leo thought for a moment. If Gaeth knew he gave Sonja some of their money, he would be furious. But he couldn't say no. Not when he could Gaeth out of the city faster.

"I'll give you the money." Leo reached in his pocket for the metal chip. "Ten you said?"

"Yes."

He pulled the chip out and carefully pushed the up arrow on it until the screen said ten.

Gaeth would hate him for this, he knew it.

He carefully handed the chip to Sonja, then stuck his hands back in his pockets. Sonja slid the chip into the caller.

Please enter coordinates.

Sonja typed, and a long sequence of numbers appeared, filling up the screen. After a moment, a flat line flickered.

"New Star City has the worst technology." Sonja rolled her eyes.

The caller buzzed and clicked. A female voice answered. "Hello?" The flat line bounced up and down with the inflections.

"Ava. It's Sonja."

There was a pause. "Sonja. How long has it been?"

"Too long. But that's good for you. I've been gathering intel."

"I'm all ears."

"I've been stationed at a spa just outside New Star City. Lots of high-profile targets visited, but I never had a chance to take any of them out." Sonja smiled. "I got a lot of information for you, though."

"Hold on a second." The bar bounced slightly as there was a soft typing sound. "Okay, my terminal is open."

"Enzu Ruba visited a lot. She's making too many moves for my liking. She has too many friends in Sentrum, and I know for a fact she thinks what Onyx is doing is useless. If we do anything to get in the way of building Bisekt on more planets, then she'll use her money to shut us up."

"What if we take out Enzu Ruba? Do you think it'll help our chances?" Ava asked.

Sonja forced a laugh. "With all that money surrounding her, do you think it would go unnoticed if she just disappeared one day?"

"You're right. Let's sleep on that one." More typing. "Send me the names, we can start there. I'll pass this along. Anything else?"

Sonja smiled. "Just that you're doing a great job."

"Aw, thanks," Ava said. "You keep up the good work too."

Sonja cut the call and turned to Leo. "You probably have questions, right?"

"A few." He crossed his arms.

Before Sonja could answer, someone tapped him on his shoulder. He turned to see a red-faced Gaeth, inches from his face.

"Really?" He was breathing heavily. "After what we did to get that money?"

"There's a reason. It's for us."

Gaeth's hands shook. His shoulders rose and fell with every breath as he stared Leo down intensely. Leo wasn't sure if he might punch him or run away.

Leo leaned forward so only Gaeth could hear him. "She needed to make a crucial call, and I gave her money to use the caller."

He thought Gaeth would say something along the lines of *Oh, that makes sense, I'm sorry for the misunderstanding.* But when his brother took a step back and gave him a look of confusion, Leo's stomach dropped.

"Why would you be contacting them?" Gaeth asked slowly. "They're trying to bring down the Empire."

It was Leo's turn to be confused. "We *want* to bring down the Empire."

Neither one said anything.

Scril ran up to them so fast, he bounced off Gaeth's legs. "Vanish wants us back in her office."

"That was really fast," Leo said.

"Hey, you don't question it, you just follow orders," Scril said as he walked away.

Gaeth threw a look at Leo and followed Scril, clutching his index finger.

"Is he alright?" Sonja asked Leo, her eyebrows knit together.

"I'm not sure," Leo murmured, watching Gaeth disappear into the crowd.

13

The sun filled the halls of Bisekt with warm light as Tank walked to breakfast. He walked with a much bigger bounce in his step now that he knew a ship sat behind the mansion, but he couldn't dwell on it. If he wanted to get out of this place, or even make contact with his mother, he needed to keep his head on straight. He rounded the corner and spotted Arby gazing out the window.

"What are you doing?" Tank asked, getting closer.

"Oh, good morning, sir." Arby smiled. "Sometimes the droids don't come in at night, and we need to round them up. I'm making sure they come in."

"Is that normal?"

"Yes, nothing to worry about. They patrol the grounds for me, and if they detect anything out of the ordinary, they'll send me a message instantly. There's so many it's a wonder more of them don't get lost."

Tank looked around to make sure they were alone before speaking. "Arby if I wanted to fix up a spaceship, would you be able to help me?"

The motors in Arby's faced whirred as his eyebrows furrowed. "Pardon me for asking, sir, but why do you want to fix up a spaceship?"

"After your lesson, I thought it would be an interesting way to teach Myca more about how ships work," Tank sputtered.

Arby seemed satisfied with his answer. "It all depends on the spaceship, of course, sir, but I'll be glad to help any way I can. I'll be happy to take a look after Mr. Ruba's day is done."

Someone tapped Tank's shoulder. He turned around and came face to face with Enzu's assistant nervously looking up at him. She gripped her clipboard tightly against her body.

"Tank, Miss Ruba needs your help with another meeting," she said. "If you could follow me please." She didn't bother waiting for an answer as she turned and walked away. She led him down the hall to the back of the mansion and stopped in front of a large wooden door with intricate carvings of spaceships, stars, and planets. The assistant knocked three times, and the door opened.

Enzu sat inside at a monstrous desk with nothing on top of it except for one pen. Bookshelves stuffed with volumes of books in different languages lined the office walls. Tank walked across a fluffy carpet to stand in front of the desk. Everything reflected what the mansion looked like. But for some reason, he felt a lot smaller in this room.

"Tank, perfect." Enzu smiled. "I need you to stand behind me again when our next meeting comes in. It's a big one this time."

Tank walked around the desk and stood next to her giant red, leather chair. Enzu's assistant sat in a chair in the corner of the room, writing quickly on a notebook. The seconds ticked by as they watched the door, waiting for the guests to arrive. Tank glanced at Enzu. Her knuckles were white as she clasped her hands together on her lap. It was the first time Tank had seen her nervous since he had arrived at Bisekt.

"Who's the guest?" Tank asked.

"Two significant people." Enzu smirked. "From Sentrum."

"Sentrum?"

"Yep," Enzu said. "Anything you want to change in Whukogantu? You could ask them at this meeting if you want."

Tank gave half a laugh. "There's so much. I can't imagine having that much power."

It was Enzu's turn to laugh. "I let them think they have all the power. Just wait until things really kick off."

"Let me guess, that's why you wanted me here?" Tank asked.

"You're catching on quick," Enzu said.

There was a knock on the door, and Enzu's assistant answered it. "The Sentrum councilmembers are here Miss Ruba." She pulled open the door to let them in.

Two figures stood in the doorway, in what looked like white sheets flowing from their head to the ground, leaving every inch of them covered. Each one of them wore a matching white mask with no facial features tied around their heads.

Tank's tail twitched. He forced himself to keep it still.

They floated in the room as their cloaks billowed out from behind them and sat in front of the desk.

Enzu held her arms out in greeting and sat in her chair. "I'm so happy we were able to welcome you to my home. I trust you were able to make it here without any trouble?"

"Of course," one of the councilmen said. "Our trip was uneventful."

"I'm glad to hear it." Enzu leaned forward in her chair. "Let's get right to business then."

"Yes." The councilman's deep voice carried throughout the room. "We've been discussing among ourselves where we should acquire our next spaceships. It was a long debate, but we finally decided we want Bisekt spaceships for every councilman in Sentrum."

"So you're here to buy?" Enzu asked.

The councilman's heads turned toward each other ever so slightly.

"After many discussions, we agreed it's your duty as a galactic citizen to help Sentrum in any way you can," said the one on the left. "That includes building ships for us."

Enzu leaned forward, putting her elbows on the desk. "Why wasn't I invited to these meetings? With all due respect, there's easily more than one hundred of you at Sentrum. The materials I need to build one Bisekt ship takes a while to collect."

"We understand, but you also have the most durable ships," the councilman said. "If anything were to happen to one of us on a trip, we know we would be safe. It can be dangerous traveling through the galaxy, and what message would that send to the people if we didn't have safe ships?"

Enzu shrugged. "Councilman, I would love to help you, I really would. But I also need to run a business, and giving away over a hundred ships eats into my bottom line. I wish I could do something for you." Enzu's eyes shifted between them.

The other councilman spoke up. "What if we only took fifty? All of us aren't out in space at the same time. We could share."

Enzu pressed her hands together. "Councilman, I need you to understand that these are luxury spaceships that take hours upon hours to build. I can't simply give Sentrum fifty of them and expect to hit our goal for the year. The production isn't there."

"Twenty-five. We'll send you extra workers to help with labor," the councilman said.

"Deal." Enzu smiled. "When do you need them?

"Ideally, as soon as possible."

Enzu nodded. "I can do that. We might need to increase production a bit, but that's not a problem for Bisekt."

They all stood and shook hands. "I'll let you know when to expect the shipment," Enzu said.

"Wonderful. We'll tell the others. The Sol Empire thanks you," the councilman said.

Enzu's assistant escorted them out of the office, leaving Tank and Enzu alone. She seemed to be thinking about what just happened.

"I don't think you needed me for that." Tank said. "You handled yourself just fine."

"Production can handle one hundred ships no problem. But convincing the people who control the galaxy they can't?" Enzu looked up at him. "You were needed."

———◆———

Tank brought Arby to the ship in the yard. With the sun down, it took a little longer to find his way. It hadn't moved, still in the back buried in the dirt where no one could find it. Tank wondered why no one had tried to fix it up before. He didn't care, though. He would be the one to do it.

"Ah yes, I remember when we put this back here," Arby said, running his hand over the ship. "One of the older models."

"You think you could fix it?" Tank asked.

Arby rubbed his chin in thought. "We have a maintenance room. Let's look in there to check if we have any parts for it first."

They made their way back into the mansion, where Arby led Tank to a room labeled Maintenance. Inside were shelves stuffed with parts for all different types of robots and spaceships. Every section had labels, but Tank still didn't think he would be able to find what he needed. At the end of the row sat a monitor with a blinking cursor.

"I can check the entire inventory from this monitor. We'll know in just a few moments." Arby sat down at the monitor and typed furiously at the keyboard. Tank could barely tell what Arby typed. Different ships flashed on the screen for a second before disappearing again. Arby didn't seem to even be looking as his hands danced across the keyboard.

Tank spotted the ship. It flashed by for a second. "There." He pointed.

Arby went back and pulled it up. It looked exactly the same as the one outside. "We have most of the parts. As long as there isn't any long-term damage, we should be able to fix it from out of this room."

Tank's heart soared. "Great. When can you start?"

Arby typed on the monitor again. "Well, we are usually helping Mr. Ruba, but I think I can find time in our schedule to have the droids inspect it. How do you want to teach the lesson to Mr. Ruba?"

Tank froze. He forgot the reason he told Arby he wanted to fix it up. "Let's fix it up first. Then we can go through everything with him."

Arby tilted his head. "Wouldn't it be more logical to show him the inside of a spaceship as it's being fixed, sir?"

"I don't want him to get hurt while the droids are fixing it."

Arby turned back to the monitor. "Very well. Perhaps I'll ask Miss Ruba what she prefers."

Tank tried to act calm. He didn't want Enzu to know a spaceship was being rebuilt in her backyard. "You know what, Arby? You're right. Having Myca watch a spaceship be built would be the best way to learn about them."

"Excellent, sir. I'll send the droids to work on it immediately."

14

"So remember we're going to Covernia to find information on Enzu and, if we're lucky, the Sol Empire," Sonja said as Scril climbed on her shoulder. "If you see anything strange or hear anything you think could be beneficial, then tell Scril or me. Mostly me."

Leo piloted the ship with Gaeth sitting in his regular spot as Sonja sat on the floor in the back with Scril.

Scril scoffed. "Hey, I'm just as good at taking information as you."

"Yeah, but you aren't as discreet about it." Sonja turned to Leo and Gaeth as she read a holo-pad. "Just tell me, it'll be easier."

Scril rolled his eyes. "So what's Covernia like?"

"Lots of trees," Sonja replied. "Not much else really, but still beautiful. The Volnea are lucky to live there."

"Have you been there before?"

"No, but I've done enough research to see all the pictures."

"You've seen every picture of Covernia there is?" Scril crossed his arms.

Sonja shot him a glare. "You know what I mean, Scril."

"We should be there any minute," Leo called back as he typed on the dashboard. The ship beeped as they flew closer to the planet. A massive forest came into view, stretching in all directions. Leo followed the computer to a small clearing in the woods and carefully set the ship down. "Everyone out."

Leo moved to push the button for the hatch, but Sonja stopped him. "You should know something about the Volnea. They only talk in questions."

"Do we have to only talk in questions?" Leo asked.

"No, but it's more polite," she replied. "Let me do most of the talking." She pointed at Gaeth and Scril. "That goes for you two as well."

They opened the hatch where a Volnea stood waiting for them. Leo was surprised they had sent a greeter. She towered a few feet above them, with a long thin neck and small eyes. Her hands were folded at her waist as she waited for them to approach.

"How do you do?" she asked. "How was your trip into Covernia?"

"Great," Gaeth said, taking in the view. "Your planet is beautiful."

"Isn't it wonderful to listen to the youth take such pleasures in the simpler things?" the alien asked.

Sonja stepped forward. "My name is Sonja. This is Leo, Gaeth, and Scril. We would be honored if you showed us your village."

The Volnea smiled at her softly. " Did you know my name is Hihna? Follow me, please?" she asked, turned, and walked down the path in front of the ship. "Don't the trees look beautiful this time of year? When was the last time you saw bark this dark or leaves this thick?"

As they walked, Leo fell into step next to Gaeth, who glared at him before crossing the path to walk next to Scril.

What's his problem?

The trees shaded them from the sun as they followed her through the woods. They were much bigger than the trees back on Earth, the brown trunks stretching so the tops were barely visible. After being in New Star City for so long, the forest was a welcome change. The woods seemed to be alive as the different noises of the wildlife surrounded them. They came to a stop at a group of trees, and Hihna knocked on an unusually large tree trunk.

"What's the reason you've come here?" she asked.

"We want to speak with Iri," Sonja said.

"Why do you want to talk to her?" Hihna asked.

"We have some questions," Sonja smiled.

"Will you wait here, please?"

"Yes."

A wooden platform attached to the bark by gears lowered from the tree, and Hihna stepped onto it. She didn't say anything as it ascended into the treetops.

"I can't stand it," Scril said. "Only talking in questions makes me want to scratch my ears off."

"Maybe you should, so when we talk to Iri, you don't make a fool of yourself," Sonja mumbled.

"It won't make a difference," Scril said. "Why don't you just let me do the talking?"

"You have to pay attention long enough to figure out what they're actually saying. You think you could handle it, Scril?"

"I think I could, Sonja." Scril straightened his coat.

She raised an eyebrow at him as she sat down.

They sat against the trees waiting for Hihna to come back. Leo sat next to Gaeth. "Are you good?" Leo asked. "You've been acting weird ever since you went off by yourself in New Star City."

"Yep." Gaeth bent his index finger a few times. "Just tired." He didn't look at Leo as he talked.

Leo nudged him. "You know you can tell me anything, right?"

"I'm fine. Honestly," Gaeth said.

"Is it about what happened with Sonja?" Leo whispered.

"I mean, I'm the one who killed Felgi. Then I turn the corner, and you're giving away our money." Gaeth shot a glare at Sonja who knelt down next to him.

"Gaeth, don't blame your brother. I convinced him to give the money to me," she said.

"I get why you're mad. I even said it wasn't a good idea," Leo said. "I should have asked you first."

"Yeah. You should have," Gaeth said. "I feel like you went behind my back."

"I'm sorry," Leo pled. "It was to get us out of New Star City faster. If anything like that ever comes up again, I'll talk to you first, okay?"

"I'm sorry too," Sonja said.

"It's alright. You thought you were doing the right thing." Gaeth kept playing with the grass.

The sound of rope and gears turning startled them. The wooden platform descended and stopped in front of them. Leo stood and wiped the dirt off himself.

"Are you ready for your meeting?" Hihna helped everyone onto the platform, touched a button, and they slowly rose up the tree trunk.

As they got closer to the canopy, Leo thought they would emerge from the treetop. Instead, they broke through the canopy, the massive branches of the trees had grown up and wrapped themselves around each other above the tree, creating a round enclosure. Copious amounts of vines curled themselves around the branches so they could walk in it. Hundreds of trees grew taller, surrounding them in green.

Hihna led them off the platform and into the tree where the sun poked through the branches. A bridge connected to the other side of the tree, where it crisscrossed with hundreds of others, connecting all the trees in the vicinity, creating a village in the sky. Hihna walked across the bridge without hesitation, not looking back to check if they were following.

"Is this safe?" Gaeth whispered to Leo.

"Now you're speaking their language," Leo said with a smirk.

Scril snickered from Sonja's shoulder, and she shushed them all.

Hihna led them across several bridges, some more rickety than others. Leo tried his best not to look over the edge. Even though the branches stopped him from seeing the ground, he was still very aware of how high up they were. They passed several other Volnea on their way, all of them saying "How are you?" as they walked by.

How was Leo supposed to find something out of the ordinary here? What was considered normal in the first place? Should he go snooping around and ask random Volnea if they were acting strange?

Hihna took them over a well-worn bridge to a tree much bigger than the others, in the center of the village. A group of Volnea sat in the center of the tree, listening to a much taller one talk.

When she saw Leo and the others, she held out her arms and greeted them. "Who have you brought to me today, Hihna?"

"Couldn't we use some company from someone who isn't from our planet, Iri?" Hihna replied.

Iri walked around the group sitting on the floor and stared hard at Leo, her blue gaze staring right through him. Leo glanced at Sonja, who kept her eyes on Iri, waiting to be spoken to, so Leo did the same.

"Did you come here to relax, or is there something important you need?" Iri asked.

"Isn't it always something important?" Hihna asked with a hint of humor in her voice.

"Should I even ask when humans visit?" Iri chuckled.

Gaeth sighed next to Leo. He elbowed him in the arm, hitting metal instead of flesh. Leo hissed but tried to not make much noise. If they had to sit there all night going around in circles until they got their answer, he would do it.

"Are you alright?" Iri asked.

"I'm fine," Leo said.

Iri smiled at Gaeth.

"How troublesome is it to have metal bones? Are you in any pain?"

Gaeth stiffened next to Leo. "It's fine."

Sonja stepped forward. "We came here to ask you about Enzu Ruba. We were told you might have information on her."

Iri rubbed her chin thoughtfully. She stared into the forest. "Isn't Enzu Ruba the one who builds the spaceships?"

"Yes," Sonja said. "She went to the New Star spa a lot."

"Don't I see everyone there?" Iri closed her eyes. "Is she so important she would stick out to me?"

"Would she have said something to you that could jog your memory?" Hihna asked.

Iri turned to them. "If I did talk to Enzu, what would you want to know?"

"We need to know what she's scared of. There is something she did to Vanish that needs to be repaid," Sonja said.

Leo tilted his head at her.

"Isn't everyone scared of something?" Iri said. "Do you think she told me?"

Leo could feel Scril banging his head on the back of his leg. He felt the same. Talking to the Volnea was getting ridiculous. Were they going to get out of here before nightfall?

"I think you had a lot of talks with her. She probably trusts you since you only speak in questions," Sonja said.

"What do I get out of it?" Iri said.

"A direct line to Vanish. No tricks. Your bridge out there looks a little worse for wear, we could help you," Sonja said. "It'll be better than the business we had before."

Iri looked over her shoulder at the group who had gone back to talking among themselves. She bent down a little so only they could hear.

"What is every mother's fear?" she asked. She straightened up and dusted off her robes. "When can I expect that direct line?"

"As soon as we report back to Vanish," Sonja said. "Thank you. We need to get going now."

"Isn't is quant how they come and go as soon as they have what they want?" Hihna asked. "Won't you stay for a little longer? Is our village so unwelcoming you would rather leave right away?"

Without hesitation, Sonja said, "We would be delighted to stay overnight if that is your wish."

"Hihna, could you show them where they'll be staying tonight?" Iri said. "And will you make them your special soup as well?"

Hihna bowed and motioned for them to follow her again. They were led back over the bridge to a treetop nestled on the edge of the village. Hihna lit a fire in the middle of the treetop and set a large pot of bird soup on top. As night crept in, Hihna poured each of them a hearty filling and passed the bowls around. Scril had a bit of trouble holding his own bowl until Sonja made him sit it on the floor.

After they were done, Hihna came back with stitched blankets made of leaves for everyone. She gathered the bowls and took the pot away, asking them to have a good night.

"This is a nice place. I wouldn't mind living here." Scril burrowed under his blanket, his arms behind his head.

"Earlier today you were complaining about how they only talk in questions, and we hadn't even met Iri yet," Gaeth mumbled.

"That's before I knew how good their soup is."

"This might be a little personal, but what did she ask you about metal bones?" Sonja asked.

Leo and Gaeth glanced at each other. Leo nodded at him, encouragingly.

"I have Steel Elbow. It turns my bones into metal. It can be pretty painful."

"Oh." Sonja stared at the fire in the middle of the treetop. "I'm sorry."

"Don't be," Gaeth said. "It's not your fault."

"We've been used to it for a while," Leo said.

"So you're turning into a robot?" Scril asked.

"Scril!" Sonja shoved him, and he fell over.

"It's fine. Honestly, it's not the worst I've heard." Gaeth shrugged.

"Yeah, I've had to put a few people in their place when we were younger," Leo said. "Kids can be cruel."

"How did you find out you had it?" Scril asked. "Did you start beeping one day?"

"Scril, I swear I'm going to throw you in that fire," Sonja said.

"When I was young, my fingers became really stiff one day. My mom took me to the doctor, and he did some tests that came back positive. It was weird because they weren't telling me how I should deal with it; they were telling my mom how she should hide it from other people. It felt like my whole world had shifted. Friends looked at me differently. Meeting people for the first time became a new experience. Some of my mom's friends found out and treated her differently too. It's crazy what people think is okay to say to someone who has a disease." Gaeth stared into the fire as though it was pulling out everything he had been holding back for the last few years of his life.

"And then the whole town knew I had it and suddenly I had to be shipped off to a planet where I'm not allowed to see any of my family or friends. Like I'm some sort of experiment. I wouldn't wish this on my worst enemy. It's hard to get out of bed because I'm so stiff, and people make fun of me for how I move. They think they're funny making jokes about loose screws. Fuck 'em, honestly."

The fire continued to crackle as Leo patted him on the shoulder. For the first time, Scril didn't have anything to say.

"So how did you end up here then?" Sonja asked.

"I was sent to Oblurn, but the place was the worst, so Leo got me out," Gaeth said. "We've basically been on the run."

"I would do the same if I thought my family was in danger," Sonja said.

Scril stood on Gaeth's knees. "If anyone tries to make fun of you, I'll knock their knees out."

Gaeth laughed. "Thanks for the support."

Leo slept soundly that night, the silence of the forest lulling him to sleep. He was glad Gaeth had finally opened up about what bothered him.

The next morning Hihna came back and brought them to Iri.

"You enjoyed your stay?" she asked.

"Of course," Sonja said. "Your village is beautiful."

"Will you be coming back?" Iri asked.

"I'd love to," Sonja said.

Iri said her goodbyes as Hihna led the group back over the bridge and through the village. Leo didn't hesitate walking over them this time. Hihna brought them to the wooden platform.

He couldn't believe Sonja had actually pulled it off. How had she been able to talk to the Volnea without getting frustrated? He couldn't take Gaeth asking him questions for more than ten minutes.

Hihna helped them on the wooden platform and asked, "Can you find your way back to your ship when you reach the ground?"

Sonja smiled. "It might be better for you to come with us since this is our first time here."

Hihna rode down the cart with them and walked through the woods back toward the ship. She bowed as they waited for the ramp to lower.

"Thank you for your hospitality," Sonja said.

"Of course," Hihna answered.

Everyone froze.

Hihna waited with wide eyes, watching them all stare her down. Leo took a careful step toward her. Without warning, she darted into the forest.

"Get her!" Sonja yelled.

Scril ran after her, using his legs to jump ahead of everyone else. Leo ran behind them, doing his best to keep up. He pulled out his blaster, and a shot rang out through the quiet forest. Hihna's long legs helped her stay ahead of them.

"She's getting away," Gaeth shouted, trying to keep up.

Leo pushed himself to go faster. Hihna glanced back at him and pushed forward. Leo lunged, managing to grab her around the ankles. They both fell in a heap on the grass.

Gaeth, Sonja, and Scril caught up to them. Gaeth helped Leo hold her down. Sonja already had her blaster out and pointed it at Hihna's face.

"Why did you run?" Gaeth asked.

Hihna struggled against Gaeth, but she was no match for his metallic strength.

"The Sol Empire sent me here." Hihna spat. "I'm not a Volnea. They disguised me as one in case Onyx ever tried to get the Volnea on their side." She glared at Gaeth, talking faster. "You should be scared. They told me who to call. They're on their way now."

"Who?" Gaeth shook her.

"Oblurn."

15

Tank and Myca sat in the classroom, waiting for Arby. He usually showed up right on time, but today they had been waiting for him longer than usual.

Tank had half a mind to go searching for him when the door flew open, and Arby walked in, a big smile plastered on his face, his typical pile of textbooks he carried with him nowhere in sight.

"Hello, Mr. Ruba," he said. "How would you feel if I told you we were going on a field trip today?"

Myca's face lit up, and he jumped out of his chair. "Anything to not have to go to school."

"Please meet me at the front door in a few minutes." He left without another word.

"A field trip?" Tank asked.

"Yeah." Myca was already heading for the door, his books forgotten on his desk. "It's still school, but you don't have to do work."

Tank followed closely, making it to the front door where Arby had already called a rover. Just then, Kirk walked up the stairs.

KATHLEEN CONTINE

He sneered when he noticed Tank. "Heard you boys were going on a field trip today. You sure you don't need me to come along?"

"After watching you train Myca, I know I don't need you to come along," Tank snarled.

Kirk glared at Tank before patting Myca on the shoulder. "Why don't you go play on the grass down there with Arby while you wait for the rover?"

As soon as Myca and Arby were out of earshot, Kirk took a step closer so he and Tank were inches from each other. "Careful there, lizard. You think you're tough because of that cannon attached to your arm. You haven't even used it in a real fight."

Tank straightened to his full height. "I don't need a cannon to kill you."

Kirk grinned. "You worry about Myca staying safe. But I'll have Arby send me regular updates to make sure you're doing your job." He patted Tank on the shoulder and slammed the door behind him.

It took every ounce of strength to not send a blast through the door.

"So where are we going?" Tank called to Arby as he joined them on the grass.

"We're going to visit a specific type of plant that goes into making Bisekt ships," Arby said. "Very fascinating."

"Anything else in the desert we should be worried about?"

"There are some predators out there, but they're mostly nocturnal, so we should be fine, sir."

"You have your cannon. We'll be fine," Myca said.

Tank still wasn't convinced.

152

"If anything happens—"

"Nothing will happen, sir. We've gone on field trips many times," Arby said as he opened the door. "The rover is here, so let's hurry along before it gets to be too late."

They walked down the front stairs to the rover and climbed in. It wasn't the same as the one Tank had ridden in with Enzu, but it was just as nice. It raced through the desert, kicking up sand in its wake.

"So what kind of plant is it?" Tank asked as they bounced around in the carriage.

"I can't tell you yet, sir. It would ruin the fun," Arby said.

Myca watched the desert roll by, kneeling on the cushions as he stared out the window. He pressed his face against the glass, his wide eyes filled with wonder and amazement, ignoring Tank and Arby's conversation.

"How far away is it?" Tank asked.

"Not too far." Arby's eyes narrowed. "You almost don't seem excited to go, sir."

"I just want to know how long I'll be trapped in this box," Tank grumbled.

They rode for a while, Myca becoming increasingly excited until they finally stopped. A guard unlatched the hatch and helped Myca out first before Arby and Tank climbed out after him.

"It's only a short walk from here," Arby said.

They began their walk, and the rover sped away, kicking up sand and dust in their faces.

Tank wiped the sand from his eyes and checked on Myca. "Kid, you okay?"

Myca coughed, sand falling on the ground. "Yeah, I'll be fine."

Tank rounded on Arby. "Did you know they would drive away?"

"No." Arby put his hands up. "They must have thought they would pick us up later. I was under the impression they were staying all day. It's what I requested."

"If we end up out here at night, I'm blaming you," Tank grumbled, a slight growl rising in his throat.

"I still want to see the plant," Myca said. "Can we?"

"Of course we can." Arby took Myca by the hand and led them toward a sand dune. When they reached the top, Tank was surprised at the small collection of plants all growing together, overlooking the desert. Arby walked into the middle of them and pulled one out of the ground.

"This is called Dyver's Bite. Very dangerous if touched the wrong way. Since I'm a robot, it doesn't matter how I touch it, but if a living organism touches its needles, then its poison will travel through their system at an alarming rate and could possibly kill them in a few hours."

Tank and Myca took a step back.

"You don't have anything to worry about now. It's daytime, so the needles have retracted into the outer shell. But I would still advise to not pick them up on a whim." He set the plant back down. "Can anyone guess what they're used for when it comes to building spaceships?"

Neither Tank nor Myca said anything. Tank concentrated on where Myca walked in case he took a wrong step. Of all the places Arby could have brought them, it had to be the place with the poisonous plants. Kirk had to be bluffing about Arby giving him updates.

"They're used as screws to keep the metal together. These needles are as strong as steel and can withstand forces from traveling through space," Arby said. "Useful."

"Why do they use those and not actual screws?" asked Myca. He was starting to take an interest in what Arby was showing them and took a step forward. Tank grabbed his shirt and pulled him back.

"Metal rusts over time, but these needles have proven to last much longer," Arby said. "Bisekt has its own patch of these. They grow for the purpose of harvesting them later."

Tank glanced back at the cloud of sand, still heading back toward the mansion. He didn't like this at all.

"Arby, when's the rover coming back?" Tank asked.

"I can call for it when we're done with the lesson, sir," Arby replied. He continued on about the different types of Dyver's Bite and how to spot them, what different colors mean, and what kind of antidote works best on its poison.

"However, Bisekt has some of the best doctors in the galaxy. You don't need to worry about any of that," he reassured them.

Myca and Tank exchanged worried looks anyway.

Entranced by the lesson, Myca asked, "So I could use the needles on someone if I wanted to?"

"That's a pretty good idea," Tank said, thoughtfully.

Arby frowned. "I suggest not using any means of violence, Mr. Ruba. Your mother wouldn't be happy. And I highly suggest not encouraging him."

Tank rolled his eyes. The rover still hadn't turned around. He rubbed his hand over his snout. Myca wandered through the plants, studying them closely but being careful not to touch them.

"Arby, you should call the rover now so it's here when we're done," Tank said.

"If it makes you feel better, sir." Arby held up his arm and typed on his wrist. His face wrinkled in confusion. He typed again, but the same expression stayed on his face. "It seems we're too far out for the signal to reach, sir," he said at last.

Myca's head snapped up. "We're trapped here? Forever?"

"Not forever, kid. We just need to figure out how to get back," Tank said. "It'll be best if we start walking now."

Arby shook his head. "The nocturnal creatures will be out before we can make it all the way back to the mansion, sir. It will be better to stay here and wait for the rover."

"Arby," Tank said slowly, "if the rover doesn't come, we'll be spending the night in the desert."

Myca stood next to Tank, chewing on his fingernails.

"Either way, it seems we'll be spending the night in the desert, sir," Arby said.

"So it would seem," Tank replied.

As the sun traveled through the sky, Arby continued the lesson. He taught them how the Bisekt scientists took the needles out of the plants and even demonstrated on one of them. He held it up for Myca and Tank to examine, careful to not get it too close. Tank regularly checked if the rover was on its way, but the cloud of sand never appeared.

Eventually, darkness settled in, the plants blossomed, and their needles shone in the moonlight.

"If we stay in the middle of these, anything that comes around won't be able to get to us," Tank said.

They sat in the center of the patch. Arby had built a small fire. Myca yawned and leaned against Tank, his soft snores soon filling the air.

"You know, even though you might not be fond of the boy, he really likes you," Arby said. "Every night, he tells me something you said or did that day. 'Arby, Tank is so funny. Arby, you'll never guess what Tank did.'"

"Could've fooled me," Tank mumbled.

"Pardon me for stepping out of line, sir. This may just be a job to you, but try humoring him. Enzu is always in her lab, and he only had me for a long time. It might do you both good. Maybe start with telling him your name?"

A growl in the distance pulled them out of their conversation.

"What was that?" Tank raised his canon.

Arby squinted into the darkness. "I don't see anything."

By the light of the fire, an animal appeared. It crawled on all fours, its back covered in spikes. It paced back and forth on the edge of the patch, baring its massive fangs, its eyes bulging out of its flat head. It leaned back on its hind legs and in one smooth jump, cleared the patch, landing in front of them.

Tank grabbed Myca, holding him close to his chest. His cannon glowed brightly as he backed away.

Arby ran at the animal, but it swatted him out of the way.

Myca clutched onto Tank's claw.

Tank's cannon illuminated the desert. The animal leaped and Tank shot. It hit the animal right in the chest, and it landed in the sand, where it didn't move. The blast knocked Tank backward.

Right onto the open Dyver's Bite.

His foot landed directly on top of the plant, and it felt like an unleashed beehive. Tank yelped in pain and surprise as the needles pierced his scales. A hot flash went through his foot as he pushed Myca forward to make sure he didn't get hurt.

The searing hot pain traveled up his leg, pounding in his blood. Tank took several deep breaths, trying to calm down. He didn't want to worry them.

"Sir, can you hear me?" Arby was at his side. "Does it feel hot or cold?"

"Hot. Really hot," Tank said through gritted teeth. The desert heat didn't compare to the agonizing sensation in his leg.

Myca was next to him. "Are you okay?"

"I'll be fine," Tank said.

"Will he be okay?" Myca asked again, his voice getting higher.

"Yes, we need to get him back to the mansion as quickly as possible," Arby said. He put one of Tank's arms around his shoulder and started walking.

"Don't let anything happen to him," Myca said.

But Tank was fading. The desert swirled in front of his eyes as his vision narrowed. He concentrated on walking with Arby as they made their way toward the edge of the dune.

Tank could barely hear Myca. "He better be okay. Why did you bring us here if you knew this would happen?"

Tank took one more step before the hotness made its way up his whole leg. He collapsed into the sand and couldn't move. As he tried to keep his eyes open, he saw Naf's feet walk in front of him before stopping.

That isn't right.

He tried to say something, but all that came out was a grunt. His ears stopped working as he stared at the feet. His body suddenly shivered. A hand grabbed his shoulder as someone tried to move him. Tank tried to move his body, but it wouldn't listen to him. He stayed still in the sand as the voices around him started to muffle.

---◆---

When Tank awoke, a bright light blocked his view. Was Naf still there? He had to ask if he was okay. He tried moving, but Enzu appeared at his bedside. She pushed him back down. It was only then he realized his arm cannon was gone.

"Stay down. The poison is still wearing off," she said as she examined his foot.

"What happened?" Tank asked. The burning had evolved into pinpricks. He tried his best to ignore it, but he couldn't help moving his foot to get more comfortable.

"You stepped on the Dyver Bite and almost died from the poisoning. You're lucky Arby and Myca were able to get you back here as fast as they did," Enzu said.

"Are they okay?" Tank asked.

"Perfectly fine." Enzu smiled.

"My friend Naf was there too. I saw his feet when I fell," Tank said, trying to sit up again. "Where did you put Naf?"

"Naf? No one else came back with you. It's just you, Myca, and Arby."

"How did they get me back without getting themselves killed?" Tank asked.

"Looks like the protector was the protected in this case," Enzu said. "It's alright, everyone needs someone to care about them."

Tank couldn't help but be annoyed by her words. He was supposed to be the one watching out for others; he wasn't the one people took care of. They would start thinking he was weak, that he couldn't do his job. He tried not to dwell on it as Enzu checked his foot.

Tank suddenly felt someone's presence next to his bed. He looked up, expecting Myca or Arby, but his face fell when he saw Kirk standing over him with a giant smirk on his face.

"So you stepped on a Dyver's Bite, huh?" he said. "Haven't you lived in the wild your whole life?"

A spark of anger flew through Tank's body. He took a deep breath. "I lived in the forest my whole life, Kirk. Never the desert."

"I see. I just figured since you haven't ever lived in civilization, you would be an expert," Kirk said.

He wouldn't last one day on Whukogantu, the coward.

"Well, since you weren't there Kirk, you should keep your mouth shut about it," Tank said.

Kirk huffed. He leaned in close so no one could hear. "Interesting how you threaten me, and then you end up stranded in the desert."

Tank's lip curled. "You think I won't tell Enzu what you did? You almost killed her son."

"Will you tell her, though? It doesn't sound very plausible that her son's defense teacher would set him up like that. And you're new here. How do we know we can trust anything you say?" Kirk smirked and walked away without another word.

Enzu finally finished looking at his foot, writing something down in her notebook. "Myca and Arby have been distraught since you got back. Do you want me to tell them you're awake?" Several lab assistants shuffled back and forth from Tank's side, taking notes and checking his vitals.

"That'd be good." Tank closed his eyes. He couldn't admit his embarrassment. He was just getting used to the light in the room when someone appeared at his bedside. Myca and Arby. Myca's eyes were red, his face puffy.

"I didn't know if you would be okay," he said, wiping his face. "Arby and I carried you all the way back. And the whole time you were talking funny. It was scary."

Tank ruffled Myca's hair. "Don't be scared. I'm fine, kid." He paused for a moment. "How did you carry me back? I'm bigger than both of you combined."

Arby cut in, "I used my backup power. I needed to be serviced once we got here, but I'm alright now, sir."

Tank nodded. "I don't know what to say."

Arby smiled. "A thank you usually suffices in these situations, sir," he said while Myca sniffled.

"Well, thank you then," Tank said. "I mean it. And you don't have to call me, sir. My name's Tank."

16

A spark of rage ignited in Leo as he pulled out his own blaster and pointed it at Hihna.

"Why would you call them?" he shouted.

"You think I'm going to let someone with Steel Elbow walk around on their own?" Hihna said. "If you don't want them to capture you, then I suggest you leave now."

Leo glanced at Gaeth.

His face had twisted into one of rage. "I'm not contagious anymore."

"Do you realize what you've done?" Leo yelled, the blaster shaking in his hand. "I could lose my brother."

Sonja grabbed Leo's arm. "We need to leave." She pulled him away from Hihna.

The spark in Leo's stomach yelled at him to punish her for what she did, but he knew Sonja was right. They had to get Gaeth out of here.

He pulled Gaeth off Hihna, and they ran back through the forest. Leo was sure at any moment the roar of Oblurn ships would descend on them, but he refused to let Gaeth be taken back to that place. They raced onto the ship, and Leo jumped in the pilot seat as everyone climbed on board. He flipped switches and pushed buttons, and they suddenly lifted above the ground, flying away.

No one dared say anything to Leo as he concentrated on flying. He regularly checked between the motion detector and the window, hoping against hope they wouldn't run into anyone. They zoomed through space in silence until finally, Scril spoke up. "If we're going to outrun them, the best place to go is back to New Star City. They can't touch us there when they have to answer to Vanish."

Leo finally pulled his eyes away from the dashboard. "You're sure?" he asked.

Scril shot him a side-eye. "You know what she's like."

Sonja glanced at the dashboard. "Are you sure we'll be able to outrun Oblurn ships if they do come after us?"

Leo hadn't thought of that. His dad's ship was so old it would never be able to outrun newer vessels.

"The computer will tell me if something locks on," he said. "We should be fine as long as they didn't follow us."

She arched an eyebrow at him. "And I'll be dry as long as I don't get wet."

Scril snickered in his corner.

"You want to pilot the ship if it's so funny?" Leo said to Scril.

"Leo, calm down. We don't even know if they're following us," Gaeth said.

Leo took a deep breath. It was true they might have got out before Oblurn got there. But if they were able to somehow find them, he didn't know how he would be able to pilot the ship out. It was so old.

Beep.

The jarring sound pulled Leo out of his thoughts. His stomach dropped as one lone blinking red dot taunted him on the screen.

Right behind them.

Stupid piece of shit.

"Gaeth, I need your help."

As though waiting for Leo yell his name, Gaeth jumped out of his seat. "What's wrong?"

"They're following us. Dad's ship is so old, it didn't detect it until they were right on top of us." Leo pushed the lever forward, but the ship didn't do anything. He swore under his breath. "The engines aren't heated up all the way. Why did I agree to take a hand-me-down ship?"

The red dot inched closer. A low rumble traveled through the ship as something white flew in front of them. It was the same size as Leo's ship with a red flag painted on the side.

"It's Oblurn," Leo said.

Gaeth ran to the back, pushing Sonja and Scril out of the way.

"Watch it," Sonja yelled.

Leo ran back to where Gaeth stood next to the wall. He had taken the panel off, and different colored wires stuck out at odd angles. It was hard to tell where one cable started and others ended. Leo ran his finger over the wires, searching for one he could connect to make the engines heat up faster. He hadn't had to do it in so long he couldn't remember how.

"Which colors do I connect?" he yelled to no one in particular.

Gaeth pulled his gloves off and shoved Leo out of the way. He punched the panel, the metal clang echoing in the small space as the engine roared to life. Before Leo could run back to the cockpit, Sonja pushed the lever down.

The ship shot forward, sending everyone back. Scril fell onto Leo's feet, clinging on with his feelers. Leo kicked him off and made his way to the front. The radar still showed the red dot right behind them. He should have known the ship couldn't outrun an Oblurn ship. If they could follow them when they sped up, then there was one other option.

"Gaeth, close the panel," Leo called back.

"What?" Sonja said, "We're supposed to let the engines warm up to escape the ship you freaked out about."

"Yeah, and they followed us, so now I'm trying something else," he replied. "Buckle up, guys." He reached above him and pulled a lever. The ship's brakes activated and Gaeth and Scril strained against their harnesses. The Oblurn ship flew ahead of them, barely missing the top of their ship. Leo watched as it slowly became smaller and smaller.

"I'm turning everything off. Leaving only the essentials on and running at minimum power," Leo said. The ship went dark and eerily quiet. "The only way they'll see us is if they look out their window."

"We don't have any sort of shields up, they could just blow us up and call it a day," Sonja said.

Everyone held their breath as they watched the white ship. It had turned back around and slowly made its way toward them.

"Maybe they're using the window," Gaeth said, going to the back of the ship and dropping to the floor, his head in his hands.

Leo kept watching the ship, hoping somehow they wouldn't notice them, but it still drew closer. He and Sonja backed away from the window as it got closer. Perhaps they would think they had abandoned ship?

The Oblurn ship passed, still going the same speed and Leo let out a deep breath. He looked down and realized Sonja held tightly onto his arm. She must have realized it too because she let go as if he burned her.

Leo cleared his throat. "They're gone." He went to the back of the ship and knelt next to Gaeth. "You okay?"

Gaeth shrugged him off. "I'm fine."

"Gaeth, if they're trying to capture you, we have to get back to New Star City," Leo said. He patted Gaeth on the shoulder and slumped in the pilot seat. He rubbed his face a few times, taking a deep breath and trying to calm himself down.

Sonja sat in the copilot seat and took a deep breath. "Good job, Leo. That was impressive what the two of you just pulled off."

"Yeah, well I'm just glad we're all okay," Leo said. " Let's get out of here."

Leo put in the coordinates for New Star City, and they shot off toward the space station.

17

After Tank had recovered from his poisoning, Myca grew closer to him than before.

Before Tank's injury, Myca would walk ahead of him to class, not talking. Now, he walked next to Tank and asked him how he was feeling and if he slept well. Throughout the day, he'd periodically check in on his bodyguard. Eventually, Arby had to intervene because it took time out of their schedule, but it made Tank happy to have someone caring about him.

Bisekt, in general, seemed to be more accepting of him. When he walked through the hallway, different lab technicians said hello, some asking if he felt better, while others gave a simple wave or nod. Even when he trained with Enzu, the technicians didn't keep their distance as much as they used to.

The only person who still acted like they didn't care if he lived or died was Kirk. Every time they saw each other, Kirk looked the other way or shouldered past Tank without saying a word. Tank refused to take the bait. After finding out that it was Kirk's fault they were stranded in the desert, he knew he had to do something to get back at him. But if he started something or hurt Kirk, he didn't know what Enzu might do to him.

He still wanted to find a way to reach his mother. She'd feel better knowing he was trying to get home. With all the ship parts lying around and the money and technology Enzu liked to brag about, there had to be a way. He walked up the stairs into the dining room as he thought on it. Enzu had to have a way to communicate with people outside of Bisekt. He wasn't very good at talking to people, but since everyone came up to him now, perhaps it would be easier to ask them about it.

"Tank, you almost missed breakfast," Myca said as he sat down. Myca had almost finished his own meal.

Arby rushed out with Tank's food and placed it in front of him.

"How are you feeling today, Mr. Tank?" Arby asked.

Tank smiled. "Arby, it's alright to call me Tank."

"If that's what you wish"—Arby paused—"Tank."

He left Tank to his food, but before he could take a bite, Myca piped up, "Sit with me. You don't need to be all the way down there."

Tank picked up his plate and carried it down to the other end of the table, setting it next to Myca. Arby pulled up a chair and sat it down for Tank. Myca moved his food out of the way so he would have more room.

"This is better," Myca said. "It's no fun talking to you at the very end of the table."

Tank ripped a large piece of meat off with his mouth while the young boy finished the rest of his breakfast. Myca took a deep breath and asked Arby to leave for a moment. Tank eyed him as Arby shut the door.

Myca put his silverware down and turned to Tank. "How has your morning been?"

Tank raised an eyebrow. "It was good, kid. I trained with your mom like I always do." Why was he asking?

"Do you like the arm cannon?" Myca asked. He eyed the cannon as he talked. Tank pulled it back under the table in case it made him nervous.

"I wouldn't say I like it. The reason I have it isn't anything to be happy about." Tank scoffed.

"But if you forget that for a second, do you like the arm cannon?" Myca asked.

Tank glanced down at it. For all the times he had fired it, and it had slammed him into the glass wall, he wasn't entirely sure he liked that. But if it meant he could do his job to protect Myca, then he could say it was a good thing.

"It's heavy, and sometimes I wish I could take it off more easily, but it's better than having to protect you with a couple blasters," Tank said. "Why do you ask?"

"I was just wondering," Myca said.

"You just wonder a lot," Tank said with a laugh.

Myca moved the food on his plate around with his spoon as Tank took another large bite from the meat on his platter.

Neither said anything for a moment before Myca spoke up again.

"Will you sit here every morning?" he asked, not looking at Tank. It seemed like he had finally been working the courage up to ask.

Tank smiled to himself. "If it means I don't have to sit in boiling heat coming from the window anymore, then yes."

It was Myca's turn to smile. "Good."

"Kid, if you wanted me to sit here, you could have asked. Don't be afraid to speak up," Tank said.

"Well, you're kind of scary sometimes," Myca said.

"Only to people I don't like."

Myca's head snapped up. "You don't like me?"

Tank rolled his eyes. "I like you, kid. I'm saying I can be scary when I need to be."

"Can you show me now?"

The Ceremony flashed through Tank's mind. Killing Sovichs, yelling at Naf, and running from Prylek. "You sure you can handle it?" he asked.

"Yeah, I'm not scared of anything," Myca said.

Tank straightened in his chair. Myca observed him. Tank reared his head back and let out a bloodcurdling roar. The room shook as Myca dropped his silverware, sending food splattering onto the table. Tank stood up, letting the sound take over his body. He snuck a peek at Myca, who stared at Tank with wide eyes.

The door flew open, and Arby ran in, ready to face the danger. "What is going on in here?" he asked incredulously.

"Tank's showing me how scary he can be." Myca jumped up and down excitedly in his chair.

"Well, it's disruptive to the rest of the mansion," Arby replied. It was the sternest Tank had ever seen him. "Breakfast is over, it's time to go." He herded them out of the room.

Tank followed Myca, surprised he hadn't been more scared when he roared in his face. The kid might do well if he brought him Whukogantu. But if that didn't scare the kid, then what did scare him?

He sat in the back of the classroom, watching Arby teach. It took him a moment to realize both of them were staring at him.

"Mr. Tank, I told Myca how we had a ship we can show him. We haven't fixed it up yet, so I can't show you everything. But it would be a good start. As long as it's okay with you."

Myca earnestly looked at Tank. "Another field trip?"

"I'm fine with it," Tank said. "Have you ever seen a spaceship up close?"

"Only when Mom brought me home, but I don't remember," Myca replied.

They went to the back of the mansion, down the familiar pathway, to the ship. Myca's eyes widened when he saw the mess of metal.

"How long has this been here?" he asked as he circled the ship.

"I don't know," Tank replied. "Arby and I are rebuilding it to show you what the old ships looked like."

"About that, Mr. Tank," Arby said. "Miss Enzu let me keep the Dyver's Bite needles so it will be much stronger than if we used other materials. I guess you could say your accident was a blessing in disguise."

"I guess," Tank said. "You want to go inside, Myca?"

Myca touched everything, crawling over anything he could. "You think it's ever been in any battles?"

"It doesn't have a weapons system, Mr. Ruba," Arby replied. "Bisekt doesn't make those kinds of ships."

———◆———

That night Tank stood on the stone balcony staring out toward the yard. He didn't know what he was supposed to do. The kid was growing on him, but he still wanted to go back home and find Prylek. To talk to his mother again.

It was better to just go to bed, to sleep on it.

With a sigh, Tank walked back through the doorway. He sensed the change in the air immediately.

It was too cold.

Wrong.

He activated his cannon, the orange glow being the only thing giving him light in the hallway. He froze, listening for any sort of sound, and pulled his cannon up, aiming at . . . no one. Nothing seemed to be out of place from what he could tell, but the feeling remained. Tank released a breath as he approached the stairs.

A scream erupted from Myca's room.

Tank took the stairs two at a time. As he reached the top of the stairs, he spotted movement under Myca's door. He let out a roar, smashing the door open. The window had shattered with glass everywhere. A teary-eyed Myca sat in the center of the room, a towering Sovich aiming a blaster at his head.

Without hesitation, Tank smashed his cannon against the Sovich's head as he pulled Myca away.

The Sovich's scales caught in the light. Bright orange scales.

It felt like the air rushed from the room. Tank pushed Myca behind him.

"Naf?" Tank whispered.

"Tank?"

"What . . . How . . . But Prylek," Tank stammered, trying to stay calm.

"I didn't know you were here." Naf didn't lower the blaster as he spoke. "They told me I didn't have to worry about any guards when I got here."

"Who?"

"Prylek."

Tank tilted his head. "You're working for Prylek?"

"What else could I do since he let me live?" Naf's blaster shook in his hand. "His guards brought me to the junkyard you fell in. I looked for you for days."

"Naf put the blaster down." Tank held his cannon steady, holding his arm out to make sure Myca stayed behind him. "You alright, kid?"

Myca didn't make a sound but nodded furiously.

"You want to know why Prylek sent me here?" Naf eyed Myca. "To send a message."

Tank spat. "Enzu didn't do anything to Prylek."

"You sure about that? You've been gone for a while," Naf sneered. "People from the outside came into the village and demanded we all work for Bisekt. They want Sovich guards. You must do your job really well to have them come for us."

Tank's head spun. "I don't know what to say. If you leave right now, I won't tell anyone you were here."

"No. I'm so close again." Naf's voice rose in pitch. "I can go back to the village with something to be proud of. You aren't talking me out of it this time."

"Killing a child, Naf?" Tank asked incredulously.

Naf gave a short laugh. "You killed our people in the Ceremony. What's it to you if I kill a child?"

Tank's cannon whirred and buzzed, the orange light glowing so bright the entire room lit up. He took a step forward. Naf flinched but stood his ground. He didn't lower his blaster, but the slight shake in his hand gave his nervousness away.

"You heard everything Prylek said about the Ceremony winners. You saw him cut my hand off. But you still want to work for him? Is that who you've become since I left?" He couldn't keep his voice from shaking.

"You left me to fight those guards on my own. Did you think I could have taken them out by myself? Who's the true friend here?" Naf's eyes narrowed.

"If that's what you think, then I won't feel bad stopping you," Tank growled.

He lunged at Naf with a snarl. Naf dove out of the way and Tank collided with the dresser behind him. He looked up in time to see Naf aiming his blaster at Myca.

Tank grabbed Naf's tail and pulled hard. He fell to the ground with a crash, the room shaking around them. Tank aimed the cannon and shot. The room lit up like fire as Tank was thrust backward toward the window.

Myca screamed.

Tank's arm tingled from the shock.

Naf struggled to stand, the floor wet with his blood.

"You always thought you were better than me," Naf said through gritted teeth. "I wish I hadn't missed that shot during the Ceremony."

Naf hurled himself at Tank, his blaster forgotten on the floor. He pushed Tank into the mirror against the wall, sending glass in every direction. Tank pushed Naf off him and charged with his cannon again.

"You were always trying to use me." Tank's cannon collided with the side of Naf's head, knocking him to the ground. "Even when we were on our way to the Ceremony, you told everyone I had blasters to give you an advantage." He kicked Naf in the side. "And now I'm not there to protect you from the bullies, Prylek is the next best thing. You disgust me."

He raised his cannon and pointed it at Naf's chest. The cannon sprung to life as Tank stared Naf down. Anger consumed his vision. The cannon shook as it charged in the darkness, the orange light almost blinding him. The metal warmed around his arm. Naf stared at Tank with wide eyes.

It was as if lightning had struck in the middle of the room. The cannon shot so fast Tank fell backward; when he opened his eyes, he just caught sight of Naf falling out the window.

There was a big thud as Naf's body hit the ground below. Tank glanced at Myca, who still cried on the bed.

Tank peeked his head out the window. Naf lay in a crumpled heap in the dirt.

Several staff members surrounded the body, whispering and pointing. "Another one?" someone gasped.

Naf was dead.

Tank slumped to the floor, hanging his head. He had to do it. It was his duty to protect Myca. But why had it been so easy to kill the others in the Ceremony, and he now he felt so broken?

The young boy sobbed, his face buried in his hands as he leaned against his bed. Tank sat next to him, putting an arm around his shoulder. "It's okay, he's gone."

A dull pain formed in his feet where he'd been stepping in the shattered glass. He ignored it as Myca started shaking.

He threw his arms around Tank and cried against his chest. "I didn't think you were coming," Myca managed to say.

Tank's stomach twisted. If he had been home, this wouldn't have happened. If Kirk hadn't been the one watching Myca, he might be —

"Well don't ever think that again, because I'll always get here whenever you're in trouble," Tank promised. And he truly meant it.

Myca leaned back, wiping his face with the back of his hand. "What do I do if it happens again?"

"You yell for me," Tank said. " And I'll take care of you."

18

Leo's heart rate slowed as they took the familiar elevator ride to Vanish's office. The doors slid open to reveal Vanish inspecting a holographic map in the center of her office. Blue lines crisscrossed over the map with red dots. It looked like a giant mess, but it seemed to make sense to her.

When she saw them entering, she closed the map. "How did it go?" Vanish asked.

"Well, they called Oblurn on us," Leo said, a hint of anger in his voice.

"The Volnea?" Vanish asked. She genuinely looked shocked.

"The Sol Empire disguised one of their own as a Volnea, but they slipped right before we left," Sonja said. "That's when we got her to tell us she called Oblurn."

"Well, Oblurn can talk to me if they have a problem." Vanish plopped down behind her desk. "Did you at least find something out from the Volnea?" Vanish asked. "Please tell me they didn't trick you."

"We found out what Enzu Ruba is afraid of," Sonja said. "We told the Volnea they would have a direct line to you if they told us."

Vanish raised her eyebrows. "A bugged direct line," she corrected.

Sonja smirked. "We found out her greatest fear is losing her child."

"I thought my head would explode from all the questions," Scril said.

Vanish smiled with glee. "If we can get the child, then we can finally hurt her from the inside," she said. "You all need to go to Bisekt and take him from her."

"We can't show up to someone's house and kidnap a child," Gaeth said.

"It's not a house," Vanish said, waving her hand. "More of a fortress."

Leo shifted from side to side. "How did we go from killing an alien to invading a fortress?"

"You all work so well together." Vanish laughed. "Maybe not the best team I've ever had, but pretty close."

Leo glanced at Gaeth, who rolled his eyes. They thanked her and took the coordinates.

"Are we supposed to march up to Enzu Ruba's place like we're best friends?" Leo asked.

"That's exactly what I want you to do," Vanish replied. "Go up to the door and act like you're supposed to be there. Oh, and you two"—she pointed at Leo and Gaeth—"I'm transferring more money to your chip."

————◆————

Scril stretched as they walked through the crowded street. "Can we do something fun for once? I like trying to stop the Sol Empire as much as the next Kekzin, but I need my downtime."

Leo peered down the road. "Looks like it's nothing but bars."

"Your point?" Scril asked.

Sonja pointed at a restaurant on the corner. It didn't have as many lights as the surrounding ones, and Leo peeked through the windows, and it seemed to be almost empty. "We can go here. Let's get some food, my treat."

The quietness of the restaurant was a welcome change from the business of the street. They sat down and screens flipped up from the table with different selections of food. Leo picked what he wanted, and the screen went dark and flipped back down.

"So I've meant to ask you two," he said to Scril and Sonja. "Is Vanish your boss? She hasn't paid you since Gaeth and I joined."

Sonja and Scril exchanged glances.

"Remember how I told you she caught me pickpocketing?" Sonja asked. "She pretty much raised me after that. I never got paid to do anything. She taught me how to be a thief, use a blaster, everything I know. I've always been too scared to ask for money."

"I see," Leo said.

"Don't feel sorry for me. I get by just fine, taking other jobs when things get slow. It works for me," she said.

They all turned their attention to Scril, who cleared his throat. "I lost to Vanish in a bet. The biggest game I ever played. I'm convinced to this day she fixed it, but I can't prove it. I'll owe her money forever." He straightened his suit. "Let's not get into sob stories. I bet you we can make some cash right now." He scanned the restaurant before eyeing Gaeth. "Do those metal bones of yours make you stronger?"

"Yeah. I try to keep it under control, though." Gaeth rubbed the back of his neck.

"I need you to not keep it under control," Scril said.

"I know what you're planning, and I don't agree with it," Sonja said.

"It's easy money, Sonja," Scril said. He jumped on top of the table. "Who here thinks they're the strongest alien in New Star City? Is it you? Or you over there? I have the perfect test of strength for you. Only a couple credits and you can walk away with the title."

The few aliens in the restaurant looked up from their meals.

"Arm wrestle this young gentleman right here"—Scril held up Gaeth's arm—"and walk away richer."

A ripple of laughter traveled through the room. An unusually large alien stood up. "I'll give it a go. How bad can it be?"

Leo looked at Sonja, whose forehead wrinkled. "He'll be fine."

The alien and Gaeth sat across from each other at an empty table. The alien smirked at Gaeth, who took a deep breath. They grasped each other's hands with their elbows on the table. Scril stood on the table, holding their hands still.

"I want a good, clean, arm wrestle," he said, looking from one to the other. "Three, two, one." He jumped off the table.

At first, their hands stayed in the center. But slowly, Gaeth pushed the alien's hand down toward the table. The alien's eyes went wide, his arm bulged as he tried to push back. Some of the others in the restaurant looked up at the commotion. Finally, Gaeth slammed his hand on the table. Scril clapped.

"Gaeth wins. Pay up." He held out a feeler for the money.

The alien waved it away. "I want a rematch."

Scril smirked. "Then you'll have to pay again."

"Fine." He threw money on the table.

Scril caught Sonja's and Leo's attention, rubbing his feelers together.

The alien's face turned red as he pushed against Gaeth's hand. Gaeth stayed calm, and the alien threw down money in frustration.

His friend laughed and pushed him out of the chair. "You're doing it wrong." He threw money down and grabbed Gaeth's hand. After Gaeth beat him, he called another alien over.

A crowd soon formed around the table, people walking in from the street to see what the commotion was. Leo and Sonja moved through the crowd, their food forgotten on the table, taking names of people who wanted to be next. Scril's pockets overflowed with coins as he lined up the next match.

"Think about the bragging rights if you win." He counted down and jumped off the table.

The crowd erupted in cheers, some cheering for the alien, others cheering for Gaeth. Leo's eyes went wide as the alien managed to push Gaeth's hand down toward the table. Before he could say anything, Gaeth smiled at the alien and in one quick motion, slammed his hand on the table, creating a dent. The crowd went nuts.

"Ladies and gentlemen, that's enough for tonight," Scril yelled. "Thank you for coming, we'll see you tomorrow." He motioned to the door to Leo and Sonja.

They managed to make it into the street without being stopped, all four of them laughing. Scril sat atop Gaeth's shoulder.

"Look at all the money we made." He patted his pocket, the coins clinging together. "If you guys ever change your minds about leaving, we have our business set up."

Sonja laughed. "None of them ever suspected a thing."

"I thought the last guy figured it out, but he was so shocked I don't think he knew what to do," Gaeth said.

"I'm glad you had fun," Leo said.

"Just don't give away my money this time," Gaeth replied.

A beep went off on Sonja's wrist. She tapped it a couple times, staring at the screen. "I have to make a call."

"Everything okay?" Leo asked.

Behind him, Gaeth let out a sigh.

"One of my information dealers has something important to tell me," she replied.

They made their way through the streets, following Sonja, who kept furiously typing on her screen. No one said anything as the cars zoomed overhead, flying to their destinations. Sonja finally turned a corner, and they were back at the callers.

Scril tossed her some coins, and she dialed in. A different voice from the one before answered.

"This is Sand Worm."

"I got your message," Sonja said.

"I only have a few minutes. Are you ready?"

Sonja held her hand over her wrist, ready to type. "Ready."

"Enzu is starting production on fifty ships for Sentrum. I don't know when she's shipping them, but the councilmen want them as soon as they're done," Sand Worm said.

Sonja typed back and forth on her screen. "If she's shipping them to Sentrum, that means she's working with the Sol Empire."

"Exactly."

"Anything else?"

"No. I'll update you if something else happens. Sand Worm out." The caller went dark.

"Sand Worm?" Leo asked.

Sonja raised an eyebrow at him. "We need to get to Bisekt."

19

Tank and Myca walked through the halls of the mansion, Myca rattling off about each cased item. He would point to one, naming the planet it came from and what the item was used for. As they reached the end of the row, Tank immediately recognized the item. A blade from a helibike sat behind the glass. It was broken and rusted. Whoever had collected it hadn't cleaned it properly.

"This is a blade from a helibike," Myca said, pointing to the blade with a flourish. "It's from Whukogantu, and the Sovichs use it on their helibikes." He stopped for a moment. "You must have ridden one, right Tank?"

"Yeah," Tank said.

Myca sighed. "I wish I could ride one."

"They're fun," Tank said.

"Mr. Ruba." Arby had appeared at their side. "It's time for your lessons. Mr. Tank and I won't be able to come with you today, so Kirk will be joining you."

Myca and Tank looked at him incredulously.

"Tank always comes with me to my lessons," Myca said.

Tank nodded. "Kirk doesn't know the first thing about protecting Myca."

"It's only for one day," Arby said.

Myca's shoulders drooped as he dragged his feet to the classroom.

"If you would follow me to the maintenance room please, Mr. Tank." Arby walked down the hallway.

The room was the same as they had left it. They sat in front of the monitor again, and Arby smiled at Tank.

"The droids are finally ready to start their work. I think Myca will really like this, Mr. Tank." Arby typed on the monitor, pulling up the parts for the ship came up.

"Arby, I think it's time you just call me Tank."

"That would be rude of me, Mr. Tank," Arby said.

Tank shook his head as Arby read the information on the monitor.

"My droids will take these to the ship. I want to watch them and make sure they get a good start on it." Four small droids on wheels popped out of the desk amidst a series of beeps. They raced through the shelves, darting in and out of each other, and within minutes they came back holding the ship parts.

"I have the needles with me. Let's go," Arby said.

They followed the droids through the hallway toward the yard and to the broken-down ship, where Arby instructed them to lift it out of the ground. The droids got on either side and with one easy push, the ship gave way. Dirt and muck fell away from the bottom, leaving an even layer of soil behind.

"If I scan this, it should tell me what I'm already sure of," Arby said. "There might be a crack in the frame of the door. We need to realign it." He held up a scanner to the ship, and a faint orange line traveled down the side. Arby checked the scanner on his wrist. "Just as I thought. We need to realign the door frame."

"Nothing else?" Tank asked.

"It didn't crash here, Mr. Tank. It was placed out of commission. It's from sinking in the ground. It must have fallen out of place, but we can fix it right up. Anything else we might find wrong will need to have parts sent out for." Arby walked under the ship. "We should clean the mud off as well to see if there's anything else we missed," he said.

"Is there anything I need to do?" Tank asked.

"Just keep a watchful eye on Mr. Myca," Arby said with a smile. "Thank you for bringing this to my attention. It's been back here for so long, who knows how long it would be until we fixed it up if it weren't for you?"

At that moment, Myca walked through the opening in the maze. His eyes went wide at the sight of them. "Woah."

"Myca Ruba, you should be in class right now young man," Arby said.

"Kirk never showed up," Myca said. "Can I go inside it?"

Tank shrugged. "Sure, why not?"

Myca lit up as Tank opened the hatch. It hissed open, and he ran inside, sitting in the pilot seat. He rubbed the leather as he looked around the cockpit.

"You can look but don't touch," Tank said. "Arby and I just started fixing it."

"This is so cool." Myca stood and looked at the buttons on the dashboard.

Tank held his arm out. "I said, don't touch them. We don't know how safe they are yet."

Myca nodded. Tank dropped his arm and walked back to the door. There was a rumble, and the ship lifted off the ground momentarily before crashing into the dirt. Tank whirled around to see Myca with his hand on the dashboard, exactly where Tank had said not to touch.

Tank's blood boiled so much that he couldn't see straight. Myca cowered in the chair, wide eyed.

"I told you not to touch anything when you got on the ship, how hard is it to understand?" Tank yelled, unable to help the roar rising in his throat. "When I tell you not to do something, don't do it, understand?"

Within seconds Arby flew in the doorway. "Is everyone alright?"

Myca stared Tank down, his mouth a thin line. He pushed past Tank without a word and disappeared back into the hedges.

Shit.

Tank sank into the chair and scratched his green scales with his claws. He hadn't meant to yell at the kid, but if he hadn't been there, he could have hurt himself.

Listen to you talking about the kid hurting himself. Do you really care?

No. He needed to stay focused. Make sure the ship would be repaired. What would he even do if he brought the kid with him? He couldn't bring Myca back home. This was better.

———•———

Arby and Tank checked and double-checked the ship. It looked like it had just come off the freighter, nicely packaged, and Arby had taken the extra step of spraying that new ship smell throughout it. Every time Tank stared at it, he could only think one thing: I can go home.

"Just one more thing before we try to turn it on, Mr. Tank." Arby pulled out the needles from when Tank had been poisoned and gave them to the droids. They drilled them smoothly into the outer shell of the ship before rolling away.

Tank and Arby sat in the cockpit facing the mansion. He put his hand on the starter and held his breath. He pushed it and . . .

Nothing.

The ship remained still.

Tank hung his head. He should have expected it. It was too much to hope he might get a way out of here.

Arby put a hand on his shoulder. "I know you're upset we won't be able to show it to Mr. Ruba soon, but don't worry, it's tricky with these older models. I'll put in another order and have them work on it," Arby said. "The older projects always take longer, don't they Mr. Tank?"

Tank nodded, mad at himself for expecting it to work this time. That he might have been able to go back to his village. Instead, he took a deep breath.

"What's the matter, Mr. Tank?" Arby asked as they made their way back toward the mansion.

Tank didn't know if he wanted to tell Arby what happened. Would he even understand? Was it in his programming? Or would he tell Enzu Tank could no longer take care of Myca? It was all stupid anyway.

"It's nothing," Tank said.

"Suit yourself, sir," Arby said. "But I will say, Mr. Ruba has been a little under the weather lately."

Tank's head shot up. "What are you talking about?"

"Mr. Ruba was upset after the last time you both were out here at the ship. Anything you want to say?" Arby asked.

Tank's eyes narrowed. "Are you trying to imply something?"

They stood across from each other. Arby stood one step above Tank and still barely looked up at him.

"Only the best type of bodyguard is the kind that gets along with the person they are supposed to be protecting." Arby's mouth stretched into a thin line, and even though he didn't have pupils, it still felt like someone stared into Tank's soul as he looked at him. "Please tell him you're sorry; it's so difficult to teach a child clearly thinking about other things." He walked up the stairs but not before turning back. "I think Myca also misses his friend."

Arby trudged back up the stairs, leaving Tank staring after him. He really needed to talk to Myca if it was going to have Arby coming to him and asking him to do his job for him.

Tank trudged up the stairs into the mansion. A lot of people had already gone down to the lab for work. He walked around, checking the different rooms for any sign Myca might be wandering around. Eventually, he decided to check outside.

Where would Myca have gone on his own? He couldn't have traveled far. As Tank rounded the corner, that annoying laugh filled the air that made his insides twist.

Now of all times?

Kirk was talking to Myca in their training area. They both looked up as Tank got closer.

"Look who decided to show up." Kirk raised one eyebrow.

Tank waved him off. "Not now, Kirk."

"No, I think now is a perfectly good time. Scaring the child you're supposed to be protecting doesn't reflect well on you, Tank." Kirk crossed his arms. "I don't think Enzu would take well to that."

"I don't think Enzu would take well to you stranding her son in the desert. If it weren't for me, Myca would be dead right now," Tank replied, drawing himself up to his full height.

Kirk gave a short laugh. "Your anger is going to get you in a lot of trouble one of these days." He pushed past Tank and walked toward the mansion without looking back.

Tank turned toward Myca, who sat in the grass, staring out beyond the shield. Tank wasn't sure what to say; he never had to deal with anything like this before, so he opted to sit next to him. As he made himself comfortable in the sand, Myca watched him out of the corner of his eye. A shimmer traveled up the shield as the silence hung between them.

"Hey, kid," Tank started.

"My name's Myca."

Tank paused. He was almost mad at himself. How had he out-lasted so much, yet he couldn't talk to a child? He took a deep breath.

No. If Arby was going to give him a hard time about it, then he'd apologize.

"Sorry. Myca, I wanted to talk to you." Tank sat next to him in the grass. "I wanted to apologize for what happened."

"I don't like getting yelled at," Myca whispered.

Because you don't know how to do what you're told.

"Well, that's life," Tank said. "When you do something wrong, you get yelled at. When you do something that puts you in danger, you get yelled at. The funny thing is it's mostly by the people who care about you."

Myca glared at him.

"You're the only person here I consider family," Myca said. "Enzu isn't my real mom and Arby is just a robot. I never had a friend until you showed up."

"I think you're a good friend too, kid," Tank replied. "Will you forgive me if I promise to be nicer?"

At first, he thought Myca had gone back to ignoring him, but after a moment, the kid looked up at him and nodded.

"That means you need to listen to me too, kid." Myca shot him a look. "I mean, Myca," Tank said.

Myca huffed as the bubble shield shimmered once more. "I guess so."

"How about a yes?" Tank asked.

"Okay."

"Good."

They stared at the bubble shield for some time, the sun setting in the distance. But the silence between them wasn't heavy like before.

Finally, Myca broke it. "Want to play a game?" he asked.

"Sure."

Myca stood up and brushed his pants off. "Let's play hide and seek. I'll hide first." He ran off before Tank could say anything.

"Alright, then." Tank mumbled. He didn't bother counting, just waited a few minutes until he gave Myca enough time for a head start. Eventually, he got up, shook the grass from his scales, and followed Myca into the mansion. It wasn't tough to tell where Myca had gone. Rugs were bunched up, and he had left doors wide open as he ran through them. Tank strolled along the path until he came to Enzu's office. The door stood slightly ajar. Tank checked to make sure no one was coming before barging in.

The office was dark, the only light streaming in from the window behind Enzu's desk. Gently Tank shut the door and took a tentative step forward, listening for anything that might tell him Myca was there.

Nothing.

He made his way around the desk.

"Looks like he isn't here." Tank gripped the top of the chair as he said it. "Unless he's down here." He looked under the desk, hoping to catch Myca off guard, but he wasn't there. Before Tank stood back up, he noticed a big button hanging on the bottom of the desk.

He pushed it, and a blue hologram of a woman appeared on top of Enzu's desk. Tank stood up straight at the sound of her voice. It carried throughout the office, and he was sure someone might come running at the noise.

"Welcome back, Kirk, my name is Ava. You have one new message from Vanish." The woman waited for Tank to speak.

Tank's mind raced. He didn't know anyone named Vanish. Was this how he could talk to people on other planets? Could he reach his mother? It was worth a try.

"I want to talk to someone on Whukogantu," he said.

"Whukogantu. Searching." There was a pause. "Whukogantu found. Would you like me to put you through now?" Ava asked. She had a smooth voice, but it still had the undertone of a computer, of something that wasn't alive.

Tank's heart almost beat out of his chest. "I want to talk to a specific Sovich there."

"Please state the name of who you would like to speak with," Aya answered.

"Shucah. She's my mother."

"One moment, please." Aya paused again. "Shucah on Whukogantu found. Would you like me to put you through right now?"

Tank took a deep breath. He was finally here. Would she be happy to see him? Of course she would—what mother wouldn't? He promised he would send a message to her one way or another any-way. "Yeah. Put me through."

Ava stepped back and onto the floor where she grew to the size of a normal human being.

"Calling Shucah on Whukogantu now." She disintegrated into hundreds of small blue dots that floated in the room. Tank gripped Enzu's chair tighter, the only sound a constant beeping.

What if she refused to talk to him? Or worse, what if she asked about Naf? Should he tell her what happened? Would she even un-derstand why he did what he did? So many questions ran through his mind that at first, he didn't hear Ava's voice again.

"You are now connected. Please say hello." The blue dots flew together and before him stood a hologram of his mother.

"Hello?" A voice traveled throughout the room. His mother's voice.

Tank opened his mouth to say something, but his throat went dry. He walked around the desk and stood in front of her.

Hello. Say hello.

"Hi . . . Mom."

There was a beat where he wasn't sure if she heard him or not, but then, "Tank? Was that you?" she asked excitedly.

"Yeah. It's me." His voice shook as he reached out for her hand, but he grasped nothing but air.

She fell silent for a moment. "I thought I would never hear from you again."

"I told you I would get a message to you." He half laughed.

"Where are you?" she asked. "Prylek told us you didn't want to say goodbye. What happened?"

He didn't know where to start. Bisekt, Prylek, Myca, the ship, all of it swam in his mind until it flowed over. "Mom." A sob escaped him. "It's been so hard."

"Oh, Tank."

He told her everything he'd gone through. From what Prylek did to how he was trying to get back home and finally Myca. When he finished, he looked up at her.

"The outside world hasn't been good to you, has it?" she asked.

"I want to come back. I want to kill Prylek. I'll help all of you."

She placed a clawed hand on his face. He closed his eyes trying to imagine the touch. "Tank if there's one thing I've learned, it's revenge never solves anything. It won't bring your father back, it won't bring the other Sovich back, and it won't make you feel better."

"What am I supposed to do, then?"

"Forgive. That's what I did."

"I'll never forgive him," Tank growled through tears.

His mother smiled. "Forgiveness isn't being okay with what happened. It's accepting that it happened and moving on."

Tank took a shuddering breath. "Did Bisekt really try to take everyone?"

She nodded. "They came a few days ago."

"I'm sorry."

"You couldn't have known," she said. "Don't worry about us anymore, alright? It sounds like there's someone you worry about enough there."

"I do," he replied.

"Remember what I said after you won the Ceremony?" she asked. "It's still true. I'm so proud of you, Tank. Your father would be too."

A lump formed in Tank's throat. "I miss you."

A sad smile crossed her face. "I miss you too. I know you'll do the right thing."

She disappeared, replaced by Ava once more.

"Do you need anything else today, Kirk?"

"No. Nothing else."

"Have a pleasant evening, Kirk." Ava disappeared, leaving Tank alone in the office. He slumped back in the chair, staring at the spot where Ava had been standing. The office disappeared around him. He couldn't stop thinking about what his mother had said. How could he move on from everything that happened?

20

Leo's heart pounded against his chest as he clutched the controls on the ship. It was the only thing keeping him calm as they veered toward Bisekt, knowing they were going to try to kidnap a child. If they managed to actually do it, he would never tell a soul about this adventure. How could he live with taking a child from their family?

"So what's our plan for getting the kid?" Scril asked.

"Get in his room, take him, and get back to the ship," Gaeth said.

Leo laughed. "How are we supposed to do that when we've never stepped foot in Bisekt?"

"I'll ask Sand Worm," Sonja said, going through her contacts.

"Ah yes, Sand Worm. How could I be so silly?"

While they waited, Scril went over every possible situation they could find themselves in when they got there.

"Maybe Enzu is in his room when we get there and kills us all where we stand. Or maybe he sleeps with a knife under his pillow and slices us before we get a chance to grab him."

Gaeth groaned. "Scril, you're not helping at all."

"Are you doing the deed this time?" Scril said, elbowing Gaeth. "You killed Felgi and all, I think it'd be easy for you to grab a kid from his bed."

"Whoever wants to is fine with me," Gaeth said.

Sonja gasped. "Found it. He's sending us a map of Bisekt."

A few minutes later, a hologram of a large mansion popped out of Sonja's holo-pad with several red dots scattered all over it.

"This is where we can enter," Sonja said, pointing to the red dots. "And there's Myca's room. There isn't really anything below his window we could use to climb in."

"Look how big this place is. How much money do you think Enzu has?" Scril asked.

"Selling luxury ships is good business," Sonja replied. "I wonder if there is a way we could get in through the kid's door. If we did, then we could just throw him out the window and have someone in the ship waiting for him."

"We could do it at night when no one's awake," Gaeth suggested. "Or at least when not as many people are awake."

"Good idea," Sonja said. "I like my idea of going into the mansion and grabbing him in his room and getting out through the window. But if we do, it'd be best if you two go together while Scril and I stay on the ship and pilot it under the window when you're ready."

"Wait, why do Gaeth and I have to be the only ones to go inside?" Leo asked.

"Because I can hold a ship steady better than you can, and Gaeth can throw the kid with his strength," Sonja replied.

Leo huffed. She was right. If he could have it his way, Gaeth would stay in the ship with the others. He didn't want to take a chance something could happen to him. No. He was doing this for Gaeth. Once they were done with this, they were done forever—that's what Vanish said. If he could stay back while someone else did the work, he would be perfectly happy. Leo leaned back in his chair and tried his best to fall asleep. It was the only thing he could do until they got there. The steady grumble of the ship gnawed at his ears. Why of all times, did that sound have to be super annoying now? After a while, he thought it better to close his eyes. Just for a moment.

He stood in the field where they had said goodbye to their parents. Except this time, there was no ship to take them away. The crowd jostled him around as Leo searched frantically for Gaeth, pushing people out of the way and trying to jump above the crowd to find him. He eventually made his way to the center, where people were giving something ample space.

Leo approached to see a figure in a flowing cloak standing in the open field with its back to him. It seemed to be looking for something, the crowd backing away as its gaze traveled over them. Leo made his way toward it through the rain, and his hand reached out. Just as he was about to touch it, it whipped around. Its face wasn't human, but completely metal, the rain effortlessly gliding down its sides.

Leo didn't run, his feet rooted to the ground. He couldn't pull his eyes away from its stare. A crack of lightning flashed across the sky, and a jolt rocketed through his body.

KATHLEEN CONTINE

"We're really close. Get ready." Sonja shook his shoulder. Gaeth still snored in the corner, Scril curled up against his neck.

Leo sat up and grabbed the controls. In the distance, what looked like a bubble sat on the horizon, glowing against the night sky. Leo pushed the ship closer.

"Land over there." Sonja pointed to a sand dune.

As Leo set the ship down, got up, and tapped Gaeth on the shoulder, sending Scril to the floor.

"You ready?"

"We're here already?"

Leo held out a hand to help him up. "Yeah, let's go."

"I have the map with me, and I'll keep you updated the entire time you're in the mansion," Sonja said as she typed on the holo-pad. "Tell me when you're near his room, and we'll get into position."

The ramp lowered, and Gaeth and Leo walked into the desert night. Leo shivered against the cold, swearing for not bringing a jacket.

"Why didn't we ever pack jackets for you in Oblurn?" Leo asked, hugging himself tighter.

"Because we never thought we would be walking through a desert on our way to kidnap a kid," Gaeth said, sarcastically.

They walked through the sand with nothing but the bubble to light their way. With every step they took, Leo couldn't help wondering what the hell they were doing. Could they actually pull this off?

"You think Vanish told the truth when she said this was the last job?" Gaeth asked.

"I think so," Leo said.

"I wouldn't be surprised if we get the kid to Vanish and she suddenly remembers she wanted us to blow up a planet."

Leo laughed. "Good thing I brought my book on how to blow up a planet."

Gaeth rolled his eyes.

As they continued, Leo's foot bumped into something. He looked down to see a strange plant. He held out his arm for Gaeth as he realized they were surrounded.

"Careful, you don't know what they might do," Leo cautioned.

"It's you who should be worried about it," Gaeth said. "You've got normal bones."

As they navigated the patch of strange plants, Leo tried to fill the silence. "What are you going to do when you finally get your house in the countryside?"

"Live there and never deal with anyone ever again," Gaeth answered. "I'm done with taking orders, I'm done with people feeling bad for me. I just want my own place where I don't have to worry about it."

"Are you okay?"

"Yes. You don't need to keep asking," Gaeth said. "I know you mean well, but seriously, you need to stop."

"Something's been bothering me for a bit. Ever since you went off by yourself that day in New Star City, I feel like you've been acting different. Are you sure you're okay?"

"I'm fine, I just want to get this done and go home. That's really all it is," Gaeth said.

They walked the rest of the way in silence. As they approached the bubble, Leo put his hand on its surface. It was solid, but the more Leo pushed his hand, the more it made its way through the strange substance. Eventually, Leo's entire body was through, and he walked on the other side. Gaeth quickly followed.

Sonja's voice buzzed in Leo's ear. "You need to find the closest door to you. Get inside as soon as possible."

"Do you see the door anywhere?" Leo asked. He and Gaeth looked around in the darkness.

"Let's look this way," Gaeth said. They tiptoed around back to see a broad set of stone stairs. Leo stopped Gaeth as he was about to climb them.

"Let me do it." He took a tentative step forward and started climbing, waiting for a guard to jump out at him. But the higher he got, the more he realized nothing would happen.

Once Leo was at the top, Gaeth quickly followed, making sure no one was behind them. Without hesitating, Leo grabbed the door and pulled it open. The first thing he noticed was how tall it was. Who needed this much room?

Sonja spoke in his ear again. "Up the stairs."

"Did you hear that?" Gaeth whispered.

"Yeah, it was my earbud," Leo whispered back. "Come on."

They snuck past the overstuffed furniture, toward the grand staircase. As they neared the top, Sonja spoke again. "The room on your left. We're flying there now."

Leo walked over to the door. It clearly belonged to a child, with stickers of different characters on it. Leo grabbed the handle and, holding an index finger to his mouth, pushed the door open. Gaeth nodded, and ever so slowly, they stepped into the room. It was dark, nothing out of the ordinary for a child's bedroom. Myca lightly snored in his bed nearby.

They stood over him for a moment, both not ready to be the one to make a move. The sound of their ship getting closer made his heart race. Finally, he took a deep breath. Leo grabbed Myca's arm and yanked him out of bed.

He hadn't even taken one step when Myca screamed.

He did a quick maneuver, and Leo's hand slipped off his arm. Myca ran for the door, but Gaeth was too fast and grabbed him around the middle. A low rumble sounded outside as Sonja hovered the ship just outside the window. He opened the window and waved to Scril, who stood in the doorway. He gave a small wave.

"Throw him," Leo shouted.

"Got it," Gaeth said.

Myca's eyes widened. He kicked, clawed, and scratched as Gaeth carried him toward the window. He managed to pull Gaeth's glove off, but Gaeth still held on to him. Leo grabbed his ankles to help.

"Tank!" Myca yelled.

"What tank?" Gaeth said.

There was a loud smash, and pieces of the door flew into the room amidst a terrible roar. Leo turned around to see a towering figure running toward him. Instinctively, he got between the figure and Gaeth, but that only made it angrier.

The figure stepped into the light, wielding a massive arm cannon. It was a Sovich, towering over them, baring its shiny fangs. It pointed the cannon at Gaeth.

"Drop the kid," he said in a deep voice.

Gaeth dropped Myca, who scrambled behind the monster.

"Jump," Scril shouted from outside.

Leo and Gaeth turned from the Sovich and sprinted toward the window. Gaeth was ahead, but not by much. As they got closer, Scril backed into the ship to give them room. Tank's footsteps thundered behind them, and he was suddenly in front of the window, blocking them from going any further.

Gaeth pulled a blaster out and aimed it. The monster laughed and swatted it out of Gaeth's hand, and Leo and Gaeth backed away slowly. They had nowhere to run now. Tank stood between them and the window. Footsteps pounded against the floor as a woman in a lab coat ran into the room with several guards.

"Who are you people?" she asked, hugging Myca to her.

Before Leo could speak, a loud noise erupted, and the ship outside the window flew off into the night. His father's ship was gone. He sighed and took a step forward.

"I'm Leo. I was going to kidnap your son," he said, thinking perhaps if he told the truth she would take pity on them.

"I have no idea how you got in here. But this is a high-security facility. This entire planet belongs to me. You were trespassing the second you landed," she said. "On top of that, you think you can just tell me you were here to take my child and I'll let you walk out of here?" She scoffed at Gaeth. "And who are you? You think I'll just talk to your friend and let you off?" The anger in her voice was rising.

"Well, that's my brother—"

Before Gaeth could finish speaking, she had grabbed his wrist. He winced as she pushed her thumb into his hand.

"You've escaped, haven't you? We haven't had that happen in a while." She typed on something with one hand and then motioned to Tank who walked over. "You'll be fine, we just need to get the car."

"Yes, Enzu," Tank said.

"Wait, what's happening?" Leo asked.

"I felt the Steel Bones, there's no other explanation than he escaped. If you're together, then you must have escaped as well. I'm sending you both back. Tank, please bring them downstairs to the rover waiting for them," the woman said.

Tank grabbed Gaeth's arm, aiming his cannon at Leo, and pushed them out of the room. As they went down the stairs, Leo's mind swam with any way he could possibly get them out of the situation.

"What did they say your name was? Tank?" He kept his hands in the air to show he wasn't going to pull anything. "You ever want to get out of this place? If you let us go, then you can come with us."

"Leo, he just tried to kill us," Gaeth said.

But Leo could have sworn Tank paused for a moment before he shook his head and kept walking.

"You want to leave, don't you?" Leo asked.

"It's not that simple," Tank said as he opened the front door where a rover waited at the bottom of the stairs.

"Last chance to let us go," Leo said.

"Or what?" Tank glared down at him.

Leo didn't say anything.

"That's what I thought," Tank said as he shoved them in the rover. "And I have my own plan." Darkness consumed them as the rover sped away.

21

After the night Myca had been attacked, Tank hadn't slept soundly. He kept dreaming he heard his name and jumped out of bed, ready to smash through Myca's door again, only for nothing to be there. The dreams steadily became less frequent, but Tank remained paranoid every time he went to bed.

Enzu was furious it even happened and wanted Myca to have more self-defense training. Each moment they spent in Kirk's presence infuriated him more. It took everything Tank had to not roll his eyes as Kirk explained Myca would have been fine if he had made a specific move Kirk never taught him. It didn't help Myca sleep better at night thinking he would need to use the step again.

Tank sat down at breakfast and waited for Myca, who came in with bags under his eyes, his hair not brushed.

Poor kid.

Tank picked his plate and chair up and walked down to Myca's end.

"Mr. Tank, I'm afraid protocol states Myca's bodyguard must always be at the other end of the table," Arby said.

"Look at him, Arby." Tank frowned. "He could use some company for a meal, don't you think?"

As Tank spoke, the door to the lab opened, and Enzu walked out. Her eyes shifted around the room, and she wrung her hands.

"Mind if I join you for breakfast?" she asked Myca.

Tank got up and carried his chair around so she could sit. Myca beamed.

"I'll give you some privacy," Tank said. He and Arby walked outside, where they saw Kirk practicing self-defense moves by himself.

Loathing replaced the happiness Tank felt. "Your services aren't needed anymore," he said, walking straight up to Kirk.

"What are you talking about?" Kirk frowned.

"I'm teaching the kid self-defense."

Kirk laughed. "I've been teaching him since he arrived. No one knows his stances better than I do."

"Well, your stances are shit," Tank said. "I'll let Enzu know you're not needed anymore."

Kirk's eyes narrowed, and Tank thought he might punch him for a second. He wanted him to. Please let Kirk be stupid enough to do it; he just wanted a reason to finally put him in his place. Nothing would make him happier than to show him what it really felt like to get your ass handed to you. Kirk waved Tank off and walked back to the mansion.

"Miss Ruba won't appreciate you saying those things, Mr. Tank," Arby said.

Tank watched Kirk leave. "You let me worry about that."

———◆———

Arby suggested going inside in case Kirk had gone to talk to Enzu. As soon as they walked in, Kirk's voice echoed throughout the hall. Lab assistants glanced at Tank as they passed by, some whispered to each other while others rushed by without making eye contact.

As they got closer to the noise, Arby pulled on Tank's arm. "Let's not get involved."

"No, let's." Tank shrugged Arby's hand off and stomped toward the voices.

Enzu and Kirk stood in front of the staircase. Enzu tapped her foot on the carpet, standing above Kirk as he sat in one of the fluffy chairs. His arms flailed as he talked, sweat forming on his brow.

"You think I'll let you stay here after what happened? If it weren't for Tank, Myca might be dead," Enzu yelled. "You're lucky I've been busy, or you would have been sent off planet days ago."

Kirk searched the crowd for a friend. When no one came forward, he said, "Miss Ruba, I taught him the most advanced self-defense techniques. I had him prepared for anything that could happen. The reason he almost got kidnapped must have been because he was asleep."

Enzu paced back and forth, shaking her head. She caught Tank's eye before she turned back to Kirk.

"The most advanced self-defense moves?" she asked.

"Yes," Kirk whined. He clearly thought he was getting her to see his point of view.

"Tank?" Enzu waved Tank over. "Would you please demonstrate for everyone some of the techniques Kirk taught Myca?"

"Of course," Tank replied, strutting into the middle of the forming crowd.

He paused for a moment, giving everyone a second to wonder what he would do, and then flopped to the ground without warning, his arm cannon clanging against the floor. Several people screamed from the sudden noise. Others froze.

Tank decided to twist the knife.

"I'm dead," he said.

It was impossible to stop the smile spreading across his face as gasps arose from the crowd. Tank stood up to Kirk's glare, but he just smiled.

"I think we're done here." Enzu waved a hand. "I'll be reviewing your time here at Bisekt and decide if I need your services any longer." She turned back to her technicians. "Everyone back to work. We have a shipment that needs to be ready to go as soon as it's done."

The crowd dispersed. Kirk left without saying anything, bumping into people as he rushed from the scene. Enzu had already started heading back toward the lab.

Tank jogged to catch up to her before she headed through the door in the dining room. "I want to ask you a question about Myca."

Understanding briefly flashed on her face, but it disappeared as Enzu said, "Go ahead."

"I overheard people talking about him being sent away soon. Is that true?" He watched her face intently. She didn't answer right away but sighed.

"In the coming months, Myca will be sent away," Enzu said at last.

"Why?" Tank asked.

"Because"—she pulled him closer—"because he has Steel Elbow."

"What do you mean?"

"Come to the lab, and we'll talk," Enzu said.

Tank left everyone behind, following Enzu to the lab. No one was around, and they sat in the glass chamber where Tank normally trained.

"You know Myca isn't really my son," Enzu said. "The thing is, he has a virus called Steel Elbow. It can be brutal. But when I found out he was being sent to Oblurn at such a young age, I felt terrible. A child that young can't go to Oblurn. So after giving him the antidote to make sure he wasn't contagious, I let him live here. Now that he's older I'll let him go, and if another child who's too young for Oblurn comes along, then they'll be sent here too."

"So Myca is leaving?" Tank asked.

"Don't worry, you'll stay here and keep your job," Enzu said. "When another child comes along, you'll get to guard them as well."

"What's the point of the classroom and the self-defense if you're just waiting for him to get older and leave?"

"Classroom is to keep his brain active," Enzu said. "I don't want him to be bored all day. And you should know why he needs self-defense. You've protected him from enough. Then, once he's old enough for Oblurn, we can send him there."

"Is Oblurn where we sent those other two?" Tank asked.

Enzu smiled.

22

Leo and Gaeth were jostled around in the darkness, unsure exactly where they were going. Gaeth hadn't said anything since Tank shoved them in the rover.

"Are you okay?" he asked.

"Do you think I'm okay? We completely failed our mission, Sonja and Scril took off with Dad's ship, and now we're here." The sound of Gaeth banging his head against the metallic walls of the rover echoed in the small chamber.

The rover came to a stop. Leo held his hand up to shield his eyes as light poured in.

"Gaeth and Leo, I'm so happy you were able to find your way back to us."

It was the woman in white.

Leo's body went completely numb. How had she found them at Bisekt? Voices screamed in his head.

Get out of there. Grab Gaeth and run. Escape.

"Please step out of the vehicle," the woman said.

As Leo slid out of the rover, his stomach dropped. He was in front of Oblurn. Several guards stood nearby, the woman in white motioned to them, and they grabbed Gaeth, leading him toward the dome. Leo went to follow, but another guard put his hand up to stop him.

"You will be talking to our board," the woman in white said. "They aren't happy with you."

The guards pushed them in the decontamination chamber, the woman in white following behind. Instead of walking to the tour room when the doors opened, Leo was forced past the statue of Dr. Moon, toward a large doorway.

"The Oblurn council wants to speak with you about breaking your brother out," the woman said.

They walked into a circular room with stadium seating, all facing one spot in the center. The speakers sat in the seats, wearing white robes like the woman, watching Leo intently as he walked in. When he stood in the center of the room, the woman walked up the stairs to sit at her own desk while the guard remained with Leo.

A man in black robes stood from the center of the council and walked forward so everyone could see him.

"Leo Spearman," he began. "Do you understand why we have called you here?"

"No," Leo lied.

"You are here to discuss the actions taken regarding your brother, Gaeth Spearman." He leaned over his desk. "Do you know what happens to someone with Steel Elbow who doesn't get treatment from Oblurn?"

"Well, nothing happened to Gaeth when he was with me, so I'm going to say nothing."

The council members looked at him disapprovingly. Some of them shook their heads, while others wrote furiously in their notebooks.

"When he doesn't get proper treatment, his virus overtakes his body, and he dies." The speaker paused for dramatic effect. "Do you want that for your brother?"

"My brother was fine the entire time he was with me and wasn't in any sort of pain. Am I supposed to believe he would lie?" Leo asked.

"Since his return, his virus has got worse because of your own incompetence," said a council member to the leader's side. "Even if you think he wasn't in pain, it doesn't mean he wasn't."

"We've put him in an anti-containment lab to try and reverse the damage you've done," another council member said.

"I understand you think this is best for him," Leo said, "but the first time I brought him here, he was so miserable when he found out what his life was going to be, I couldn't leave him. We've been to so many places together and made friends. He hasn't been this happy in a long time."

"Even so, you've put not only your brother but the other planets you've visited in danger," the leader said. "Not to mention one of our guards was killed trying to keep him here. You need to understand the severity of your actions."

The room heated up. Leo couldn't think of how he could argue out of having a dead body on his ship. "He got the vaccine that made it not contagious," Leo said.

"We can't just let you go home now." The woman in white clasped her hands. "You need to face some sort of punishment."

"Why don't we keep him here for a few days while we figure out what to do with him? Clearly, this won't get resolved now," a council member said to the woman in white.

Everyone nodded in agreement.

The speaker raised his hands. "All in favor?"

They all raised their hands.

"Very well. Bring him to a room, and we will give you our verdict soon."

The guard pushed Leo out of the council chamber. Leo left, unsure if he had just become a prisoner or not.

23

Gaeth opened his eyes. Blinding white light filled his vision and he blinked several times. He tried to get a sense of his surroundings. He had somehow ended up in a bed in a bright windowless room. It had to be the size of a closet.

Where am I? Where's Leo?

He attempted to sit up but stopped when restraints around his chest, legs, and arms tightened. Sweat formed on his forehead and he pulled harder. Next to him a high-pitched alarm sounded. There was a rush of heavy footsteps and the door flew open, revealing several Oblurn workers in pristine white lab coats led by the woman in white. The sight of her made Gaeth struggle against his restraints even more.

"Gaeth Spearman." She smiled. "You finally came back to finish your treatment."

She nodded at one of the lab workers, who wheeled in a machine covered in numerous tubes and bags of yellowish liquid. The woman in white grabbed a tube and flashed her smile at Gaeth.

"Since you left, we'll need to make sure you haven't been decontaminated by any outside sources."

She grabbed a syringe from the top of the machine.

"Stay away from me," Gaeth said.

Where's Leo?

He tried to sit up again, pulling with every ounce of strength he had left. The woman in white watched him for a moment, still smiling. She strolled over to him and inserted the syringe in his neck.

"Oblurn is your home now," she said. "No one is coming for you."

Gaeth's body collapsed. Only his eyes were able to follow the woman in white as she grabbed a tube from the machine. If it weren't for the syringe, Gaeth would have yelped at the prick on his arm. The machine whirred and the yellowish liquid slid through the tube. A cooling sensation overcame him, traveling throughout his body before there was another prick. And another. And another. His thoughts became fuzzy.

Leo's not coming.

24

It was almost time for Myca's defense lesson, so Tank left the ship to meet him at their training spot. Myca was already practicing different Sovich stances Tank had taught him. When he saw Tank approaching, the little boy smiled.

"Did you see how good I was doing?" he asked.

"Very good. Better than last time," Tank replied.

It was true. Two weeks had passed since Tank took over Myca's training, and the kid had improved so much it surprised Tank. Clearly, Myca didn't want anyone sneaking in his room again.

"Do you want to practice with Arby or me this time around?" Tank asked.

Tank liked to watch Myca and Arby train together so he could point out where Myca needed more improving, but Myca liked training with Tank.

"You," Myca said.

They sparred for a while, jumping, running, dodging, ducking, and having fun. Afterward, they sat down in the shade while Arby served them drinks.

Myca didn't drink his right away. He swirled the liquid around in his glass, staring at it thoughtfully.

"What's wrong?" Tank asked.

"Nothing, I just thought when I'm older, I want to leave this place and find my parents so I can show them how much you've taught me," Myca said. "I think they would be proud, wherever they are."

Tank didn't say anything. If he did, he knew he would tell Myca what would really happen to him when he was older. And he couldn't stand it.

"I think that's great, kid." Tank nudged him. "And you're right. They would be proud."

Myca smiled. "Do you think your parents are proud of you?"

Tank paused. "I know they are." Tank replied. "Before I left Whukogantu, my mother said she was proud of me. If I ever see my father, maybe he'll say he's proud too."

Myca smiled. "When will you see your dad?"

"I don't know. I haven't been searching for him because I've been here," Tank admitted.

"Well, you should go find him," Myca said.

"Honestly, Myca I don't think he's alive anymore. After what happened to me"—Tank motioned to his arm cannon—"I don't think my father made it out of the village."

"Oh." Myca took a sip of his drink. "Do you miss them?"

Tank looked out over the sand. "A lot."

"I could tell from how you said goodbye."

Tank's head snapped to look at Myca. "You were spying on me?"

"I was hiding behind the bookcase and you called her before I could leave," he said, pausing before continuing. "I miss my mom too, you know. Not Enzu. My real mom. I think about her sometimes."

Tank glanced down at Myca, who concentrated on his hands. "I'm sure she misses you too, kid. And just like my mom, I know she'd be proud of you if she could see you now."

Myca stood and wiped the dirt off his clothes. "Ready for round two?"

Tank smiled. No one at Bisekt had really taken the time to ask how he was doing. It felt like the first time someone wanted to make sure he was okay. Make sure he was happy.

"Yeah," Tank said.

25

Leo had been at Oblurn two days, and he still hadn't seen or heard from Gaeth. Every time he asked someone about him, he was met with answers that danced around the question and only confused him more. He had wandered around the plaza so many times he had every crevice and tile memorized. It was all so contained and clean and too perfect. He remembered the plaque on Dr. Moon's statue by heart, watched people come and go through different doors, and even saw someone new be brought in through the main doors. He considered warning them about what awaited them after the tour but decided it would lower his chances of seeing Gaeth.

He had been told the council was still debating what to do with him after escaping with Gaeth. Or as they like to put it, "kidnapping." Personally, if Leo had the chance to do it again, he would.

Several older patients walked by the bench where he sat. Leo couldn't help but wonder how long they had been there. He knew Gaeth would be here for the rest of his life. But until old age? Would he not have a family? Or get married? There weren't any families around, just different-aged people interacting.

An old couple slowly walked around the fountain, and Leo picked up bits of their conversation. Mundane things like what they had for breakfast and what the weather was probably like back home.

Back home.

Would Gaeth ever consider this place home or would Oblurn always be the place his town forced him to go? He would make sure that he would somehow visit. Gaeth wouldn't live to old age without him.

The couple was in front of him now. The old man had the old woman's hand in his arm.

Leo smiled. Gaeth would probably make friends. There were others his age here he could talk to.

There was a loud thud as the old man fell forward and smashed into the ground face first. The woman screamed and ran away. Leo rushed to his side and rolled him over. He wasn't breathing, and his skin was turning white.

In seconds, they numerous Oblurn guards surrounded them, pushing a stretcher. They lifted the man onto it, poking him with different instruments and asking him different questions. Leo gripped the old man's hand even though it was limp in his grasp. He walked with the guards as they pushed the stretcher toward a door.

"Tell me what happened," one of them demanded.

"He was walking around the fountain and then he fell down. There weren't any signs, he just fell." Leo held on to the side of the stretcher to keep up with them. The wheels spun over the tiled floor with a steady *ca-chunk, ca-chunk.* The door opened, and they rushed down a brightly lit hallway.

A guard pulled out a long needle and stuck it in the man's arm. He immediately started seizing, squeezing Leo's hand so tightly he was worried his fingers might break, but none of the guards reacted to it.

A nurse appeared next to Leo and injected a second needle into the man's arm. As soon as she pulled it out, he lay still once more. His hand slipped from Leo's as they approached another set of doors. One of the guards put his hand on Leo's shoulder.

"I'm sorry, but we can't allow you in here," he said. "Please go back to the plaza."

They pushed the stretcher through the last set of doors, the lock clicking into place with a note of finality.

Everything about this seemed wrong. Why couldn't he shake the feeling something else was going on here? He started to walk back to the plaza to wait for the council again, but a door in the wall caught his eye that he hadn't seen before.

Double checking for guards, Leo slid into the room. It was pitch black, and the only thing he could see was a faint orange glow on the other side of the room. He stumbled toward it, arms held out in front of him. As he got closer, a light shone through a panel of windows coming from somewhere below them.

A large warehouse stretched out before him. Workers ran back and forth with pieces of metal and tools in their arms. In the corner were half-built spaceships with the word Bisekt painted on the side.

In the opposite corner sat a large pot attached to a conveyor belt carrying pieces of metal. Workers darted back and forth from it, grabbing what they needed. A hatch in the wall above the pot opened, and the guards with the old man appeared. Sweat dripped down his face as Leo leaned against the window. They tipped the stretcher forward with a swift push, and the old man slid into the pot with a splash. The liquid in the pot bubbled and hissed.

Leo covered his mouth with his hands. Several seconds later, small pieces of metal slid out of the pot onto the conveyor belt. The workers, who acted like they hadn't even seen what happened, grabbed the pieces and rushed them over to the ships.

Leo backed away from the window.

That could be Gaeth. That *would* be Gaeth. Find Gaeth.

He raced out of the room, leaving the warehouse behind. His brain felt like it had been turned off. People with Steel Elbow were being used for spaceship parts. What was the purpose of the council? If he told them what he saw, would they believe him? He had to act. Before something happened to Gaeth.

Find him. Find him. Find him now.

He busted through the door, desperate for any sign of where Gaeth might be.

A droid noticed him. "Excuse me sir, but if you aren't in need of medical assistance, then I'm afraid you aren't allowed back here, and I have to ask you to leave."

"Gaeth?" Leo half yelled. He was in a circular room with six doors. He knew where one of them went. Was he even in the right place? What if Gaeth had already been turned into a spaceship?

"You're looking for Gaeth Spearman?" the droid asked. "He's in that room over there." It pointed to the room closest to them.

Leo rushed into the room. Gaeth lay in a hospital bed, hooked up to all sorts of different monitors and tubes. Slowly, Leo approached the bed and tapped Gaeth on the shoulder.

"Gaeth, can you hear me?"

Gaeth opened his eyes just barely so Leo knew he was awake. His mouth curled into an unnerving smile that didn't belong to him.

"Leo. This place said they were going to heal me. Now, look at me. I'm stuck to a bunch of fucking tubes, and I can't even move."

Leo grabbed his hand. "I'm breaking you out again, okay? I did it before, I'll do it again."

Gaeth's eyes rolled in the back of his head. "I don't know," he said, slurring his words.

"Gaeth, I need you to stay awake." Leo's pulse quickened. They were doing this to Gaeth on purpose. He knew it. In case this very thing happened. In case he decided to come to get Gaeth out again. "Gaeth, I need you to stand up okay?"

As if on cue, the door opened, and five Oblurn guards stormed in the room, weapons drawn.

"Let go of the patient, now," one said, loudly.

Leo gripped Gaeth's hand tighter.

"If you don't let go of the patient's hand, we will have to force you."

Leo didn't look at them. He stared at his brother as the guards surrounded the bed. They grabbed him by the arm and dragged him away. Gaeth held out a hand toward him as if trying to tell them to come back.

But as soon as he did, he passed out. Leo fought against the guards as best he could, but it was no use as he was taken back through the doors and out into plaza, where everyone stopped and stared at him.

His feet dragged as they stormed into the council chamber. The guards threw him on the ground, and some of the council members snickered.

The leader stood at the center and stepped up to the podium. He stared down at Leo like he was a bug about to be squished. The other council members sat back in their chairs as if relieved they weren't the one who had to talk directly to Leo.

"Leo Spearman, it seems we can't leave you alone for two days without you causing trouble," he said.

But Leo wasn't having it. He wouldn't take any of their shit this time.

"I'm sorry. I was trying to save my brother from being turned into a spaceship," he spat.

The air was sucked from the room. Several council members stiffened.

"You must be mistaken," a councilman said, his eyes narrowing. "We heal people on Oblurn. Anything that has to do with Bisekt is a silly conspiracy theory."

"I never said anything about Bisekt," Leo said. "But I saw an older patient fall in the plaza, and instead of helping him, I watched your guards kill him and then dump his body into a warehouse to be used for spaceship parts. And now you're standing in front of me like I'm supposed to feel bad for trying to break my brother out?"

"You have no idea what you saw," the leader said, his eyes narrowed.

"I do. How can you be okay with this when you all have Steel Elbow as well?" Leo said exasperatedly. "You won't be buried outside when you die; you're all going to be made into spaceship parts."

The leader nodded at the guards. "Throw him out. I don't want a record of this anywhere. Just throw him out." The woman in white watched as Leo was dragged out of the room.

Leo pulled and kicked and scratched at the guards through the plaza, passing several people who gawked at him. He wouldn't make this easy. They marched past the stupid statue of Dr. Moon and finally through the decontamination chamber. The second it was open, the guards threw him out into the sand and slammed the door shut behind him.

26

"I'll race you to the door," Myca said as he took off down the hall-way.

Tank ran after him, trying his best not to knock anyone down as Myca got further and further ahead. Tank took a shortcut to the right and sprinted passed a droid carrying equipment to the lab. The door to the outside was ahead. He could beat Myca if he hurried.

There was a small scurrying of footsteps, and out of the corner of his eye, Myca lunged for the door, barely sliding passed him.

"Told you," Myca shouted as his hand touched the metal.

They were about to walk outside when a lab assistant tapped Tank on the shoulder. "Miss Ruba wants you in the lab. I'll make sure Myca gets to his lessons."

Tank furrowed his brows. Enzu hadn't needed to test his cannon out for a while. The lab was still as cold and white as he remembered.

Enzu waited for him at the bottom of the staircase. "How are you doing?"

"Good." The hallway seemed to shrink. The smile Enzu gave him looked forced, almost painful.

"I want you to come in the lab for a second so I can make sure your cannon is still working properly," she said.

She led him into the lab, where a chair waited for him. He sat, removing his cannon and placing on the nearby table. Enzu ran a scanner over it that started beeping. Every so often, she would type something, and it would ding.

"So how do you like Bisekt?" she asked.

"I like it a lot," Tank said.

"Myca isn't giving you too much trouble I hope."

"No, he's been great," Tank said. "I've been teaching him how to use a blaster, and he's been getting better at self-defense now that he has a competent teacher."

"That's good." Enzu paused for a moment before continuing. "You know, I find it interesting you wouldn't tell anyone your name, but you decided to tell Myca. Why is that?"

Tank looked down at his hand. "I think it's because I saw how upset he was when I got hurt. And by then he considered me a friend so how could I not?"

"A friend," Enzu repeated. She gave him a forced smile again. "Well just remember who you work for. Myca is staying here for only so long. I can take that arm cannon away any time I want."

Tank shifted in his seat. Neither one said anything until she was done with the scanner. Finally, she backed up, waving him away.

232

"I'm taking Myca on a trip in a few days. So don't get too at-tached," she said. "We'll send you your new child's name soon so you'll know their basic information before they get here."

Alarms sounded off in Tank's head. He couldn't take care of a new child. Myca was who he took care of. He couldn't, no, he re-fused to let Myca be taken away. The only option was to bring him when he escaped.

———◆———

No one was around when he got to the main floor, so he ran outside to the ship. Arby's droids held it up, welding the bottom again.

"How much longer do you think this will take?" Tank asked.

"It should be done before tonight," the droid replied.

Tank thanked him and ran back inside. Tonight was the night. They were leaving. He didn't care; another child was coming to Bisekt, and he was getting Myca out of this place if it meant break-ing every rule Enzu had in place.

The rest of the day dragged on as Tank went about his duties. He wanted to explain his plan to Myca, but every time he tried some-one was too close, or a lab assistant happened to be walking by. It was almost like they knew what he was planning.

Finally, Arby escorted Myca upstairs for the evening. Tank de-cided to wait in his room for a bit before knocking on Myca's door. He said goodnight to Arby, making sure everyone saw him go in his room. He waited for the light to go off outside, then carefully snuck over to Myca's room. He knocked gently on the door, and a sleepy-eyed Myca answered.

"Get dressed," Tank whispered. "We're leaving."

"What?"

"I'll explain everything as soon as we're out of here. But I need you to trust me."

Myca shut the door, and at first, Tank thought he had gone back to bed, but a second later he appeared in his clothes, wringing his hands. Tank motioned for him to follow and they snuck down the stairs. The door was so close Tank was sure they didn't need to worry about running into anyone. They made it outside, and Tank grabbed Myca's hand to pull him along faster.

His heart pounded against his chest. What would happen if they actually got caught?

"Sir Ruba, what are you doing out of bed this late at night?"

Tank and Myca jumped at the voice. He squinted in the dark and saw Arby standing next to the ship. He must have gone down to check the droids work.

"Arby, you scared me," Tank said.

"You didn't answer my question." His eyes scanned them, and Tank suddenly wondered if he could alert someone where they were.

"Arby, you are the only other person in this place I trust," Tank said. "As Myca's guard, I need to get him out of here for his own safety. Will you come with us?"

"Why are you trying to remove Mr. Ruba from the premises?" Arby's eyes lit up in the darkness.

"Enzu wants to hurt him, Arby."

"But Enzu is his mother. That can't be right," Arby replied.

"She told me she's going to take him away and bring back a different child. What else would that mean?" Tank asked.

"Mom wants to take me away?" Myca looked at Tank for an answer.

"I won't let her, kid." Tank said.

Arby said. "But perhaps it would be better if I asked Ms. Ruba instead."

Myca grabbed his hand. "Arby, please come with us?"

Arby glanced between them. "As long as you don't tell Ms. Ruba I'm coming."

Myca cheered, but Tank hushed him. He waited a few seconds and then herded Myca and Arby onto the ship. He sat Myca in the cockpit seat while Arby sat on the floor in the back.

"Buckle up," Tank said.

"Wait, you didn't tell me what's going on," Myca whimpered. "I'm scared."

"If you stay here, Enzu is going to take you on a trip and not bring you back. As your guard, I can't let that happen, so we're leaving."

"Where are we going?"

"I don't know yet. We'll figure it out," Tank said.

He sat down and turned everything on. His heart soared as the ship roared to life. Myca sat wide eyed as everything glowed and beeped. Tank pushed buttons and pulled levers, and the ship tipped backward. All Tank could see were the stars. Everything around them rumbled as the computer counted down.

"Are you ready?" he asked Myca.

"I think so." Myca gripped his chair.

The ship shot up into the sky. They were going to do it. Tank wasn't sure where they would go. Probably back home. His mother could take care of him while he tried to deal with Prylek. All he cared about right now was getting Myca out of Bisekt.

Without warning the rumbling stopped. Everything went quiet. The stars weren't getting any closer. Tank knew something was wrong. In the silence, the ship's nose slowly tilted down until they were facing the ground. The ship creaked and groaned under the movement. Red lights flashed around them as alarms rang through the cabin. Tank grabbed the controls and pulled as hard as he could, but it did nothing. He held his arm in front of Myca as they hurtled toward the sand.

"Where's the eject button?" Tank yelled.

Myca didn't move; he held tightly to his seat, looking at the ground rushing up to meet them. Tank sat in his chair, grabbing for his own buckle that wasn't there. The engines blowing up muffled Arby's frantic commands. There was nothing Tank could do but wait for the crash. He closed his eyes.

Shit.

Tank slammed into the console as the ship met the ground in a thunderous crash, burying its nose in the sand.

———◆———

The smell of the smoke woke him up. Tank wasn't in the ship anymore, but lying in the sand. His brain caught up to his body, and he groaned in pain. Everything hurt. He turned over to see the ship ablaze, the smoke billowed into the sky. Fighting against the pain, Tank bolted toward the ship, his mind screaming at him to run faster.

No.

Tank could barely see inside. He opened his mouth to yell for Myca but started coughing as his throat was overtaken by the smoke. He forced himself through the door.

"Myca?" he yelled.

Only the violent fire answered, the heat bearing down on him so much he had to cover his face. Pieces of the ship bent up at odd angles, tearing at his scales.

"Myca?" he yelled again, his voice becoming higher.

He made his way to where Myca should have been sitting. The seat was empty, and the console in front of the seat had blood on it, the window smashed. Outside, he could barely make out a small body in the sand.

A pit formed in his stomach.

No. No. No. No. No. No.

Tank jumped through the window and stumbled through the sand. It burned his feet, but he didn't care.

"Myca!"

Myca didn't answer. Tank knelt down beside him.

Nonononononononono.

"Myca." He turned Myca over. His face was white and scratched up. Blood dripped down the side of his head. His eyes fluttered slightly when Tank said his name.

"Tank, it hurts." He grabbed Tank's arm so tightly it seemed to be the only thing keeping him from fading.

Tank's eyes followed where he pointed. His shirt had been torn, and his stomach was cut open, glass shards and sand still stuck in the wound. What were those metal bars?

Myca started shaking. "I'm cold."

The all-too familiar feeling settled in Tank's stomach. He knew there was nothing he could do. He held Myca tighter. "I know."

"Will you do me a favor, Tank?" Myca asked, barely able to get the words out through his chattering teeth.

"Anything." Tank forced himself to look Myca in the eyes.

It took Myca a few tries before he was able to speak. "Find your dad," Myca said. "I know you think he's dead. But I bet he's still out there."

Tank nodded. It felt like an invisible creature had an iron grip around his throat. With every word he tried to say, his voice stopped working. Myca shook more violently. Tank held him closer.

"Tank, I'm scared." Myca's eyes became distant.

"It's okay. You'll be fine." Tank said it more for himself than Myca.

"You'll stay with me, right?" Myca asked.

"Of course."

"Will you tell me about where you used to live?" Myca asked.

Tank's scales bunched together around his eyes as he forced himself to smile. "Well, there is a big forest. Nothing like this desert. And every day I would go out in it with my friends, and we would hunt together. We would play games on our helibikes and run through the village. We loved to throw big celebrations. Anytime there was something we could celebrate, we would have a party. We would probably have a celebration for you learning more about your blaster."

Tank looked down at Myca. His eyes had gone blank as he struggled to take in a breath. The desert became cold as Tank wiped Myca's hair out of his face and rubbed his shoulder.

"When you have a celebration with us, we'll parade you around the village, and you'll get to eat all the good food. I'll make sure you're the center of attention," Tank said, staring out at the horizon again. The night sky met the desert in a mix of black and brown. He took a deep breath. "I'll show you how to ride a helibike too."

Myca went limp in his arms. Something inside Tank's chest shattered and he hugged Myca to his chest and cried. Hard.

It wasn't fair. It should have been Tank. It was his job to protect Myca, and when he needed to the most, he had failed.

He laid Myca back on the ground. He had to give him a proper burial. Tank grabbed a piece of fallen metal and started digging in the sand. As he dug, thoughts clouded his mind. What if he hadn't brought Myca with him? He would have been safe in Enzu's ship, and they wouldn't have crashed. Myca would still be alive.

It was hard to dig with just one hand, but Tank managed to eventually make a hole big enough for Myca's body. When he was done, he went to pick Myca up to put him in, but he stopped himself. He pulled his necklace off and placed it around Myca's neck.

Carefully he placed Myca in the grave and started shoveling the sand back on top. When he finished, he stepped back and sat on the ground. His chest still ached, and he couldn't stop crying.

He was gone. Myca was gone.

27

Sand. It was all sand. It was in his shoes, his eyes; his skin had turned red and raw under the heat. For the first time since he and Gaeth had left Earth, Leo didn't know what to do. All he could do was put one foot in front of the other and hope he would end up where he was supposed to be.

Face it. Gaeth is going to be killed, and it's your fault.

No. He couldn't accept it until he saw Gaeth's body with his own eyes. He promised his parents he would take care of him. He just had to figure out how he would do it this time.

What are you talking about? You saw him lying in that bed. He's as good as dead.

Leo stopped walking. Gaeth's face flashed in his mind, his hands reaching for him as the guards dragged Leo away. His brother left to be turned into a machine. A fresh bubble of anger swelled in his chest. He continued trekking through the desert.

You don't even know where you're going.

He didn't know where he was going. He didn't know what he was doing. How was he supposed to protect his brother, keep his promise to his family, when he didn't even know how to help himself?

Why not give up?

Maybe he should just give up. Gaeth's bed was right next to the factory, and if he somehow made it back there, how would he even get him out? How long had he been in this desert? There was nothing behind him; he must have walked for days. He couldn't even see Oblurn anymore.

You'll probably die out here.

He would probably die out here. No one would know. Gaeth wouldn't know, his parents might wonder what happened to him, but how could they find him? He failed everyone. His parents. Vanish, Gaeth, himself.

The sand whipped around him, slapping him in the face. He tried his best to wipe it out of his eyes, but it was no use. When his vision finally cleared, he opened his eyes to see his mother and father standing in front of him.

"Why didn't you do as I asked?" his father said. "All I asked was you help your brother."

His mother fell to the ground sobbing. "My son. I want my son back."

They won't ever forgive you.

They wouldn't ever forgive him. How could he face his family? How could he tell them their youngest had become a pawn in Bisekt's plan?

His parents turned into sand and flew away, replaced by Gaeth. He stood in front of Leo, tubes still attached to his arms. His eyes remained unfocused as he reached out.

"Leo? Why did you leave me? Why didn't you take me with you?"

"I wanted to, Gaeth," Leo cried. "I just couldn't."

Gaeth's face twisted in anger. "You could have saved me. You left me to die."

You're a terrible brother.

Leo put his head down in shame. He was a terrible brother. He should have tried harder. There was no reason for him to leave Gaeth behind. When he looked up again, Gaeth was gone. He was staring at himself.

"You're going to die out here. It's what you deserve."

Leo fell to his knees, tears in his eyes. He couldn't walk anymore. There was no reason to. Why should he?

A cloud of smoke rising behind a sand dune caught his attention.

That isn't real, don't bother.

But it might be. It could be a way off the planet. He could go get help. He tried to stand, but his legs refused, cemented to the sand. "Move," he begged, but his throat was so dry it barely came out as a grunt.

He managed to get one leg up, and it shook as it supported his weight. The other leg followed, and he started the long climb up, keeping his eyes on the smoke. Several times he slid backward, but he regained his footing. The smoke was his lighthouse, and he was lost in the storm.

The top of the dune was so close, the wind pushed him, trying to stop his progress. He kept putting one foot in front of the other. That's all he could do. As he made his way over the dune, a ship engulfed in flames came into view. Pieces of metal lay scattered around it. The heat coming off it didn't help the intensity of the desert. Next to it was the Sovich, Tank, who had thrown him and Gaeth in the rover. He knelt down, staring at a spot in the sand. A broken-down robot sat next to him.

Leo walked tentatively toward the Sovich. "Hey."

Tank glanced over his shoulder, not bothering to turn around. "What are you doing here?"

"I saw the smoke." He peered over Tank's shoulder to see what he was looking at.

"Myca is dead," Tank said, noticing the direction of Leo's gaze.

"Oh. I'm sorry," Leo murmured. He truly meant it.

The wind picked up, whipping sand around them. Neither one moved. It stung Leo's sunburnt skin, but he tried not to let it bother him.

"I didn't even know where we were going. I would figure it out once we made it out of the atmosphere. I thought the ship could make it into space. But then—" Tank put his head in his hand. Leo touched his shoulder, looking at the freshly dug spot.

"His insides were metal," Tank said. "I didn't know what to do when I saw it."

Leo's eyes went wide. "He had Steel Elbow?"

Tank nodded. "Enzu told me."

"There's something I should tell you." He told Tank about everything he'd seen at Oblurn. What they had done to the old man and what they had done to Gaeth. The whole time Tank didn't say anything but stared at the grave.

"Myca would have probably ended up there," Leo finished.

"And be turned into one of Enzu's fancy ships," Tank said. He stood and walked to the ship, still burning in the sand. The cannon screeched as Tank charged it as high as it would go. He shot the charge at the ship. In a blinding flash of light, the ship exploded, sending metal and debris flying everywhere. Tank stared at the empty space for a moment before coming back over to Leo.

"We're getting your brother back," Tank said.

28

The grumble of a ship pulled them from their conversation. Leo and Tank looked up at the noise to see his dad's ship landing in front of them.

The ramp lowered, and Sonja hopped out, running to him. "We saw the crashed ship, and when we flew closer, we saw you."

A spark of rage ignited in Leo. "You left me," he said through gritted teeth.

The joy disappeared from Sonja's face. "What?"

"Gaeth and I were inside Bisekt, and you and Scril left us. Not to mention"—he pointed at the ship behind her—"you stole from me. It's because of you Gaeth is back in Oblurn."

Sonja crossed her arms. "If you had done what you were supposed to in the first place, we wouldn't have had to make a decision."

"Oh, so it's my fault you flew away with my ship?" Leo shook his head. "I can't believe this."

Sonja scoffed at him. "If we'd stayed, who knows if someone would have tried to shoot us down. You should be thanking me for saving your ship."

Scril appeared next to Sonja. "Leo. Haven't seen you in a bit."

"I don't know what to say to you two," Leo said. "Can I still trust you after what you pulled? Gaeth might die." Tears formed in his eyes.

Sonja took a deep breath. "I'm sorry, Leo. I really am. If I had known this would be the outcome, I would have tried to do it differently."

Scril's antenna drooped. "So how do we get him back?"

"What?"

"Gaeth. We're going to get him back, right?" Scril asked. "You're not leaving him there, are you?"

———◆———

"Enzu said Oblurn wasn't far from Bisekt," Tank said as he sat in the back of the ship. "Rovers travel between them so they always have a driver. We'll just take their uniform. They gave me access to everything when I was assigned to Myca, so I'll be able to get past all the checkpoints."

Arby sat in the corner, still powered down. Sonja had given Tank and Leo water, and they slowly gained their strength back. She piloted as Leo and Tank reviewed the plan. "Since you took Myca from Bisekt, how are we supposed to know they'll just let you stroll into the place no problem?"

"I have a cannon attached to my body," Tank said.

Leo narrowed his eyes. "Why are you suddenly helping me? You threw Gaeth and me in a rover a few days ago."

"Because I want one less person to end up where Myca might have ended up," Tank said. "You shouldn't have to worry about losing your brother."

"So we're going back to Oblurn, then?" Scril asked from Gaeth's seat. His head barely reached the window.

"Have you not been listening to anything I've said?" Tank asked.

Scril turned. "No, I haven't."

"Then you don't know what we're doing, do you?" Tank blew air out of his snout. "Listen next time."

He stomped to the front of the ship and stood behind Sonja, studying his cannon before pointing in the direction of the road. "That way."

"How do you know?" Leo asked.

"They put a tracker in my cannon so if I ever get lost in the desert, I could find my way back," Tank explained. Sonja flew the ship where Tank pointed until he put a hand on her shoulder. "It's best if we walk the rest of the way so no one sees the ship."

"Good idea," she agreed as she touched down.

As Tank and Leo got off, Sonja called after them, "We'll watch for you to come out with Gaeth. Just use the earpiece I gave you."

"Thanks, Sonja," Leo said.

"Just think about how we'll all be in New Star City again," she said. "You just have to get Gaeth first."

Leo spread his hands out. "Just please don't leave this time."

Leo followed Tank through the desert, Tank holding his cannon out in front of him like a compass. "I don't know how long it will take, but as long as we're heading toward the road, we should be fine."

"Won't they be hunting you down if you try to leave with Myca?" Leo asked.

"That's a chance we'll have to take. They might think we made it out of the atmosphere, so they could have sent their ships out there and not looked around the planet yet." They didn't say anything for a while before Tank asked, "What will you do when you find your brother?"

"Give him what he wanted from the beginning. A place alone where he can live in peace. And I'll protect him from anyone who has a problem with him," Leo said.

"Good." Tank paused for a moment before speaking again. "Sorry if I scared you and your brother. I had to protect Myca."

Leo shrugged. "I would have done the same. Hell, I've been doing the same with Gaeth. If you were a little smaller, I would have kicked your ass," he said without thinking.

Tank stopped and turned around. For a moment, Leo thought he was mad, but Tank smiled. "I had a friend who was small for a Sovich. Everyone made fun of his size, and no one took him seriously. But even he would have been able to squish you no problem." He chuckled to himself.

"I'd love to put it to the test if I ever meet him," Leo replied, unsure if Tank was telling the truth or not.

"Well, he's dead, so we'll never know," Tank said matter-of-factly.

"Oh. Sorry."

"Don't be."

The sound on Tank's cannon turned into one long beep. "We're getting close."

Tank motioned for Leo to get down. He didn't see anything resembling a road, only sand for miles. Tank got on his stomach next to him. "There should be a rover coming soon. They're always running."

Sure enough, the sound of an engine in the distance caught their attention. Leo poked his head over the dune. A rover raced toward them, kicking up a giant cloud of sand in its wake.

"Wait here." Tank jumped down the other side of the dune onto the road.

He stood in the middle of the road with his arms spread out. For a moment Leo thought the rover wasn't going to stop, but as it got closer, it slammed on its breaks, sending a wave of sand over Tank's head. A guard jumped out and slammed the door.

"What do you think you're doing?" the guard yelled, stomping over to Tank. Before he could say anything else, Tank knocked him out.

———•———

Leo changed into the guard's uniform as Tank threw the man onto the side of the road. Tank got in the driver seat just as Leo hopped in. It powered on, and they zoomed away, leaving a dust cloud in their tracks.

"When we get there let me do all the talking," Tank said. "If you say anything that might give them suspicion to think you're Leo, then it will blow our cover, and no one wants that."

"Got it," Leo said from under his mask.

The rover sped across the sand on an invisible path that zigzagged through the desert. After a while, the dome slowly appeared. Leo's heart pounded underneath his uniform.

"Are you scared?" Tank asked.

"Yes," Leo said.

"Me too."

The radio buzzed as a voice spoke. "Rover 415 you weren't expected back so soon. What's wrong?"

Leo held the radio button down. "I have Tank from Bisekt with me. He's been sent to inspect part of the facility. His rover broke down, so I volunteered to drive him the rest of the way."

There was a brief moment of silence before the woman spoke again. "We didn't get any memo he would be visiting us today."

"It was last minute," Tank said. "You know how Enzu can be. Nothing too formal."

"Very well. I'll open the gate for you."

The rover sped around to the front where the gate was lifting. The woman came back on the radio. "Please step out of the vehicle for the decontamination process."

As they went through the process, Leo took several deep breaths.

They can't see your face. No one will recognize you.

The second door opened, and the woman in white stood before them.

His heart stopped. *You're wearing a mask, don't worry.*

She gave them a slight nod. "I'm sorry we weren't more prepared for you."

"I'm sorry I didn't call ahead," Tank said. Leo did his best to stand at attention next to him to try and blend in. The woman eyed him suspiciously.

"Would you like me to start a tour for you?" she asked, holding out a hand toward them.

"That won't be necessary. I want to look around on my own without any input," Tank said, glancing around the plaza. "I'll let tell you when I'm done."

"Very well." She eyed them both before walking away.

The plaza looked more sinister than the last time Leo had been there. The white walls and floors didn't look clean anymore; instead they seemed to be there to hide Oblurn's dirty secret.

Leo fell in step with Tank as they made their way across the plaza. The only sound, their footsteps echoing on the tile as the other guards followed them with their eyes. The other guards nodded at

Tank as they walked by, some walking faster when they got closer, some avoiding eye contact altogether.

Leo couldn't help but notice the way the guards acted around Tank. "What did you do to the guards that made them scared of you?" Leo asked.

"Killed some people," Tank answered, staring straight ahead.

The door opened, and they marched down the hallway, not meeting anyone as they got closer to Gaeth. It was strange to Leo they hadn't been stopped. Perhaps because of Tank?

The second set of doors opened into the circular room where Leo left his brother. Tank pretended to check the counter and talked to one of the nurses.

"Do you have a patient I could see? I want to make sure they're getting the proper care before the final stage. I need to report my findings to Ms. Ruba as well, so if you could hurry it along that would be great too." Leo studied the room as Tank talked. Nothing had been moved. But the place was so clean, Gaeth could be somewhere else for all he knew.

The nurse's voice shook as she answered. "I'm afraid our only patient has been moved to a more secure location. We had a bit of trouble with him recently."

"Can you point us in the direction?" Leo asked. "Tank needs to do a thorough search of the place to report back to Enzu."

The nurse eyed Tank's cannon. "I'm not allowed to disclose information to people who don't work here."

Tank pulled his cannon off his arm and set it on the counter. "Listen," he began. "You have two options here. Tell me where the patient is, and we'll be on our way. Or I jump over this counter and you get to find out what happens after that." He leaned in closer to the nurse, who tried her best to lean away from Tank, but it was no use. "Do you want to find out what happens after that?"

The nurse stared at them, wide eyed. "He was moved to the lowest level. Take the elevator." She pushed a button on the desk, and a pair of doors opened up nearby to an elevator.

"Thanks." Tank grabbed his cannon and hurried away.

"Sorry," Leo said to her before scurrying after Tank.

The nurse watched them through narrowed eyes as Tank pushed the button for the lower level, and the doors hissed shut.

"Wasn't that a little much?" Leo asked, taking his helmet off for a moment. How did the guards walk around all day without suffocating?

"She wasn't going to tell us where your brother was. Do you want to wander around here, aimlessly?" Tank secured his cannon back in place as he watched the elevator icon plummet lower on the screen.

Leo had to give him that. Lights flashed throughout the elevator as they descended. How far down was the next level? The farther down they went, the more anxious Leo became. What if they had already turned Gaeth into spaceship parts? Or what if he was so weak when they got there, he wouldn't be strong enough to leave with them?

"I can tell you're nervous," Tank said, watching Leo.

"You think?" Leo answered.

"Just treat it like you would any other mission. We're going in to get Gaeth. We'll be leaving with him soon."

"It's the part between those two sentences that worries me," Leo said, throwing the helmet back on. The elevator slowed down, and Leo braced himself as it came to a stop. The doors didn't open right away, leaving a small moment of self-doubt where Leo thought maybe this might have been a bad idea after all. Perhaps he should have just let Oblurn keep Gaeth and accept it was what was meant to happen to him. He couldn't really control what happened to his brother, could he?

He looked over to see Tank was in a sort of trance. Was this what all Sovichs did before they went into any kind of battle? There was a beep as the doors opened and they stepped out into a brightly lit room.

A desk sat at the end of a long hallway, a woman in glasses typing on a computer. She looked up as they walked out. "Can I help you?"

"We're here to visit the patient that was recently moved to this level. Gaeth—"

"Spearman," Leo whispered.

"Gaeth Spearman," Tank said. "I'm Enzu's guard, and I've been sent to investigate the facility to make sure the operation is running smoothly."

The woman raised her eyebrows at them. "I didn't receive any notification you were coming."

She started to type something on her console, but Leo cut her off. "We've been waiting for a while. Ms. Ruba wouldn't be happy if we had to go through procedures again," he said, hoping the woman would buy it.

"Of course. Right, this way." The woman led them through a pearl-white door to the side. Tank shrugged at Leo as if to say "See? It's that easy." They followed the woman into a pitch-black room.

As the door closed behind them, Leo knew something was wrong. "Where's Gaeth?" he asked, but the darkness swallowed the sound.

He threw his helmet off to try to see better, but it didn't help at all. Tank said nothing as his cannon glowed dimly in the darkness.

The lights turned on, and they were surrounded by a dozen guards, all aiming blasters at them. Behind the circle of guards stood Enzu.

"Shoot them," she said.

Before he knew what was happening, Tank pushed Leo down, blasting the guards. Leo pulled out his own, trying to take out the ones closest to him. The sound of blaster fire rained over them. There was a roar next to him. Tank held onto his limp arm falling on the ground.

Enzu held up her hand, and the shooting stopped. "You really expected to get all the way through Oblurn without someone asking me why I decided to send a guard here on a whim? Do you know how silly that sounds?"

"It almost worked, didn't it?" Tank said.

"Where is Myca?" she asked.

"Dead," Tank replied.

She inhaled sharply. "What did you do to him?"

"Nothing. Your ship stopped working when we left, and we crashed."

"That ship you took was an old model. It shouldn't have been able to take off."

"That's why I fixed it," Tank answered.

Leo couldn't tell who wanted to kill the other more. "Miss Ruba, we're just here to get my brother out. He shouldn't be here." Leo took a step forward with his arms out.

She raised an eyebrow as if seeing him for the first time. "Yes, he should," she replied. "If he were to live on his own without any sort of treatment, then the Steel Elbow would slowly take over his whole body, and he would become a machine. If that happened, he wouldn't be able to control his actions. It's happened before, which is why Dr. Moon created Oblurn in the first place. He knew what people were becoming and found a way to take advantage of it. If you hadn't brought Gaeth to Oblurn do you realize how dangerous he could become?" Her voice lowered. "He could kill you in your sleep, Leo."

"I don't believe you," Leo said. A pit of fire formed in his chest. This woman had no idea what she was talking about. Gaeth dealt with Steel Elbow for years, and it never got bad. Leo would never think Gaeth was dangerous to be around. He would never try to hurt anyone.

Enzu smirked at him. "It doesn't matter what you believe. Gaeth was scheduled for the processing chamber a few minutes ago. I'll have some shiny new spaceship parts any minute now."

Leo's heart stopped. "You're lying."

Enzu shrugged. "Am I? I sell the most luxurious spaceships in the galaxy. The metal in your brother's body is stronger than any metal I could ever find on some planet."

Tank backed toward the door. "Leo, if you want to save him, we have to go."

Leo shot one last look at Enzu before sprinting through the door after Tank.

"Enjoy the cannon I made you, Tank," she called.

They made it to the elevator and he punched the button. The doors closed and they shot up. It seemed to take even longer to get to the first floor. What if Gaeth was already dead? How did they know Enzu was telling the truth?

The doors opened and they flew out. The nurse who was still at her station looked shocked they were both even there. Leo nodded at her as they raced by, trying to remain calm. Four guards carried Gaeth down the hallway. He was pale and could barely walk on his own.

"This way," Leo called to Tank.

"I'm ready." Tank charged up his cannon. The orange glow bounced off the walls and floor before it flickered and went out. The cannon slid off Tank's arm, clattering on the tile.

"What happened?" Leo asked.

"I don't know. This is the first time." Tank tried to put the cannon back on his arm, but it slid off again.

Leo sighed. "We have to keep going." He ran after the guards, Tank right behind him.

As they came closer, the guards stopped at a blank wall. One of them pushed it and it gave way to the production room. The giant metal pot stewed below them, awaiting its next victim.

Leo screamed.

Gaeth fought against the guards, but he was too weak. They easily pushed him onto the platform above the pot. The liquid bubbled and boiled below them, steam rising and making it harder to see.

"Target is in position and ready for extermination," the guard said into his headset.

Tank let out a roar and charged. He grabbed the nearest guards and threw them into the pot where they screamed before sinking in with a hiss. Another guard lunged for Gaeth, but not before Tank grabbed him by the collar and threw him to the floor of the warehouse. He turned and held his arm up to the last guard, who sat stunned for a moment before realizing Tank wasn't harming him. He punched Tank hard. Tank fell face first on the platform, his claws digging into the metal.

Gaeth sat at the edge of the platform, his hands digging into the sides. Leo ran by the guard and Tank, reaching out and grabbing his arm. He pulled Gaeth back, but not before glancing up to see Enzu looking down at them from the window. Her smile sent chills down his spine.

"We're leaving. Don't follow us," he yelled at her.

Tank pushed the last guard into the pot. "We're halfway there," he said. "Call Sonja and tell her we're coming."

Tank supported Gaeth as Leo pushed the button on his earpiece. "Sonja? If you can hear me, we're coming up from Oblurn now, and

I need you to bring the ship over." Static answered him as they made their way to the doors. The hallway seemed much shorter now that they had Gaeth. Before Leo could catch his breath, they were already stopping.

Tank threw Gaeth over his shoulder, not bothering to wait for Leo.

Gaeth swung loosely from Tank's back as they walked through the hallway.

When they made it to the big door, Leo stopped him.

"You're carrying my brother. Are you sure you can get him out without him getting hurt?" Leo asked.

"Trust me, you want me carrying him," Tank answered.

Leo braced himself as they walked into the plaza. There weren't any guards waiting for them. Everything was just as it had been when they got there. Had Enzu not been able to get a hold of anyone?

Tank walked as though it was the most normal thing in the world for him to be carrying someone half-conscious over his shoulder. Leo kept his head down, trying his best to prevent anyone from seeing his face.

As they got closer to the door, a realization hit him. Did they need someone who worked at Oblurn to open the gate for them? Surely they would recognize Leo if they asked for help. Before he could dwell on it too long, a guard walked over to them.

"Tank, do you need me to open the gate for you?" he asked.

"Yeah. Just doing a quick errand for Enzu," Tank said, pointing to a motionless Gaeth.

The guard laughed, making Leo's skin crawl. Leo stood on the other side of Tank to stay out of sight. The guard typed on the keypad, and the gate opened.

"You have a good day, Tank," he said. "And you too." He patted Gaeth's shoulder before walking away, laughing.

Were they really going to walk out of Oblurn with Gaeth, just like that? The familiar sound of the wind whipped around them as they waited in the darkness for the other side to open.

"Decontamination process complete. Thank you for visiting Oblurn."

Leo held his breath. There had to be a catch. Someone was going to stop them. It couldn't have been this simple. Light flooded into the room as the second gate opened, the wind blowing sand into their direction. Ahead of them, Leo's ship sat on the ground, waiting for them.

"Walk to the ship. If you run, they'll get suspicious," Tank said.

They stepped into the sunlight. Leo forgot how hot the desert was. He immediately started sweating. His ears tuned into every sound around him. Tanks heavy footsteps in the sand, the wind slapping against his face, and the occasional creak of his armor kept him on his toes.

They were halfway to the ship. Leo could just make out Scril and Sonja in the window.

They waved and disappeared, Sonja's voice buzzing in Leo's ear. "Don't say anything. They're watching you. Just keep walking."

Leo took a deep breath.

He kept his eyes on the back of Tank's head. Anything to take his mind off the fact someone might shoot at them at any moment. The ship loomed before them, the ramp lowered, and Tank boarded the ship, ducking, so he didn't hit his head on the roof.

As Leo went to get on, there was a shout and guards rushed out of Oblurn. They ran toward the ship with their blasters drawn, yelling for them to stop. Leo jumped onboard. Tank had already put Gaeth in the back of the ship next to Arby. Sonja punched the engines. They took off, leaving Oblurn and Bisekt behind.

"How did you get out of there alive?" Sonja asked over her shoulder.

"I have no idea," Leo replied, kneeling next to Gaeth. He was still sleeping, his breaths coming in short. "I don't know if she let us go or if we're somehow the luckiest people alive."

"Enzu doesn't let people go," Tank said, crossing his arms. "Something had to have happened for her to let us just walk away. Or she has something else planned."

"I don't want to think about it right now." Leo leaned against the metal wall and put his head in his hands. He just broke into Oblurn and got Gaeth out. Why did he feel like a terrible person? "Vanish has someone who can take care of Gaeth, right?"

"Of course. We'll get him to one of her doctors right when we land," Sonja said. She typed in the code for New Star City, and Leo and Tank fell asleep in the back of the ship, neither one waking up until they landed.

METAL BONES

29

Gaeth barely remembered being at Oblurn again. He thought he saw his brother. And maybe the Sovich that attacked them when they tried to kidnap Myca? But that couldn't be possible. Leo would never work with him. Gaeth opened his eyes. This was the back of his father's ship. But why was he lying down?

The pain hit him all at once. He winced, grabbing his arm. Now he remembered. Numerous tubes pumping him with medicine. Leo trying to get him out. Tank had thrown him over his shoulder, no wonder he felt sore. He tried to move, but his body refused to let him, his metal bones weighing him down.

A familiar voice was suddenly next to him. "Gaeth, are you okay?" It was from Leo. He kneeled next to Gaeth, concern plastered across his face.

"No," Gaeth groaned. His entire body still fought him to fall back asleep.

"We called one of Vanish's doctors," Leo said. "You're going to be better in no time."

Gaeth sighed. *I'm always going to be the one who needs taking care of, aren't I?*

The rumbling ship intensified his headache. His bones ached. How could something he had been used to for so long make his head hurt so bad? He covered his face with his arm. A stomp near his feet forced him to look up. Tank stared down at him.

"What?" Gaeth tried to crawl away, pushing his body as hard as he could. "Leo, how did he get on the ship?"

"It's okay, he's with us," Leo said, patting Gaeth on the shoulder. "He helped me get you out of Oblurn."

Gaeth eyed Tank, still unconvinced. This was the alien who had put them back in Oblurn. Why should he believe he suddenly changed his mind?

Tank snorted. "I'm not going to shoot you if that's what you're worried about. I have my own reasons for leaving Bisekt."

Scril jumped to the back of the ship. "I'm glad you're okay, Gaeth. I thought I might have to knock someone's knees out on your behalf."

"So how exactly did you get me out?" Gaeth asked Leo.

"Leo come look at this." Sonja called over her shoulder.

"Hold on one second, Gaeth." Leo jogged to the front of the ship.

Gaeth glared after him. He had just been through hell and back and Leo was already ignoring him for Sonja? *Some brother.*

———— ♦ ————

"So not only did you not kidnap Enzu's child, but you brought a robot and a Sovich back with you?"

It was the first time Gaeth had seen a hint of surprise on Vanish's face.

"Why did I think I could send you four on a mission together after only being on a few?" She sat back in her chair, taking several deep breaths. "How am I supposed to expect you to get anything done after this?"

"Vanish"—Sonja held her hands up in defense—"Leo and Gaeth aren't as experienced as your other workers. They don't know how to think quick on their feet like the rest of us."

"Hey!" Leo and Gaeth said but stopped under Sonja's stare.

"I wish I had realized that before I had decided to send them on one of the most important jobs I've ever handed out," Vanish said. "I got too caught up in how well they were doing, and I put too much trust in them."

Gaeth backed away so he was slightly behind Leo. The glass walls and doors didn't help his nervousness.

"To be fair, we've never kidnapped anyone before. We didn't really know what we were doing," Leo said calmly.

"I don't want to hear your excuses," Vanish scoffed. "I send you on one of the most important missions for Onyx, and you couldn't get any information?" She slumped in her seat.

 Gaeth snuck farther behind Leo.

"Does this mean you won't give us money to leave?" Leo asked.

"What do you think?" Vanish said, her eyes bulging. "You did nothing I asked. You could have called me when you were having problems, and you didn't."

Tank stood off to the side, trying to be as inconspicuous as he could. But given his size, trying to hide just made him much more noticeable.

"And who are you?" Vanish snapped at Tank.

"I'm Tank, and I used to work for Enzu."

Vanish raised an eyebrow at him. "And she just let you leave with them?"

"No, I left without asking."

Vanish laughed. "This is getting better and better. Are you here to work for me?"

"No."

Her eyes narrowed.

"But I do recognize your name. Kirk had a message from you," Tank said.

"Sand Worm?" Sonja asked. "You knew him?"

"Yeah, but I wish I didn't," Tank replied.

Upon hearing it, Vanish almost instantly relaxed. "So you lived in Bisekt for a while, then? You have information no one else would have?"

"I suppose so."

"What can you tell me about a shipment Enzu agreed to?"

Tank tilted his head. "If I tell you, what's in it for me?"

"I don't kill you," Vanish said. The surrounding guards put their hands on their weapons.

Tank rolled his eyes. "Fine. She's sending fifty ships to Sentrum. They're going in a freighter. Last I knew they'd be done pretty soon."

Vanish rubbed her chin in thought. "We've put more people on watch. I'll put a few more just in case. If any of you hear anything tell me. I want that shipment stopped, and this is how you can make it up to me."

———————◆———————

Gaeth didn't want to be around anyone. It was too much to handle.

Vanish suddenly didn't want to let him and Leo go anymore because they didn't kidnap Myca. Tank was suddenly working for Onyx? On top of that, his bones ached from Vanish's doctors healing him. It was too much. The city was calling his name.

"Good job, Tank," Sonja said. "That information you gave is vital to Onyx."

"Yeah, but I didn't do it because I wanted to, did I?" Tank asked.

"Vanish definitely has her ways," Leo said.

"I don't like her ways," Tank said.

Gaeth slipped away as Leo and Tank argued.

The lights glowed against the street as he wandered down an alleyway, letting his feet carry him where he wanted to go. Several cars zoomed overhead, causing him to duck as he walked. He wished they had never shown up at New Star City in the first place.

He didn't realize where he was going until he was at Sebastian's table. Gaeth looked around for any sign of the man with the newspaper. It was empty, the man nowhere in sight. Why did he come here in the first place? Just as Gaeth was about to turn around, the curtains flew back, and Sebastian walked out. He lit up at the sight of Gaeth.

"My boy, you've come back!" He rushed around the table and gave Gaeth a pat on the back, grinning genuinely. "I knew you would come to your senses."

"I was wandering around, and I ended up here," Gaeth said, vaguely aware of where he was. There were fewer people around than before; the whoosh of cars in the distance only amplified how far away he was from everyone.

"Of course you did," Sebastian said. "Have you eaten today? We should eat something together." He grabbed Gaeth's upper arm and herded him to a nearby restaurant.

It was poorly lit and too loud for Gaeth to hear himself think. No one noticed them as they entered. The tables were so close together, the backs of the chairs were almost touching. Sebastian led Gaeth to a table near the back where it was much less crowded. It looked like it hadn't been cleaned in years. They sat across from each other.

Menus popped up from the table, and Gaeth studied his carefully. He pushed a couple buttons and "okay" at the bottom, and the menu receded back into the table. Sebastian hadn't stopped smiling, and Gaeth was still unsure what to say.

"I'm glad you came back, Gaeth," he said, typing on his own menu. The other diners threw glances their way. "I know we only talked once before, but what made you change your mind?"

Gaeth immediately thought of Leo giving Sonja money. *Their money.* That they had promised they would save for his house in the country. He had never quite let it go. If he had to go out on his own instead, then he would. Even if it meant leaving Leo behind.

"You were right about Leo," he said at last. "He gave away our money. I think it would be easier if I joined you and got the money myself."

"Without your brother?" Sebastian asked, leaning forward.

"Yes. Everything you've said has been true. I wouldn't be surprised if he took all the money for himself," Gaeth said, talking himself more and more into it.

"Not to mention, when you join, you get to go to Sentrum." Sebastian's eyes were bright with excitement.

"That too." Gaeth paused for a moment. "Speaking of Sentrum, I think there's something you should know."

He explained what Onyx had been planning. How they wanted to stop Bisekt from sending their ships to Sentrum. Sebastian leaned back in his chair.

"We knew they were watching us, but I didn't know they knew that much." He clapped his hands together. "Change of plans, Gaeth. Do you want to prove to us you'll do whatever it takes to be part of the Sol Empire?"

Gaeth nodded.

Sebastian checked around the restaurant before leaning forward. Gaeth leaned forward too so he could hear. "If you stop them, then I'll bring you straight to Sentrum and cure you," Sebastian said with a smirk. "How's your finger doing?"

Gaeth touched it subconsciously. "It doesn't hurt anymore," he said.

Sebastian grinned. "See? The Sol Empire is the right choice."

Time stopped. On the one hand, Gaeth saw himself getting up from the table and walking away, never thinking about what he might have done. Going back to Leo and Sonja and apologizing for disappearing. Yes, he would be yelled at for walking away, but at least he wouldn't have made a major mistake.

But on the other hand, he saw himself saying yes and making his own decision. Not having to wait for Leo to come around and save him every time he was in trouble. All he had to do was say yes, and he could have the money he needed on his own. Leo had no problem giving away their money he had worked hard for, so why should he have a problem going his own way?

"I'll join. I want to take care of myself from now on," Gaeth said, and he truly meant it.

Sebastian's eyes flashed. Gaeth tried to ignore how unnerving his smile was.

"You've made a good choice." Sebastian rubbed his hands together as a robot on wheels pulled up to their table. Its compartment opened, and their food slid onto the table.

"The freighter is passing through the Missile Region in the next few days. I'm sure Onyx has already found out about it. They're probably going to try to destroy the ships somehow. That's where you come in."

"You want me to blow up a ship?"

"I want you to blow up all of Onyx ships. If they can't fly out, they won't set off their bombs." Sebastian reached into his coat and pulled out several small squares with a button in the center and a detonator. "You stick these to their ships and push the detonator, and it will all be gone." He mimicked an explosion with his hand.

"You just carry those around with you?" Gaeth asked.

"You still haven't learned this is New Star City, have you?" Sebastian chuckled.

"What about the ships for Sentrum?"

"They're made of the finest metal in the galaxy. A little detonator like this won't do any damage to them." He slid the detonator across the table. "All I'm asking is for you to prove you really want this," he said, digging into his food. "If Onyx ships get destroyed, it would be a massive blow to them. They're like a small bug we haven't been able to squish."

Gaeth's eyes narrowed. "Why should I help you if you're working with the people who wanted to kill me in the first place?"

Sebastian's eyes flashed. "Because I can make your Steel Elbow disappear."

Gaeth eyed the detonator. The whole reason he and Leo had come to New Star City was to find a cure. If he could get rid of Steel Elbow, then he wouldn't have to worry about anything. Gaeth wouldn't have to worry about Leo taking his money, and Leo could live wherever he wanted. It would be perfect. And all he had to do was join the Sol Empire for a few years.

Gaeth grabbed the detonator and put it in his pocket.

Sebastian smiled. "Do you still have the mask I gave you?"

"Yes." Where did he put the mask? Somewhere on the ship, he just couldn't remember.

"Wear it when you do it. It'll be easier to find you among the people." Sebastian took a big bite of his food. "I'll make sure someone is there with a personal ship. You won't be leaving with your friends."

Gaeth tilted his head. "What happens if my brother or my friends get hurt in the explosion?"

Sebastian raised an eyebrow at him, his food dripping off his fork. "Who cares? You're part of the Sol Empire now."

The detonator sat heavy in Gaeth's pocket. He needed to put it in a safe place.

They finished their meal in silence.

Sebastian gave him a final pat on the back as they left the restaurant, telling Gaeth over and over how happy he was Gaeth had finally joined the Sol Empire. As Gaeth walked back to the ship, he couldn't help but feel dirty.

I made the right choice.

Had he really? He was going against everything Leo and Sonja were fighting for. What would they say when he told them he was going to blow up the only thing giving Onyx a fighting chance?

But if I can use Sentrum to get rid of Steel Elbow, why should I care?

No. This was all so he could be cured. He didn't care about anything else.

He arrived at New Star City with Leo to look for money and a cure, and now he found a way. That way happened to be blowing up the ships his friends needed.

30

Gaeth sighed as he stepped onto the elevator. His mind swam with thoughts about what he just agreed to. A hand grabbed his shoulder, and Leo stepped on after him.

"I was calling your name, but you didn't hear me." He leaned against the railing as the elevator shot up. "Can you believe it, Gaeth? One last job and it will all be over. You'll finally have your house, and we won't have to worry about New Star City ever again."

Gaeth tilted his head. "But you'll be there with me, right?"

Leo rubbed the back of his neck and laughed nervously. "I mean, I'll visit you. I wasn't planning on living there too."

Gaeth didn't say anything, so Leo continued, "After everything we've been through, I want to fly around the galaxy. It's so much bigger than I thought. Plus we have Dad's ship, and Tank and Sonja are with us. What will they do?"

Gaeth's eyes narrowed. "Are you anxious about Tank and Sonja, or are you just worried about Sonja?"

Leo tensed. "Gaeth, we talked about this already."

"I still care that you did it."

"Gaeth"—Leo sighed—"I gave it to her because she needed to get information to Onyx. What else was I supposed to do?" He waved his arms around.

"How about telling her you needed it for your sick brother?" Gaeth's fists clenched, his shoulders tensing. Why couldn't Leo understand what he did was wrong?

Leo shook his finger at Gaeth. "Don't play the sick card. She needed—"

Gaeth swung a punch toward Leo, who ducked out of the way and fell. His fist smashed into the side of the elevator, leaving a small dent. Neither one said anything. Both were breathing hard.

How dare Leo say that? How dare he think Gaeth would ever use Steel Elbow as an excuse? Leo still lay on the ground, gawking at the dent.

Gaeth stood over him. "Never. Say. That. Again." His shoulders heaved with every word. His voice was soft but carried such anger and hurt in it that Leo stood on the other side of the elevator. Gaeth crossed his arms to keep himself from shaking, staring out at the city, the detonator still in his pocket. He glanced at Leo.

"If you're going to come on this mission, then you need to stop acting like a child and grow up." Leo's brows furrowed. "You can't be like this when we actually get out there."

"Look at the big man talking." Gaeth scoffed. "This is your fourth mission, how would you know?"

Finally, Leo turned to him. At first, Gaeth thought he might try to hit him back, but Leo simply said, "Quit with the 'poor me' attitude. It won't help anyone when we actually go on the mission, alright?"

"Yeah, sure."

"We're both under a lot of pressure. After this, let's take a break. Get that house and lie low for a while." Leo was still leaning on the other side of the elevator, as though he was waiting for Gaeth to punch him again. As though he was afraid of him.

The doors opened, and they walked into the hangar, where Tank was inspecting the ship. He ran his hand along the surface, bowing slightly every time he stopped. Gaeth had never seen someone check a ship that way before. Only when they were right behind him did he notice them.

"It's a good ship," Tank said.

"That makes me feel better," Leo replied. "She flies well, and my dad took care of her since before I was born. It's too bad that you're seeing her for the first time like this—she's definitely seen better days."

"It makes her special," Tank said.

Gaeth walked onto the ship.

Sonja sat in the copilot seat, eyebrows furrowed as she talked to Ava on a monitor. "The freighter is passing through the Missile Region. I don't want to put our people in danger for a bunch of money."

"It's strictly a volunteer mission," Ava answered. "Anyone who wants to go has been notified about the risks."

"If anyone is injured," Sonja said, "then it falls on me. I was the one who found out about the cargo and notified you. I don't know if I can handle losing people."

"Sonja, everyone going wants to be there. You can't worry about every single person, it will drive you insane," Ava said. "I'm sending you the details."

A small chip slid out of the bottom of the monitor. "Use this to cloak your ship so they think you're a patrol ship. There's a map inside there as well that you can download. Use it to get to the cargo hold and find the boxes with the green X on the corner. Our second team will have their ships there ready to take them. You'll get away in that ship as well. Do you have a way to get your ship out of there?"

"Tank and Gaeth can fly it," Sonja said.

Gaeth's stomach dropped. How was he supposed to get on the freighter if he was flying the ship?

"Good. If you need anything else, just call me." The monitor went dark, and Sonja grabbed the chip.

Gaeth followed her as she went to the bridge. "I don't think it's a good idea that I stay on the ship," he said. "I'm not good under pressure, and I don't think I'll be able to fly normally and talk to the guards on the radio without arousing suspicion."

"If you're not good under pressure, you should stay on the ship," Sonja replied. "The mission is crucial; I can't let anything go wrong."

She pushed the chip into a slot in the panel, and a map popped up.

Gaeth took a deep breath. "I really want to help. I haven't contributed a lot, and I think if I did, I would be a valuable asset to the team. You saw how I killed Felgi."

Sonja turned to him. "I saw you get so freaked out you pulled out your blaster in the middle of the spa without thinking," she retorted, clearly annoyed. "It wasn't exactly wise thinking on your part."

"He might have been able to tell that I have Steel Elbow." Gaeth's hand shook. "Who knows what he would have done."

"I would have stepped in." Sonja didn't bother looking at him.

"Scril said the same thing. You were some receptionist at the spa I barely paid attention to." Gaeth took a step back and exhaled. "All I'm asking is for you to let me come on the mission."

"I can't take any chances." Sonja left, leaving Gaeth alone.

Gaeth scoffed. He went to the back of the ship and moved some boxes aside, pulling up a loose floor panel where the white mask waited. If he weren't allowed on the mission, then he would have to invite himself.

Tank and Leo were talking in the hangar when he joined them.

"We're taking off soon," Leo said. "When we touch down inside the freighter, you and Tank will fly the ship out of the Missile Region. Stay on the radio in case we need you to come back."

"Got it." Gaeth's throat had dried up. It felt like he was watching himself from another place. Was he really doing this? Did he really want to do this?

Sonja walked around from the other side of the ship. "Everything's set up so if you're not willing to go, tell us now and we'll leave you here."

No one said anything. Gaeth's heart beat faster and faster. He wanted to say something. To tell them what he planned to do. But he kept his mouth shut and sat down.

"Leo, hop in the cockpit, and we'll go." Sonja boarded the ship.

Gaeth didn't pay attention as they flew through the air toward the Missile Region. Or as they avoided several stray missiles left over from past wars.

Tank patted him on the back. "It'll be ok. We're just flying the ship, but keep your blaster with you just in case."

Of course, he thought Gaeth was nervous about flying. He took several deep breaths and closed his eyes.

This was the right choice.

"Freighter in view," Leo said.

Gaeth looked out the window and couldn't help gasping.

The freighter moved slowly through space like a whale, with hundreds, if not thousands, of tiny ships flying around it. Lights sprinkled its surface as it housed thousands of people. It had to be bigger than New Star City. As they drew closer, it loomed over them, casting a large shadow.

"Honestly, I'm not worried about being spotted anymore," Tank said, staring at all the ships flying by.

"I wouldn't be too sure," Sonja said. "All those ships have a specific number and are constantly being tracked. If we didn't have this code, we would easily be noticed."

Tank looked at the freighter in awe. His mouth moved, but he didn't say anything. Sonja flipped a switch on the console, and a buzz swept through the ship.

A voice spoke through the radio. "Please state your number and reason for boarding today," a man stated, his voice bored.

No one said anything until Gaeth realized they waited for him to speak. Sonja handed him a piece of paper, and he read it into the radio. "Eight one seven. We're bringing workers aboard."

The man didn't answer for a while.

"Your ship is small for worker transport. What kind of workers do you have with you?"

Gaeth glanced at Sonja, who silently encouraged him.

"We were told there's a water leak in the living quarters. It doesn't take many people to fix."

"We have our own men to do that. You may leave," the man said matter-of-factly.

Gaeth leaned forward as though the closer he spoke to the radio, the more believable he would sound.

"If it's alright with you, we would like to refuel before leaving. Our ship can't make the trip back without it."

More silence.

"Very well. We're sending you to docking bay twenty-seven."

They flew through the traffic of ships to the docking bay. There was no one around, and as they landed, the ship went dark. Leo and Sonja turned everything off and ran back to grab their blasters.

"We'll leave the ship and head for the cargo. You guys fly around the outside of the freighter until we tell you we're gone," Sonja said. "We need to actually refuel first before we can leave."

After the ship refueled, Leo and Sonja stood at the exit with their blasters in hand. Sonja checked and rechecked her map while Leo said goodbye.

"We'll see you again before you know it," he said. "Take good care of the ship. I really like it."

"Spacejunk," Tank said.

"What?"

"Sonja named it Spacejunk when we left Bisekt, don't you remember?" Tank asked, "You can't rename a ship."

Leo gave Gaeth a hug. "I'll see you later."

He knows. He knows what I'm about to do.

Gaeth smiled. "I'll be here with Tank if you need anything."

The detonator and his mask pushed up against his side in his pocket. This was his last chance to tell him. But the heaviness of the detonator stopped him. The reality set in like he was watching someone else do it.

Leo and Sonja left the ship and Tank hopped in the cockpit. "The sooner we get out of here, the better."

Gaeth poked his head out of the ship. Leo and Sonja were already gone. The freighter workers had already packed up and left, their ship the only one remaining in the bay. He glanced inside where he saw Tank going over the console of the ship.

"I think something's on the ship. I'm going to check it out real quick," Gaeth said.

"Don't take too long. I don't like being here," Tank yelled over his shoulder.

Gaeth rushed down the ramp and headed for the nearest door.

The footsteps of Leo and Sonja echoed off the walls as he walked down the hallway, hunched over and trying to make sure he stayed out of sight. The interior matched Oblurn. Everything was spotless and white, polished until it shone brightly under the harsh lights of the freighter. He pulled the mask out of his pocket and tied it around his head.

He stood tall and continued walking down the hallway, trying his best to act like he belonged. He ducked in an open door along the wall. The footsteps became louder as he drew closer. Gaeth picked up his pace to make sure he didn't lose them, the small hallway not helping his nervousness.

As he neared the end, he realized he didn't know which way Leo and Sonja went. He checked both directions but couldn't see anyone. There was a sudden sound echo of footsteps, and he backed into the doorway. Several guards walked down the hall. "Did you hear someone boarded the freighter? Apparently, they let an expired code dock in the station. The ship just got away, but everyone's keeping their eye out for anyone who doesn't belong," one guard said.

"I'll be sure to keep an eye out as well. I know how important this voyage is," the second guard said. "Should we check on the cargo hold?"

"Let's do a sweep of the area first. There's no way they've had enough time to make it to the cargo hold yet." The two continued walking past the doorway Gaeth stood in. So the cargo hold was a little ways off, then? He waited a couple minutes before sneaking out and continuing on. Another door tucked away in the corner caught his eye.

He opened it and in front of him was the cargo hold filled from end to end with Bisekt ships. The room stretched far back, the ceiling tall enough for a ship to fly around in. He couldn't imagine what the freighter might be carrying that was too big to fit in here. As he walked forward, he made sure his mask was secure.

Find Onyx ships.

The holes were big enough for his eyes making it easy to see out of, but he wasn't sure if Leo would still recognize him. Voices were coming from the other side of the cargo hold. Gaeth moved in between the ships

"It should be around here somewhere," a voice said.

"Keep looking, we don't have much time."

"What about the corner?"

Gaeth stumbled and fell against a ship. The bang echoed in the room, causing the voices to stop.

"Who's there?"

"They won't answer you, dummy."

Gaeth's heart raced as footsteps got closer. He ducked behind a ship and snuck around the other side.

"Found them," someone whispered.

Gaeth poked his head around the ship. Leo and Sonja stood with a group of resistance soldiers. Sonja and a Volnea, who seemed to be the leader, had their noses in a paper while Leo talked to the others. When someone yelled they had found it, Leo jogged over and looked at the ships.

He threw a thumbs-up to the others.

Those are it.

They were too close to their ships. If he had to stick them with bombs, he would need to get close to Leo. The only way to do it would be to take his mask off. He put his mask in his pocket and came out from behind the ship with his hands up. Several people pulled their blasters on him.

"Who are you?" one of them asked.

"Gaeth?" Leo walked back to them. "Why aren't you on the ship with Tank?"

"He has it under control, and I thought you could use the extra help," Gaeth said, trying to be as casual as possible.

"Whatever," Leo said. "Go get more detonators. They're in the ship."

Everything slowed down as Gaeth walked toward Onyx's ship.

Leo called after him, "Hurry it up."

Gaeth's heart was about to leap out of his chest. He had to keep them here a little longer. As he went on the ship and bent down to pick up the bombs, he pulled out the bombs Sebastian had given him and stuck it to the side of the ship. He pressed the button on the center, and it lit up.

He ran out with the bombs for Leo, who gave him a strange stare. "Let's go. We can't be here too long."

They stuck the last few bombs on the Bisekt ships.

"Get on, and we can get out of here," a woman said. She stared pointedly at Gaeth.

She's the plant.

He put his hands in his pockets as they walked back to Onyx's ship, the detonator was warm in his palm from being in there for so long. It was time. But no matter how many times Sebastian's words rang in his head, he couldn't let Leo be hurt by the explosion.

"Hey, Leo."

"Later." Leo kept walking.

Gaeth wracked his brains, trying to think of any reason to get Leo to stop walking.

"Come look at this, I think this one didn't stick right."

"It'll still go off." Leo had no intention of slowing down.

I'm sorry, Leo.

Gaeth opened the top of the detonator. For a brief second, he considered not pushing it. He could close it and go help Leo instead. But he had made up his mind. Gaeth shut his eyes and pushed the button.

The sound was deafening. The explosion threw Gaeth to the ground, his body sliding across the metal floor. The heat from the fire was almost unbearable as it engulfed everything around them. The ringing in Gaeth's ears finally subsided. He turned over. Leo was on his back several feet away, motionless.

"Leo!" Gaeth ran to him and shook him. "Leo, are you ok?" Leo blinked as he opened his eyes; burns covered his face. He tried to sit up but winced in pain. "What happened?"

"I don't know. You were walking toward the ship, and then it blew up. Someone might be here." Gaeth looked about frantically.

But Leo wasn't listening.

He stared at the detonator still in Gaeth's hand.

METAL BONES

METAL BONES

METAL BONES

31

They had been set up.

When the ship exploded, Leo barely had enough time to cover his face with his hands before he hit the ground, his body screaming in agony. He felt better when he saw Gaeth. As Gaeth talked, Leo glanced over his shoulder at Onyx's ship writhing in spreading flames.

I'm going to die here.

Gaeth was still talking, pointing somewhere. In his hand, unmistakably, was a detonator, its top open.

Leo's mind went blank.

Gaeth couldn't have done that.

Gaeth realized what Leo was staring at. He dropped the detonator as if it had burned him.

The blank spaces in Leo's mind filled with boiling rage.

"Why?" Leo choked out, tears welling in his eyes.

"Leo, listen to me, this is the best possible solution for us." The ship behind them let out a rumble as the fire engulfed it.

"This is the best solution?" Leo laughed as the freighter's fire alarm went off. He pushed Gaeth away and stood up. He didn't even know who Gaeth was at this point.

"I was doing this all for you." Leo clenched his fists.

"The Empire can get me the money now. We don't have to worry about Onyx."

Leo punched him. Gaeth fell backward, slamming on the floor. Leo got on top of him and didn't stop.

"After everything I did to save your ass."

He punched Gaeth again.

"I got you out of Oblurn."

And again.

"I found us a place to stay while we did those stupid fucking missions."

And again.

"Who put these ideas in your head, huh?" Leo screamed. "After we got the money, I would have taken care of you."

Gaeth managed to reach up and grab Leo's fist. He squeezed until Leo's hand broke under the pressure. Leo screamed and kicked Gaeth in the face. Gaeth rolled away and ran toward the other ship in the cargo hold where the Sol Empire pilot waited for him.

"That's right! Run away!" Leo held his crumpled hand as they took off, leaving the flaming mess of trash behind.

Sonja ran out from behind a Bisekt ship. "Leo, I radioed Tank, he says he can be here soon."

He leaned on her for support and called Tank on his radio. "Please tell me you're not far away."

"Thirty seconds," Tank said.

Alarms blared as a sprinkler shot on. The water rained downed, the fire hissing as it fought to be put out.

"I don't know what happened," Leo said to Sonja. "When did he even get the bombs? I would never think he was capable of something like this."

Before Sonja could answer, Spacejunk pulled into the cargo hold. They stumbled aboard, and Tank flew swiftly out of the freighter, weaving between smaller ships.

Sonja carried Leo down to the med bay while Tank and Arby piloted Spacejunk. She laid him on the medical table and pulled open different nearby drawers, searching for bandages.

"I'm sorry we couldn't stop Bisekt," Leo whispered, water dripping off his hair onto the floor.

"Sometimes it's not all about the money." Sonja carried over a cloth and some rubbing alcohol. "What happened to Gaeth?"

"I keep replaying it over and over in my mind, everything he said to me. All I can think of is when he went off on his own. Who knows who he talked to in New Star City." He winced as Sonja rubbed the cuts on his face.

"Sorry," she said. "There are so many people in New Star City, it would be impossible to find who he talked to even if we wanted to."

"I failed as an older brother." Leo stared off into space. "When we left Earth, the one thing my parents told me was to keep him safe. Now he's trying to kill me."

"I bet if you guys could talk face to face, then you could work it out," Sonja said. "That's how it always works with siblings."

"No. I don't care if I ever see him again. I'm done taking care of him. It's time I take care of myself." He clenched his jaw.

Sonja gave a smile that didn't reach her eyes. "What are you going to do now you're taking care of yourself?"

"Explore? More jobs for Vanish? I have money saved up already. I can figure something out," he said. "First I'm going to give you and Scril the money from this job. You guys deserve it."

"You don't have to do that, Leo," Sonja said.

"You're right, I don't. But I'm going to."

"Hmm." Sonja finished cleaning his face and put the cloth in a bin.

"What?"

"I can tell you're really hurting."

Leo's throat tightened, and his eyes stung. The world became fuzzy as his vision blurred. He blinked a few times, running his fingers through his hair.

"My brother—" He could barely get the words out before the first sob broke free.

For Gaeth, for himself, for what happened, for all of it.

Sonja wrapped her arms around him. "You don't have to explain yourself to me."

32

Gaeth took several deep breaths as he tried to control his excitement. He had done it. He had proven himself. All for his cure. His freedom.

The woman flying the ship glanced at him. "I wasn't sure you would go through with it," she said. "I thought I might have to kill you."

"No," Gaeth replied. "I had made up my mind."

"Good. There's no turning back now."

They didn't say anything more, and Gaeth eventually fell asleep. He awoke when she tapped him on the shoulder. "We're almost there."

He peered out the window to see nothing but fluffy white clouds. The ship bounced and flew lower until there was nothing but a vast ocean below them. An island appeared the horizon as they sped forward, surrounded by smaller islands.

A large white stadium stood atop the island, ships flying in and out of it. The woman typed a few numbers into her monitor, and they flew lower onto the island.

The waves crashed against the rocks as they landed. Sebastian waited for them, his coat billowing in the wind. As Gaeth got off the ship, it took off almost right away. Gaeth turned back to Sebastian, still smiling his strange smile.

"You did so well," he said, putting a hand on Gaeth's shoulder. "How do you feel?"

"I wish my brother didn't have to see what I did," Gaeth admitted. "But it can't be undone."

"It can never be undone," Sebastian said. "He's probably glad you're gone."

"When will I be cured?" Gaeth asked.

"All in good time. But think about where you are." Sebastian motioned to the stadium above them, pulling out a new white mask, this one much more excellent quality than the first. A servant ran forward and threw a purple robe over him, while Sebastian fastened the mask.

"You're in Sentrum now, Gaeth. You did it."

ACKNOWLEDGMENTS

If it weren't for the following people, this book wouldn't be possible. I can't thank them enough for all they've done for me through this process.

First are my parents. My mom is the reason for my love of books. She brought my sister and I to the library every weekend when were little. I still have my library card from when I was five.

We spend hours in Barnes and Noble together and I know I wouldn't have found a love for writing if it weren't for those hours spent with books when I was younger. Thank you, Mom.

While my mom showed me books, my dad is the storyteller of our family. He always has the talent of pulling people in with whatever he's talking about. I remember when I was younger and he would make up a story about something on the spot and I would be so sure it was real until he had to tell me it wasn't. Thank you for giving me a love of storytelling, Dad.

I want to thank my boyfriend Brandon who supported me through the ups and downs of Metal Bones. Our phone calls and texts talking through its problems (when I was ready to throw in the towel) to brainstorming crazy ideas means so much to me. I'll always appreciate them. Thank you for always being there to keep my head out of my ass. I love you.

To Jordyn who I call the writing Dumbledore, thank you so much for everything you have done for me. For creating an amazing cover and also helping me whenever I came to you with questions about writing or selling a book. You truly go above and beyond and I'm forever grateful.

To Dave, after one conversation about fauna and animals in the desert, you're the reason chapter 15 exists haha. Thank you for reading Metal Bones in the beginning when it was still a baby and reassuring me it wasn't a complete mess.

To Josh, for cheering me on and always being supportive any time I had a Metal Bones chapter for you to read. You always have wise words when it comes to book advice. Thank you so much!

To Kim, thank you for getting my butt in gear to write. Because of you, I had a writing schedule I used until Metal Bones was done. If it weren't for your graphs and getting us on call all the time, this book would have taken a lot longer haha.

To my editor Sydney, without your work, Metal Bones wouldn't be half the story it is today. You helped me shape it into the book I saw in my mind. Thank you.

Thank you to Krisitin, Brittany, and Sammi. Your friendships have shaped me into who I am today and I'm thankful for all of you.

Finally, thank you to You the reader. You're the reason I write. Thank you for picking up Metal Bones. I hope you enjoyed it!

ABOUT THE AUTHOR

Kathleen Contine is a New York-born NA Sci Fi Author.

Inspired by her love of reading and frequent trips to the library with her mom as a child, Kathleen graduated from Saint Leo University with a B.A. in English with a concentration in professional writing.

When Kathleen isn't writing, she enjoys playing video games, spending time with friends, and playing with her dogs, Freddie and Pepper.

FOLLOW KATHLEEN

Kathleen Contine   @KathleenContine   @KathleenVContine   @Kathleen.contine.author

CPSIA information can be obtained
at www.ICGtesting.com
Printed in the USA
BVHW031731110320
574751BV00001B/24

9 781734 231601